D0764703

Brooke Carter

THE STONE OF SORROW

RUNECASTER BOOK ONE

ORCA BOOK PUBLISHERS

Library and Archives Canada Cataloguing in Publication
Title: The stone of sorrow / Brooke Carter.
Names: Carter, Brooke, 1977- author.
Description: Series statement: Runecaster ; book 1
Identifiers: Canadiana (print) 20190173041 | Canadiana (ebook) 2019017305X |
ISBN 9781459824393 (softcover) |
ISBN 9781459824409 (PDF) | ISBN 9781459824416 (EPUB)
Classification: LCC PS8605.A77776 S76 2020 | DDC jC813/.6—DC23

Library of Congress Control Number: 2019947366
Simultaneously published in Canada and the United States in 2020

Summary: In this young adult fantasy novel, seventeen-year-old Runa embarks on a dangerous journey to recover a magical runestone and save her sister.

Orca Book Publishers is committed to reducing the consumption of nonrenewable resources in the making of our books. We make every effort to use materials that support a sustainable future.

Orca Book Publishers gratefully acknowledges the support for its publishing programs provided by the following agencies: the Government of Canada, the Canada Council for the Arts and the Province of British Columbia through the BC Arts Council and the Book Publishing Tax Credit.

Cover and map illustration by Song Kang
Author photo by Laura Housden
Edited by Tanya Trafford
Design by Rachel Page

ORCA BOOK PUBLISHERS
orcabook.com

Printed and bound in Canada.

23 22 21 20 • 4 3 2 1

ONE

Stay with me.

A voice finds me in the forgetting place. I was supposed to be casting a spell, but I can't remember which one, and now I'm lost, surrounded by a swirling fog so dense it reminds me of the mist that obscures the sea on cold mornings. Frigid air bites into my lungs. My bones ache and I feel brittle as an icicle. If I fall now, will I shatter into shards? I must find my way through, or I may never get home.

Stay here. Stay now.

I recognize the voice. It belongs to Sýr, my sister, and it reaches out to me with a warmth that begs me to follow, and I do, clinging to its sound the way a lost navigator might listen for a bell that rings a ship to shore.

At last the fog clears and I see her face. It's then that I realize I'm not walking at all. I'm lying on my back, half-frozen on the glacial slopes above our village, and Sýr is looking down at me with concern.

"Where was I?" I ask, but I already know the answer. I was deep in my sickness again, having lost my hold on this realm. When that happens, I see things—sometimes terrible things—that aren't there. I don't know what's real and what's not. The sickness comes when I'm scared, and it's happening more and more often. Sýr is worried that one day I will not emerge from the confusion in my mind, although she would never say this to me. But I feel it. I feel it in the way she tries too hard to reassure me.

"Don't worry. I will never lose you, Runa," she says.

"Well, how could you?" I say, trying to lighten the mood. "I've been right here, stuck on the ice, the whole time."

"Ah, you blend in so well," she teases, a reference to my white hair and pale skin. She's not wrong. With my coloring and my gray cloak, it would be easy to miss me among the stones and patches of ice. Right now I feel like one of those stones. Cold, stiff, and lifeless.

"Help me up," I say. "I can hardly move. It's so..." I trail off, not wanting to sound weak. I know Sýr has spent many days lying on the ice patches, trying to connect with the powers of Ís, the ice rune.

"Cold?" she finishes for me, a glint of amusement in her eye. "Ice has a way of doing that." Sýr doesn't make me feel bad for failing or for being a coward when it comes to casting runes from the cold embrace of the ice.

The wind blows her dark hair around her face, and the thick, warm fabric of her green cloak billows, reminding me of the rolling hills and forest beyond our home. What spell would I have to cast to be as beautiful as Sýr? I wonder.

She cocks her head at me as if reading my thoughts. "It is a bitter cold," she says, "and I hated doing this too when I was training."

She extends a gloved hand to me and I take it, letting her pull me up. Despite her willowy appearance, Sýr is strong, and I have the feeling she could easily lift ten of me. Sometimes I wonder if she could use her magic to lift an entire warship, or one of the horned whales that swim in the cold waters, or even one of our mountains—the ones that spew lava when the gods are angry. How it came to be that I am her sister, I will never know. The gods are not without a cruel sense of humor.

Though we're sisters, we're nothing alike. Sýr has the long, dark hair of our mother, so I'm told, and the tall body and deeply tanned skin that some say is a sign of elven blood in our lineage. I must not have been blessed by our ancestors, because I am short and skinny and pale. Light hair like mine is common in our clan, but mine isn't just light. It's an icy, wild, wiry mess, like a bursting cloud. I was born with all this hair, born looking old, as my grandmother, my amma, says.

"My eyes are causing trouble again," I say to Sýr. "I was fine on the ice. I think I was even connecting to the cold and could feel it powering through me. But right before I cast the rune of Ís, my eyes started hurting, and I got lost in that strange fog. After that I was so confused that I couldn't find my way. I'm glad you were here, Sýr. I don't know what I would do..." I'm too scared to complete the thought. I don't know what would happen if I stayed lost in the fog. Would I remain inside it for eternity? Would I die?

"Don't worry, Ru," my sister says. "One day you will find a way through that fog on your own. And your eyes, well, perhaps they're just special. Maybe we can find a salve for them in the spring, when the clans gather to trade."

My eyes are the thing I detest most about myself. I wouldn't mind being so fair, or even so fragile-looking, if it weren't for my eyes. I long to have the sharp green eyes of my sister. They can pierce you with a look that recalls the wilds of the ocean. But I've been cursed with watery blue eyes that don't work right. They are sore most days and tinged with pink, and sometimes I can't tell how far away things are. They make me clumsy. I drop things, fall, trip. People and objects are always moving without me seeing it happen. One moment here and the next gone, only to reappear again in a different spot.

My eyes jump around as if quaking in my head, and I know it makes others uneasy, because no one other than Amma and Sýr ever looks right at me for long. I asked Sýr about it once, and she told me that maybe my eyes shake because the person I'm talking to is so boring that I'm secretly looking for a way out of the conversation.

"A salve would be helpful," I say, forcing a smile. "New eyes would be even better."

"Well," says Sýr, "perhaps you should study your runes more often, and then you could find a spell to fix them."

I give her a playful shove. "If you cannot, what makes you think I will ever be able to?"

"One day, Ru," she says. "One day." Sýr smiles her kind smile, though I'm not sure my sister has any other type. She's the one person I've met who never has a mean word to say about others, and she doesn't wear her bitterness on her face as so many do. Maybe that's why she is so beautiful and I'm not. I have nothing but bitter thoughts. Sýr has her share of hardships, me being one of them, but she never lets it show.

"You will learn to cast all the runes," she says. "You will learn to make their shapes and sounds in your mind's eye, and you will learn to connect with the powers of the island. I did, and you will too."

We walk at the base of the massive glacier that has bordered my family's settlement since our people first journeyed here. It's where we come to practice the ice runes. I know that what Sýr says isn't true. I know it because I hate casting runes.

I can never say this out loud. After all, I should have inherited my family's magical gifts. My female ancestors have all been powerful runecasters, but despite extensive training under Sýr's watchful eye, whenever I cast a spell I screw something up. I have my sickness, or something breaks, or someone falls ill, or the exact opposite of the spell's purpose occurs. If I want something to float, it sinks. If I want to heal a wart, it grows bigger. If I want to increase the yield of a crop, I kill all the plants. I hate to think what would happen if I was in charge of important things like Sýr is. She is responsible for helping to birth babies, for blessing the dead on their way to the afterlife and for curing the clan of their ills.

After all, my sister is the keeper of the moonstone—a magical runestone that grants its possessor the power of prosperity. A talented runecaster like Sýr can use it to provide for our clan by harnessing its power to cast spells that help us. It can grow food, aid us in catching fish, or even heal us from sickness. In the hands of the right caster, the moonstone can ensure that we will flourish for years to come. Without it, there would be many hard years ahead, for life on our island isn't easy. We must be strong, or powerful, or lucky to survive. I am none of these things. Without Sýr I would perish.

"You cannot grow too frustrated, Ru," Sýr says, "for this is a difficult path. The way of the runecaster is lonely, and it is hard. No one will understand."

"But you do," I say, reaching out to grasp her hand as we walk.

She smiles. "You think you are a difficult pupil, but you're my favorite."

I laugh. "I am your only pupil."

"Exactly," she says.

I know why I'm not succeeding. Instead of holding tight to the runes and their sounds when I cast a spell, my mind drifts to all the times I've messed things up and to all the ways I'm different. Some people don't belong in the lives they were born into, and I am one of them.

I feel this truth in my heartbeat and in my breath. I feel it crawling underneath my skin, like a worm making its way into my soul. This truth always says the same thing. *You're a fake. Give up*. The runes will not listen to a voice like mine. They don't trust me, because I do not trust myself.

I know it takes a lifetime to master the basic runes, but I was not blessed with patience. A runecaster must be gifted with imagination, a born dreamer, and while Sýr says I have this gift, I'm not so sure. My feelings are a mystery even to me, and my dreams often feel like they are not the right dreams.

Sýr never chastises me, and she never lets on that she knows I'm a fraud. She's the gentlest and fiercest person I've ever known, and as much as I hate training to be a runecaster, I hate letting her down even more.

"Tell me, Runa," Sýr says, reaching over to brush snow from the back of my cloak. It's one of Sýr's old working cloaks. She has promised me that when I complete the next stage of my training, she will present me with the colorful cloak of a runecaster. I am ashamed to say I care more about the garment than I do about the achievement. "What did the ice feel like to you before you got lost in the spell?" she asks.

I want to say that it was cold and leave it at that, but I know Sýr wants me to think deeply about my training, even if I struggle to find the words to explain myself. "It felt... deceptive," I say at last. "At first the snow on top of the glacier feels soft and comforting to lie on, but after a while it grows harder, and all the softness turns slippery and so cold that it aches to lie still. I roll over into an impression that no longer fits, and then I'm forced to turn back and settle again into the same aching contortion. It's like trying to sleep in someone else's footprint. It's never going to fit."

Sýr nods, looking at me with an odd expression. "Good," she says.

"Good? How is that good?" I ask. "I failed."

Sýr waves her hand as if swatting the idea away from the air between us. "You understand now why change is necessary. You can't stay in one place forever, Runa. You've got to move forward in life. And I won't always be here." She looks away from me to the horizon.

"But Sýr, what if I can never make the spells work? Half the time they don't work, or they work in reverse, or I have my sickness. And what do you mean you won't always be here?" Imagining village life without Sýr around is enough to send me into a panic. She must notice me starting to shake, because she reaches out a strong gloved hand to steady me and then wraps her arm around my shoulders.

"That's enough," she says in her calm way. "We don't worry about things that have not come to pass. I'm just saying that nothing lasts forever. People change, move, grow, journey, and they die. We know this. We can't be afraid."

We do know this. We have proof. We've both already lost so much.

"Runa," Sýr says in her gentle voice. I realize we've stopped walking and I have become lost in my thoughts again. "Stay here with me."

"Sorry," I mutter, pushing away my dark thought. We continue walking. "When will my casting improve?" I ask. "I try, but I'm always messing up and getting it all backward."

Sýr nods. "It's hard to remember every nuance of each rune. When I started, I could never tell the difference between the bright-staves and the murk-staves," she says, raising a questioning eyebrow at me.

I sigh. "You're always quizzing me, big sister. A bright-stave is the positive side, and the murk-stave is the negative."

"And why does it matter?" she asks.

"It can change the reading of the runes entirely," I say. "When I'm doing a spell, if I get them mixed up, I could start a fire when I want to put it out, or I could make someone sick instead of helping them heal."

"Consequences," Sýr says. "We have a responsibility, Ru. If we make mistakes—and we will—then we will have to deal with it."

I can only imagine what it is like for her. I don't want to ruminate on the endless mistakes I've made, and I always have my sister to help me out when I mess up.

Sýr kicks a black lava rock, and it bounces and skids across the frozen earth. "But you know, when things seem dark there is always a brightness waiting on the other side. There is always a choice. There is always something you can do."

Sýr is eternally positive and has a way of walking through the world as if she's not tethered to it like the rest of us are. It's the thing I most admire, and envy, about her.

"So there is hope for me?" I ask, cracking a smile.

Sýr fixes her steady gaze on me. "Of course. You'll be the greatest runecaster this clan has ever seen. Perhaps even the best on the island."

I roll my eyes at her. "In our dreams."

"Let's get home," she says. "The sky is growing dark."

I follow her gaze out from where we stand high on the ice-covered clifftop just beyond the glacier. I can see our seaside village from here, and I long to get away from the ice and move toward the sea. A wind is brewing, blowing waves with white crests toward land, where they crash against the rich black soil of our homeland.

"I wonder where Father is now," she says.

The ocean's horizon is a swirl of gray, and there is no sign of a ship's sail. Our father, one of the head warriors of our clan, has been on a long expedition with his fellow warriors. It's not unusual for him to be gone a long time—navigating distant waters to find new lands and settlements takes many seasons—but it is unusual for him to be away this close to the coming of the red moon.

There have been murmurs and grumblings in the village that our father's ship is lost on the great ocean. Some say that he and his warriors met an enemy they could not defeat. Sýr dismisses these musings as simple fear.

"I hope he comes back soon," I say, but that's not entirely true.

We reach our dwelling as the sky is turning red and orange and gold. The sight of the modest hut fills me with relief.

Hot soup will chase the chill away. I push open the wooden door and step down inside, my heart swelling with the comforting pleasure of home. Sýr has kept our fire burning with a longevity spell, and our home radiates warmth.

"There's fish soup in the pot by the hearth," Sýr says, knowing me well.

"Want some?" I ask over my shoulder as I drop my cloak on a chair before rushing toward the fire to warm myself. Pulling off my leather gloves, I see that my fingers have turned blue from the cold.

"No," says Sýr, frowning at my fingers. She grabs one of my hands and gives it a rub, trying to get the blood flowing. "These fingers of yours," she mutters. "Like ice. Even when you were a baby." She pauses and lets go of my hand. Her face is troubled.

"Sýr?" I ask. "What's wrong?"

"I'm tired, Ru," she says. "Perhaps I'll have soup later, so save me some. I have work to do now. Get warm."

She disappears into the darkened cupboard where she keeps her hundreds of tiny pots of herbs and salves and who knows what else. Sýr is most herself when she is growing herbs in her garden, harvesting them for her tinctures, and cooking and nurturing at home.

"More for me," I mutter as I scoop a large portion into a bowl. "Is there any bread?" I call.

Sýr emerges with the flat crust of an ibud loaf, places it on the table and then sprinkles it with a few grains and some water. She moves her lips in a silent spell and then draws the shape of Ár, the harvest rune, on the table before placing a bowl over the bread.

With careful fingers she produces a blue stone from a leather sack she wears around her neck, close to her heart. The moonstone. It used to be a brilliant, shimmering blue but has since dulled. Its powers are waning, and it must be refreshed in the sacred pool at moonwater at the time of the red moon's eclipse. The stone is said to have fallen from the moon when Odin created the nine realms, and that it carries within it the power of creation—as long as it recharges when the moon does. The strongest runecasters from all the clans compete to gain possession of it. The last time the red moon came, it was the year of my birth, and this is one of the longest intervals between moons we've ever had. Right now the stone is drawing power from Sýr herself, and I can see it wearing on her.

Sýr whispers to the stone, and it glints blue before growing dull again. She places it back into the sack around her neck and takes a deep breath, steadying herself against the table.

"Sýr," I start, but she holds up her hand, and I know not to continue.

"I'm fine." She nods at the bread. "Wait for it," she says, disappearing back into her cupboard.

"How long?" I whine, embarrassed at my own impatience.

"Wait," she says.

I slurp my soup, drinking from the bowl, and use my cold fingers to put pinches of tender flakes of cod and chewy bits of eel into my mouth.

"Now," Sýr calls in a faraway voice. She's distracted and will remain that way for the rest of the night. Once she gets working, she loses sight of all else. At least that means I won't have to do any more lessons tonight.

I lift the bread bowl and see that the tiny crust has tripled in size, growing from a morsel to a meal. A few years ago the moonstone would have turned this tiny crust into a feast for the whole village.

I use the ibud loaf to sop up the rest of the soup and bits of fish from my bowl. It's satisfying to my hungry belly, and I'm grateful for it, but it also tastes a little strange, as if the bread is more illusion than grain. I suppose that it is.

Once I'm full of soup and bread, I head to my sleeping area. It's a little triangular-shaped nook at the back of our dwelling, made private by a ragged sheepskin Sýr hung across the opening for me. Pushing the soft curtain aside, I climb onto my sleeping ledge under the small window that looks out to sea. I open the shutter, knowing Sýr will admonish me for letting the cold air in, but I must look at the sky. Every night I gaze out over my cliff side at the stars.

I love living up here. It's high enough that the water doesn't reach us, but our dwelling and my little window jut out over the water in such a way that when the ocean is full, I am able to look straight from my window into the depths.

Our clanspeople are seafarers, and I dislike being too far from the water, for I always feel too dry, as if I could turn into an empty husk at any moment. I like the privacy our enclave offers, and the way the sounds of the great ocean echo against the stone walls. It is as if I live inside a giant shell, and the whooshing of water lulls me to sleep at night like the great rhythmic heartbeat of eternity. It's a timeless feeling, like I've always been here and always will be.

Looking at the stars relaxes me but my mind inevitably drifts to the worrisome questions that plague me these nights. Can someone like me ever have a great destiny? If I tell Sýr I dream of sailing across the great ocean, will she be angry? Would she ever let me go?

What about my mother? Everyone tells me she was wild and free. Would she be proud if she could see me now? My memory is long, but of course I can't remember her. She died giving me life. If I try to conjure my birth, there's nothing there except a blackness without end. It's like trying to conceive of infinity. As soon as you think you have a handle on it, it slips away, like sand pulling under your feet as the tide rolls out toward the horizon.

"Runa?" Sýr says, her gentle voice reaching me before she pulls aside the sheepskin. She looks at me and her face softens. She knows my thoughts. Can she see that, for me, this good life, the one she's been so careful to provide, feels like a trap?

I turn to her, exhausted by my own thoughts and the failures of the day. "Do the sleeping spell, Sýr, please. I cannot rest without it."

She reaches out to pluck a single hair from my head. I feel the strand pop free, and I watch as Sýr moves her lips in a silent spell. With the flame of a candle she singes the hair and then presses its remains into her hand before using one elegant finger to draw a series of runes in her palm. Next she draws the same runes on my forehead as I lay back on my bed. I feel myself growing heavier, as if roots are growing from my body to anchor me in place. It's a comforting weight, and I shut my eyes to welcome it.

As I breathe, I feel Sýr slip away from me, closing the window and then the curtain behind her. From a distance she whispers, "At the end it will be the two of us, Runa."

I'm so tired, and her voice is faint. I don't know what she means. "The end of what?" I whisper back.

As I drift off, her voice comes to me as if from a great distance. "The end of time, Ru," she says. "Always us. Until the end of time."

TWO

In times gone by, a runecaster was a revered witch, and she had the ability to roam wherever and whenever she liked, encumbered by nothing and no one. Now it is rare to leave the village you've grown up in unless you are a warrior. For Sýr, and for me, our destinies are tied to our clan because we are needed on home soil to help our people. My mother was the last of us to voyage, when she won at the moonwater competition and secured the moonstone for our clan so many years ago. Even though I hate trying to make the runes, I envy Sýr's chance to travel to find moonwater when it is time.

When we wake this morning, the red moon is visible in the sky, peeking above the horizon. We have perhaps a day or two before it moves higher and Sýr must gather her runes and set off to moonwater for the competition. She won't go alone, perhaps taking a warrior or two with her, for the journey can be dangerous. No one knows exactly where moonwater is, for its location changes with every generation of the eclipse.

To find it, Sýr will have to follow the path of the moon, her own intuition, and the great guiding lights to the north.

I will need to stay here because our amma needs me, and it will fall to me to cast runes for the clan while Sýr is gone. If I have my sickness, I will be on my own to deal with it.

Our people are anxious about winning the runecasting competition, and I am no exception. We must win to retain possession of the moonstone and ensure our clan's prosperity, but I'm more worried about how I will survive back at the village without my sister. I'm hated enough as it is. Without Sýr around I'll be like a fish caught in a tide pool, praying the ravens don't come to peck my eyes out.

The smell of porridge bubbling draws me to the hearth, where Sýr has left the black pot simmering. I use the lifting stick to remove the lid and scoop a portion into my bowl. Sýr has left something else for me—a treat wrapped in moss next to the hearth. Its smell gives it away. Hákarl. Fermented shark, my favorite. Where did she get it? Hákarl takes a long time to ripen, and we haven't had much whey to cure it with, as our clan has a shortage of goats. There's a shortage of everything now that the moonstone is waning, and with the big ships gone, our fishing practices are limited to shoreline nets and traps. In my nets I've only caught little sharks that are not worth preparing in this way. Not enough meat.

For hákarl, it's best to use the big, mottled green shark. Its flesh can withstand the fermenting process without falling apart. It must be aged a long time, for green shark is poisonous when fresh but safe and delicious to eat when rotten. But catching a green shark takes a huge net or a long line with a large hook, and I am not strong enough to haul those in on my own. I've always wanted to spear one from atop an ice floe, as father claimed to have done once. Perhaps I will in my dreams.

Unwrapping the hákarl, I take a nibble of its pungent, tender flesh. Sýr must have known this morning would be tough. I hope she saved some for herself. In case she did not, I wrap the rest and place it in my pocket. I slurp my porridge, then find my woolen leggings and socks and pull them on under my dress, the same one I was wearing yesterday. I'm not fond of dresses, and this is not my favorite. It is made of scratchy wool and is the same muddy brown color as sheep dung, but at least it is warm. Once I find my boots, I pull them on and note how they pinch in the toes. I can't bring myself to tell Sýr they are too small, as it seems we only traded for these ones a couple of months ago. When I wrap my gray cloak around me, my boring look is complete.

A loud squawk interrupts my thoughts. Núna, my raven, flies toward me in the early-morning dim, barely visible until the glint of her black eyes is upon me. She flies through the window and alights on my ledge, ruffling her wing feathers and snapping her beak at me in pleasure. I open a little pot beside the window and pluck out a dried worm. It's one of many I've harvested for Núna over the years.

Sýr likes to say that Núna is my fylgja, a guardian spirit connected to me and to my destiny, because fylgjur show up when babies are born, and Núna has been with me since the moment I arrived in this world, breathless and still. My amma likes to tell the story of how I was born dead, but then Núna flew down through the roof and brought my soul to me. She has visited me every day since.

When I was a little girl, Núna was young too, and she was always hungry and squawking. I would say, "Now, now," as I fed her, and that turned into "Núna." We are "Runa and Núna," Sýr likes to say. Very best friends.

Núna has gotten rather fat from stealing bread from the villagers. She used to fit in my cloak pouch, but now she likes to rest on my shoulder. It's a pleasant weight that I miss when she's gone, off on her bird adventures, and I feel incomplete without Núna's claws in my shoulder. I have permanent marks where her talons dig in.

I like to pretend that Núna isn't a raven at all and that my mother sent her to me. Sometimes Núna brings me sticks and pebbles as gifts, and one time she even brought me the carcass of a white hare. I look at these gifts as signs from my mother, and I do my best to interpret them in case my mother is trying to warn me of something. So far I haven't been able to divine anything, but I did manage to use the hare's soft white fur to line some gloves for Sýr. Like Sýr, Núna has always been with me, and I hope she always will be.

Once Núna finishes her little feast of dried worms, she sits on the sill and watches over me. I am grateful for the company, because I am scared for Sýr. Today I will go down to the village with Sýr to assist her while she does rune readings and simple spells for the villagers, and I will seek out our grandmother. I can always count on my amma to help. She likes to live in the action, shunning our clifftop hideaway. One time, when he was still around, Father tried to convince Sýr that we should live among the rest of the clan. He argued that we should do it for safety and because we were already outcast enough. I don't know what Sýr said to him, but he never mentioned it again, and ever since he has regarded me with a strange expression, part wonder and part something else. Fear? But what would a powerful warrior like Father, Unnur the Axe, have to fear from me? I'm the village strangeling who can't seem to be useful. I am never the bright star in the sky, never the girl they want me to be.

Núna chitters at me from the window.

I hold my arms out and spin in a slow circle so she can see my garments. "I won't need an invisibility rune," I say to her. She cocks her black head at me. "These clothes take care of that."

Núna ignores me, preens her chest feathers, and then flies away. I pull the shutters closed after her, grab my set of wooden practice runes from the ledge, and head out to walk the cliff path to the village.

Aside from the red cast to the sky caused by the rising moon, this day is much like any other. Crisp air, breath billowing out from me in cloudy puffs, the icy crunch of semi-frozen pebbles and lichen underfoot, gusts of salty wind that whip up from the black sands below. As the path winds downward, I look out over our lands. The village sits to the left in a protected alcove beyond the beach, where it is surrounded by natural rock walls that buffer the winds. It's flanked by a collection of stone dwellings on one side and by green hills and grazing lands on the other. Beyond are clusters of cultivated land, where we grow crops, and forest, where we forage for wild berries and mosses. As I walk down the path, I can see plumes of smoke from cooking fires and hear the clangor of our people living and toiling and surviving.

The clan is hard at work. People clad in leather, wool, and fur trudge about. No one is spared of responsibility. Children fetch water while their mothers scrape hides, weave new ropes, and care for horses and sheep. The men who've stayed back at the village dig to create a new waterway from the nearby river, as they are going to make a trough that runs under the heavy stones and into our longhouse. That way we'll be able to lift the stones to collect fresh water.

To my right is the sea, my one great love, though I have never sailed far from home. As I look at the endless expanse of ocean, it seems like I can feel the power of the tides flowing into me. It's an ancient power, pushing and then pulling deep within, and I have to resist the urge to run down the path into the waves.

Is there an end to the world's waters? Will I ever see the unknown lands beyond? Will I discover the mysteries I dream of? Father and his fellow warriors returned from long journeys with wild tales of sea monsters, endless fog, and strange villages with creatures and people I can't believe exist.

A girl like me cannot hope to conquer lands or wield a battle axe. I'm not large and strong like some of the women in our clan. To join the warriors on a quest, I would have to be free of my destiny as a runecaster and skilled in the ways of battle. I am neither.

A girl like me can never leave, so I will have to be content to dream. It's not so bad, I suppose. There are worse things than having to dream through life. I could be like the banished ones, sent to wander alone in our island's dead zone, scraping out a meager survival among the glacier's caves and deep crevasses, haunted by the ghosts lurking there. There are always worse things, I remind myself, trying on Sýr's optimism. Still, the sea calls to me.

Down at the beach I pick my way across the black sand, my boots sinking in the wet pools, and hop around the outcropping of black rocks and lava formations from centuries ago. Every now and then a new eruption springs forth offshore, the sparks and lava shooting into the sky and sizzling the ocean. Once I hauled in a huge net of cooked fish, and the clan had no choice but to eat it all at once. There was no preserving it. The fish tasted of both the sea and the earth, at once salty and stony, and it had a burnt flavor. We could almost taste the island's anger. We took it as a warning from the gods, and we were careful to increase our offerings and thanks.

I make my way to my traps, nestled beyond the tide pools and moored with heavy stones and strong ropes, and flip them open to see that I've managed to catch spider crab this day. I've also collected a lot of seaweed, which will please Sýr, for once dried it provides us with the nutrition we need for long winters.

Sýr's girlfriend, Frigg, will give me some goat's butter in exchange for crab, I'll bet. Frigg is a square-shouldered, steel-haired woman who reminds me of a wall in more ways than one. She raises horses and sheep in the foothills and keeps a stand in the village for trading her skins, meat, milk, and butter. I know why Sýr likes her so much—and it's not for the delicious sheep wares. It's because Frigg is gentle and generous, much like my sister herself. I have asked Sýr if they're in love, and she always says love isn't something you're "in" but something you "do." I think they do it a lot.

Cramming all of the catch into one trap, I reset the others and then hoist my full trap over my shoulder and scramble back across the rocks and up toward the village. Icy seawater drips down the back of my cloak, soaking me, but I don't care.

Sýr will tease me, saying I've turned into a sea creature stinking of fish and covered in strings of seaweed, and Frigg will laugh. The crabs scuttle in the trap, clacking against each other. I jostle the trap to shock them a bit and keep them from killing each other. One of them reaches its long claw through the trap net and gives my thumb a pinch.

"Ow." I draw my hand back and see dark red blood running from the gash in the fleshy part of my thumb. It drips onto the black sand and mixes with the seawater before running back down the shoreline to the ocean.

"At least a part of me will journey with you," I whisper to the water as the waves retreat. I look at my hand, noting that this will hurt for some time and make it difficult to haul traps.

No matter. My hands are scarred and thick from work and fishing. They are not the hands of a runecaster.

When I walk up through the village, no one speaks to me. "See? No invisibility rune needed," I mutter to myself.

I pick my way through the working crowds, past men driving stakes into the ground, past children sifting seeds into sacks, past young women sewing clothes. Some men stare at me as I go by, and I avoid their gazes. I know I am odd and look different from the other girls. Sýr says it appeals to men the way a rare bird or wild game does. They want to hunt it, kill it, wear its feathers or hide. They want it for what it will mean about them. They don't want it for its own sake. I don't really want to find out if what she says is true.

I pass four older women weaving in a circle. They pay me no mind, as is typical, for the elder women in our clan don't figure young ones like me have anything to offer. They guard their wisdom like their gossip, hoarding it and doling it out when it will have the most impact. They are the ones who set up marriages, start fights among brothers, and have the power to shun the unwanted from our shores. Sýr warns me to always be polite to the women. As I walk by I try to make myself even more invisible. They cackle to each other as I pass, and I wonder if it's to do with me. They continue their weaving, intricate patterns and scenes designed to influence fate and bring their warrior husbands back from the great sea. I've wondered whether it would help to bring Father home, but I am a terrible weaver, and in my heart I fear it is a waste of time. No amount of dreaming has ever brought back someone I lost. Whether my father comes back alive or at all has nothing to do with my desires. I wish it did.

Sýr is set up and giving readings at Frigg's stand. This way they can visit with each other while Sýr reads fortunes for the villagers and Frigg sells her wares.

When I walk over, I see Sýr and Frigg deep in whispered conversation. Sýr looks upset, and Frigg reaches out and brushes my sister's hair from her eyes. Sýr's expression brightens as Frigg gazes at her in adoration. They kiss, and I turn away to give them privacy.

"Girl!" I hear Frigg bellow to me. "Have you brought me spider crab?"

I spin back around and heft my trap onto the trading table.

"Maybe. Have you got any butter?" I ask, and Frigg chuckles. "I'll trade a crab for some."

Frigg waves me off, her arms well-muscled from shearing sheep. "Bah, never mind. You can have it." She dips into a bin and gives me a wrapped parcel of butter.

I hesitate for a moment. She's giving it to me for free? I look at Sýr, who nods.

"Thank you, Frigg," I say. "If you come over later, we can all eat crab tonight," I offer.

Frigg sniffs. "Yes, of course. Later," she says, turning her back.

Something isn't right. I look at Sýr. "What is it?" I ask. "Is it time?"

"Not now, Runa," Sýr says, pausing to look at my hand as I hold out one of the crabs for Frigg to admire.

Ever the mother to me, she, of course, notices my injury. Sýr, twenty-seven years old now, took on our mother's role at age ten. I try to imagine what it would be like to lose your mother as a child and to have to raise your baby sister yourself. It's not as if she had a lot of help. Our grandmother is around, yes, but she is old and eccentric.

"What have you done now? That cut is deep," Sýr says as she takes my catch of crab from me and tosses it into a large earthen pot next to her. It's filled with seawater and the various mussels and limpets I collected on shore. What we can't sell we'll eat. She grabs my wrist. "Sit down."

I obey and try to stay still as Sýr rubs a thick paste into the wound. At first it stings, but then the throbbing pulse of pain in my thumb subsides. She wraps a piece of clean woven cloth around it and then makes the rune of Úr, for healing, on the back of my hand with a mixture of ash and burnt moss.

Frigg looks on, always in awe of Sýr's ability. "Can you use the moonstone to heal it faster?" she asks.

Sýr shakes her head. "No, I cannot afford to use the stone for small things. It's almost empty of power. And every time I use it..." She trails off, looking tired.

Frigg and I both know what she was going to say. The stone is drawing her power and strength. When people demand that Sýr use the stone, what they are asking is for her to give up a piece of her own soul. There was a time when the moonstone would have healed my cut in mere minutes, but Sýr can't risk using it now.

The red moon is rising. Soon we will have to contend with the desperation of other clans and the race to win control of the moonstone. Sýr needs to save all of the stone's strength.

"It's okay," I say to Sýr, fibbing a little. "It feels much better already, and I've had worse cuts."

"You'll need to care for it. Who knows what gunk lives on those dirty hands of yours?" she teases with a smile.

"Even my sheep take baths sometimes, Ru," says Frigg, joking along.

"Oh yeah?" I ask. "When do you bathe, Frigg?"

She shrugs. "When it rains."

We all laugh at this, but I notice Sýr's smile crumble, and her serious look returns.

The looming competition isn't all we need to fear, and I know Sýr is concerned. Without Father and his warriors, our clan is vulnerable to attack so close to the red moon coming. If other clans, such as our closest neighbors, the Jötnar, find out we're low on defenses, they could decide to raid us.

The Jötnar are not our enemies, but when the survival of an entire people is in question, even neighbors can become foes. Descendants of powerful giants, they used to possess the moonstone a long time ago, until my mother's mother won it for our clan. My mother won it again during the moonwater of her time. Sýr, the one living person in our clan capable of possessing it, now holds the stone, having inherited it upon our mother's death. That is the strength of Sýr. A ten-year-old girl inheriting a powerful moonstone and a baby all at once.

"Troubled, love?" Frigg asks, placing a comforting hand on Sýr's arm. She has noticed my sister's downcast face too.

Sýr pats her hand. "I'm fine. I wish…" She doesn't finish, and I suspect that if I wasn't here, she would tell Frigg her troubles.

"If you're worried about the competition, don't be," I say.

"Runa," Frigg starts, trying to cut me off. "Not now."

"What? I think she needs to know that she is the only one worthy of the moonstone." I look to my sister. "It's you, Sýr," I say.

She casts a quick glance at me. "I'm not worried," she says, but I know this is a lie. "We don't have to speak of this now."

"No," I say. "I see the red moon coming. I know it will happen soon. And I want you to know that you are the one who will win the moonstone."

"What will be is in the hands of the gods, Runa," she says, gazing up at the sky.

"Sýr, I know it the same way I know the stars. They do not lie."

Frigg grunts and starts sifting through her piles of wool, ignoring me now.

"Have you been listening to the villagers?" Sýr asks. "Or talking to the elder women?"

I shake my head. "Not really," I say. "But I guess I have heard some of them whispering as they do. They're concerned about keeping the stone in the clan, but I'm not. I believe in you."

Sýr nods, quiet now. It's true that there are villagers who are nervous that Sýr is not the chosen caster, having only inherited the stone from our mother on her deathbed.

I have never asked Sýr whether she is scared, because I already know the answer. I hear her crying when she thinks I am sleeping, and I know she longs for a simpler life with Frigg, raising horses and growing food and tending to animals. She longs for a home life free of pressure.

While I have longed to travel, Sýr has longed to stay, to root herself into the soil of our homeland even further. And yet soon she will have to go. I wonder if everyone's destiny is as confused as this. Is life just a trick the gods have played on us all?

Sýr scrunches up her face. "Oh no," she says, looking at someone behind me.

I turn to see a village woman, Hekla Vondursdóttir, walking over to us. She regards me with contempt and focuses on Sýr. She's a malicious person, with a hardened heart and demeanor to match. She never hesitates to use Sýr for anything she wants. I am too tired to deal with her today.

"Sýr," Hekla says, approaching with a noticeable limp. "I need a cure for my foot rot." She sits down with a thud and hefts her wide foot onto the table, banging her muddy boot into Sýr's tinctures and supplies. She then pulls off the boot. The stench turns my stomach. Her foot is green, as if moss is growing all over it. I look away.

"You know," says Hekla, her loud voice booming for all to hear, "I never had this foot problem until now. As well, my little horse died—the one we used to help carry our seeds—and we've had to live off the meat because my husband is still away with your father. Some are saying their ship has been lost in the great fog."

Sýr casts a sharp glance at me and shakes her head. She's warning me not to intervene, although all I want to do is smack this woman.

Hekla looks at me. "I won't say anything about the weirdling you have here. You are bad luck, eh, girl?"

Sýr bristles but continues mixing her potions together in quiet. If I had Sýr's power and ability, I'd punish this ugly woman. Maybe I'd make the foot rot spread to her face, so everyone could see how vile she truly is.

"We all think this bad luck has something to do with you," says Hekla to Sýr, who fumbles a small pot and spills green powder on her skirts. Frigg lays a calming hand on Sýr's shoulder and shoots a look at Hekla as sharp as any sword I've seen.

"Is that so?" Sýr asks, pinching the spilled powder from her skirts back into the jar with an unhurried grace.

"Yes," says Hekla. "It's the moonstone, isn't it? It's failing."

Sýr takes a deep breath. "The red moon is nigh," she says. "According to custom, the moonstone must be charged at moonwater to render it powerful again. You know this. It is the natural cycle of things. We've been through this before."

"No, that's not it, not like this," says Hekla. "It's you," she says, pointing a craggy fingernail at Sýr. "*You* never won the moonstone. You only inherited it from your dead mother.

It is ill-gotten." She leans back and crosses her arms, her mouth curled up in smug contempt.

Sýr stills at the mention of our mother. I want to grab the pot of crab and throw it at Hekla's head. But I do not, because we promised Father we would keep peace while he is gone, and because I know it would only cause more trouble for Sýr.

Hekla will not give in. "Why not let us see the moonstone, hmm?" she says, her voice taking on a forced kindness, as if she's speaking to a child. "See it? Give it a little touch? Hmm? Why not, eh?"

"Because you'd die," says Sýr, looking deep into Hekla's eyes.

Hekla recoils but continues ranting. "Why don't you use a wand? Or make sacrifices? We hear the Jötnar witch is powerful, maybe so powerful she will win the moonstone. Then where will our people be? We'll all starve."

I scoff at this, and Sýr shoots me a look. The Jötnar don't stand a chance of winning it back from us, as they don't have a runecaster as powerful as Sýr. Their head witch, a mysterious newcomer named Katla, is rumored to be obsessed with dark arts and animal magic. Our older kinfolk claim our two clans could be friends and even work together to ensure our mutual survival, but the witch Katla is said to have poisoned the minds of the Jötnar leaders and elders. Tales of atrocity and violence follow the witch, and those who encounter her say she's a nightmare in the flesh.

Some of our clan fear the evil Katla will win the moonstone, and clearly Hekla is one of them, but a caster who is not powerful or honorable enough to hold the moonstone will perish. It doesn't sound as if Katla has pure intentions for the stone.

"You are fools not to worry about the Jötnar's caster," Hekla says.

Sýr stands, her fury evident. "The Jötnar witch is not a runecaster," she says through gritted teeth. "*I* don't kill for my magic. *I* don't wear the skins of dead people like the Jötnar witch does. I am not a wand-weaver. I am a runecaster, and I will win the stone." Sýr is glowing with anger now, and I see her fingers trembling toward the moonstone around her neck.

I cast a nervous look at Frigg. Though its powers have lessened, the moonstone can still cause great harm, especially in the hands of a powerful caster like Sýr. And in the hands of an angry Sýr, it could be downright murderous. With my sister pushed to her limits and under the pressure of her obligations, I'm not sure what's going to happen.

Frigg steps in, her large frame coming between Sýr and the now-irate Hekla. Frigg is holding a stick, a thick sheep staff she calls Trollbonker. That is all she needs to do. The tension is broken. Hekla hobbles off in the mud, carrying her boot with her and casting nasty backward glances. I can hear her cursing us.

Sýr lets out a deep breath, her hands dropping to her sides.

Frigg turns to me. "Runa, go play," she says.

"*Play*?" I ask, incredulous.

Sýr's voice is weary. "Frigg, she doesn't play. Runa is almost a woman." She looks at me, seeming wistful for my long-past childhood years.

"She needs to go find a man then," says Frigg.

"You're one to talk, Frigg Baldersdóttir," exclaims Sýr.

"I'm all the man we'll ever need," says Frigg, and I take this as a sign to wander off.

Still, I can't help but sneak a look back. I like it when Frigg kisses Sýr, because she does so with the look of someone who can't believe their good fortune. I once asked Sýr if she had love-spelled Frigg to get her to behave such a way, but Sýr just laughed her quiet, shy laugh and said that it was genuine, and that Frigg was the luckiest thing ever to have happened to her apart from me.

As I walk away, I clutch my runes in their pouch and wish with all my love that Sýr has even better luck than that. *Please*, I beg the runes, *give my sister everything she dreams of.*

THREE

I spend the next couple of hours down at the shoreline, using the wind from my beloved sea to cool off my anger and blow away my worry as I reset some of my fishing lines. Hekla's ongoing disrespect is difficult to swallow, but hers is just one voice in an entire clan of people terrified to lose the moonstone.

I used to think that all a person needed was power, and then everyone would respect and care for them and treat them as they deserved to be. But I have learned through watching Sýr that having power can turn you into a slave of sorts if that power serves the needs of many. Our clan is lucky that Sýr isn't selfish, for she could use the moonstone to satisfy her own worldly desires. Instead she uses it to cure foot rot while her own feet go untended.

Despite my protests, we never require payments or trades to cast runes, as that is against the runecaster code. Instead we rely on our patrons to offer us things in exchange for our services. In older times, a caster would be a guest of honor and treated to fresh milk, organ meats, and a place at the head of the table. She would be bestowed with fine woven wool and gloves and hats. Those customs of the past are from a more prosperous time. Many of our clients are poor, though they are grateful for our services. They'll bring us a heel of bread, dried fish, a pinch of herbs, a bit of wool, whatever they have.

We don't often go hungry, for Sýr is talented at stretching what we have with her spells and the moonstone when needed, and I am decent at fishing and setting traps for small game. Our family is resourceful. Sýr eschews weapons in favor of her runes. I use my lines and traps. My amma uses her wits, and my father is fond of the axe.

No one I know uses a bow and arrow, as they are the domain of the wealthy and the elves, and my eye problems make it difficult to use the sling. My aim is terrible. Instead, like Amma, I use my smarts to trap things, setting deadfalls and snares for rabbits, creating basket traps for eel and crab, and pulling in nets of smallfish. So much of survival is preparation and patience.

I walk to the edge of the water and watch as it advances and then rolls away, over and over. Lately, I've been dreaming of deep water and of something circling me. Every time I have the dream it gets closer. I wonder how long I have left before it strikes.

There's something else about the dream. I keep seeing a face in the water. A face much like my own except older and sadder. She appears for a moment and then disappears into the depths so fast I'm not sure what I saw. It's as if my heart knows her. She isn't me, not the me I used to be, but she's someone important. My mother? I wish I had the courage to grab hold of her in the dream and follow her down into the cold, black water, but I'm afraid of what I'll find. I'm afraid I'll never wake.

My lungs fill with the salty air as a gust of wind blows over the bluff and hits me full force in the face. For a moment it feels as though I am deep underwater. I shake my head, willing the dreamy feeling away. I don't want to have an episode of my sickness right now.

Images of Sýr flash in my mind, and I keep seeing her face as if it is underwater. I'm dizzy, and I feel a hard lump form in my throat.

"No," I say aloud. "Don't do this here. Not now." I clench my hands until my fingernails dig into my palms. Sometimes the best way to stop the sickness is to hurt myself. I live inside the pain and focus on it until the sickness goes away.

When I feel calm again, I continue along the shoreline, passing by piles of broken clamshells and buzzing insects and stacks of kelp. A seabird circles overhead and cries out. I look into the reddening sky and squint at its brightness. The sky feels like a great, open mouth, widening to swallow us all.

"Hey!" a voice calls out.

The sudden noise shocks me enough that I can get out of my head for a second, and I look down the beach. Two girls are walking toward me. They are my age, and that's where the similarities stop. They are both tall, with golden blond hair and bright eyes that do not wiggle around in their heads like mine. They're smiling and waving at me, and for a second I wonder if there's someone standing behind me. I look over my shoulder, but there's no one there. I raise my hand, but I don't wave. They walk toward me, chattering to each other. Their apparent happiness makes me suspicious.

"Hallo," they both chirp in unison. They look at me as if expecting something. From afar they look like twins, but up close they have different features. One has a sharp nose and brown eyes. The other has an upturned nose and green eyes. Haraldr the Elder's daughters, Gerd and Siv. Haraldr is one of our clan's oldest people, and he fathered his children late in life. Some say that is why his daughters have an odd countenance.

"Um, hi," I say. In my drab clothing, I feel like a dark cloud that has invaded their sunshine.

Their eyes dart up and down my frame, taking in my garments, my hair, my eyes.

"You're Runa," says Gerd, in her absent way.

"Yes," I say. I don't remind her that we've spoken several times in the village. She would not remember, as it seems her thoughts fly away as soon as she has them. Amma would describe a person like this as having the spirit of a bird. I think that might not be so bad.

"We've heard your sister will travel to moonwater tonight," says Siv. "It's so exciting. Don't you wish you could go?"

"Tonight?" I say, as much to myself as to them.

"Yes," says Gerd. "The Jötnar have visited our father this day. Look, they are here in the village now."

I follow her gaze up the shore to see two large men, both of them with the square faces and immense stature of their legendary ancestors, standing guard outside a dwelling. Moments later a young man emerges. He is much taller and slighter than the guards, and he carries himself with an uneasy energy, as if he's expecting something to jump out at him. I wonder why he seems so nervous.

"Who is that?" I ask.

"That is Einar Ymirsson. He is the son of Ymir, the chief of the Jötnar," says Siv.

"Why is he here?" I ask, hoping these girls have paid close enough attention within their own dwelling to have useful knowledge beyond commonplace gossip.

"I don't know," says Gerd. "But I hope it's a marriage proposition." They both giggle.

I can't bring myself to join in their enthusiasm. I never want to be married.

I cast a glance to Frigg's stand but don't see my sister or Frigg. Where did they go? I hope Frigg stole Sýr away for a break.

Siv continues to admire Einar from afar. "He is gorgeous, isn't he?" she asks.

"Oh yes," says Gerd. "But can he be trusted?"

"Why wouldn't he?" I ask, confused. "Because he's Jötnar?"

"No," Gerd replies. "Because he's half elf."

I shrug. “Everyone has a little bit of elf blood in them. I do. I don’t see what that has to do with anything.”

They laugh. “No, not everyone has elf blood, Runa,” says Siv.

“And certainly not half,” her sister adds.

“Well,” I say, “I have never met an elf, so I wouldn’t know.”

Done with me, the girls both smile and then turn to scamper back up the beach, giggling the whole way. I know these are nice girls, but they are different from me, and a dark part of my mind suspects they are plotting to humiliate me. I try to push these thoughts away, but they are second nature. I’ve never understood how to make friends.

I feel the dreamy darkness start to take hold of my mind again. I walk to the water’s edge and again watch the waves break and pull back, over and over.

An image flashes in my mind. Sýr. Her face underwater again. I feel as though I am somewhere deep within the ocean. The water is cold and dark, and the current swirls, tossing my body like a limp strand of sea kelp. Then I feel the water shift around me, like something large is circling. Terror floods through me, because I know this thing is death, and it’s toying with me, waiting to strike. I close my eyes and wait for it, but it never comes.

I open my eyes, waking from my dark dream, and find I am up to my waist in the water. I step back and stumble on some rocks, falling into the lapping waves. Shocked by the cold, I run from the water and up the beach, soaked through. I rip off my icy cloak and am wringing out the front of my dress when my amma appears, holding a blanket.

"My girl," calls Amma, hurrying to take my arm. "Have you gone into a dream again?"

"I'm sorry," I say.

"Hush. Come on," she says, handing me the blanket. "You should be more careful at high tide. The undertow is strong here."

I nod. "I know, Amma."

"Besides," she continues, "you never know what might be out in that water."

I look at her and see a knowing expression on her face. It is kind but has a glint of amusement to it.

"Like what?" I ask, testing her.

"Oh," she says, "all manner of creatures, and not just green sharks. Strange things. Dark water spirits."

"Spirits?" I ask, thinking of the face I saw in the water.

"Yes," she says. "Did you see something? During your sickness?"

Amma is looking at me so intently, it feels as if she's staring into my soul. I want to give her an answer that will make sense, but I can't find the words.

"I..." I pause. "I don't know. My mind doesn't work the right way, I guess."

Amma nods. "I know, child," she says. "I know."

She reaches out her hand, and I take it. She turns and leads me back up the path.

"Come then, my ocean girl," she says, pulling me toward her dwelling.

I smile and follow her through the village. My amma has a way of making me feel like I belong to someone, and she never makes me feel bad about having my sickness. Amma thinks it is a gift that has yet to reveal itself. She always tries to see the good in everything. I can't bear to tell her that I don't think there's anything special about me. The truth is, I was born into a body that doesn't work the way it should, and wishing it was different or pretending I'm special doesn't help me. I have to learn to live with what I have.

We step inside Amma's hut, and I breathe easier. Her house always feels like home to me. Perhaps it's the scent of all her special herbs lined in neat rows. Or maybe it's the translucent stones she strings from strips of leather and dangles from the roofbeams. They clink together in a gentle music that calms me. As my father's mother, she benefits the most from the spoils of his adventures, collecting trinkets from faraway lands.

Amma's most treasured possessions are her scrolls. She has many of them, all written by people who lived long ago and in languages none of us can decipher. Sometimes she lets me touch the pages and feel how soft and thin their papers have become. I love the idea that these scrolls, with the ancient spells and potions contained within, are both strong with wisdom and physically vulnerable. My favorite ones are maps of strange lands and drawings of the sea and its currents. Our people come to Amma when they seek answers to questions about the world and about the vast realms most of us never get to see. A large scroll that seems to contain a map of all the waters of the world sits in a special place on Amma's hearth. One day I will ask to borrow that scroll and use it to sail the sea. As I daydream, I can almost feel the salt spray and wind on my face.

"You have such a sweet, brave *hugr*," says Amma, "the soul of a traveler." She loves to speak about these things, and can spend hours doing so.

She has arranged herself on a pile of furs, her short legs curled under her so that she becomes one with the soft folds around her. Amma always seems so in control, so calm, so unlike me, and I wonder what I inherited from her side of the family. These days I have begun defining others by how they are different from me. It seems the ways are limitless.

Amma notes my expression and my downcast eyes and makes a familiar clicking sound of disappointment at the back of her throat.

"My girl, I won't allow any self-pity in my home," she says, shaking her long silver hair. "Come," she says and extends a tattooed arm toward me.

As usual, I am hypnotized by the mysteries of Amma's skin and by the ink adorning it. Images of vines and roots and thorns and leaves curve and curl around her fingers, her wrists, her forearms and underneath her flowing robes. Her neck bears many fine thin lines, etched into it like the circles of a tree. She claims she has not had these lines applied but that they have appeared over time as she has aged.

I sit next to Amma on the hides and breathe in her earthy smell. I meet her eyes and feel like she is staring into my soul.

"My girl, you have questions," says Amma.

I nod. "I have these dreams. During my sickness. Of my mother, I think. They seem more confusing than before."

Amma purses her lips. "Of course," she says. "So much is changing now. You remind me of your mother." She speaks softly, as she always does when discussing this subject. "Your mother was also brave and sweet, and she was the most talented runecaster I've ever seen. I always wished for a power like that, but I am me, and my part in the great story of life is to be keeper of the dreams." She holds up a small scroll. "So many wonders within."

Amma leans forward and takes my hands. "Soon your sister will be leaving to find moonwater. But you needn't be afraid. You are special, and you will find your own way."

I sigh. As much as I would like to believe what Amma says, I cannot.

"You don't believe me," says Amma. "Well, that makes it hard to harness your own power, now doesn't it?"

"I'm sorry," I say.

"You mustn't be sorry. *You* decide your fate," she says. "And maybe a little gift will help."

Amma turns around and then produces a small bundle. She hands it to me, and I don't know what to say.

"Open it," she says.

I unfold the soft fabric, and inside is a golden cloak clasp in the shape of the vegvisir, the magical rune compass our people use whenever we embark on a sea voyage. It helps you find your way.

"Oh, Amma," I say. "It's beautiful. But why? I'm not going anywhere."

"Why not?" she says with a smile. "Maybe you can use it to find your way out on the sea." She winks at me.

Amma is the only one I can confess my desires to. She knows I dream of sailing on the open ocean.

"Seafaring is on my side of the bloodline," Amma says, the pride evident in her voice. "You get that from me."

I smile back, happy to share this with her.

"You are more than just one thing, Runa," she says. "More than a runecaster. More than your hair and your eyes. You are my granddaughter. Perhaps you will discover the next great land. And then take me with you!"

I laugh. She always knows just what to say. I suspect she has learned a lot from her many scrolls.

"Get rid of that old ugly pin and wear this new one," Amma says. "Don't save it for a special day. Perhaps today is the special day, já?"

"I will," I say. "Thank you, Amma."

"Now go change clothes before you freeze," she says.

I stand and walk to the door.

"Runa," says Amma. "Walk through the village with your head high. Show those other girls what they don't have." She smiles her wicked smile and waves me on.

Stepping out into the cold air, my wet clothing sticks to my body, and I feel eyes on me. I feel the wind in my hair, and then a sudden grip on my arm.

I spin around. It's Sýr. "There you are," I start, but she shushes me.

"I'm sorry, Runa. There's no time," she says. "I need you to go home as fast as possible and go into my cabinet and look for a blue pot with Bjarkan, the rune for *secret* etched on it."

"Why?" I ask. "Can I change first? I'm freezing."

"Why are you wet?" she asks, casting a furtive glance around her.

"What's wrong, Sýr?" Her manner is making me uneasy. Something isn't right.

"Nothing," she says. "I need that jar. Please go now."

"Okay, fine," I say. "I'll go." I shake her hand off, annoyed to be an errand girl.

I make my way back up the path to our clifftop home, my leather sack of wooden runes jangling. I imagine the carved pieces tumbling over one another, speaking to each other and casting the spell that would grant me the gift of freedom. The power to go anywhere. Yes, that would be something.

Sýr gave me these practice runes. A long time ago, when she was younger than I am now, she cut them from the bark of a birch tree and carved them in moonlight. At night I put them to bed under my pillow, and each morning I wake them. When I become a runecaster—if I ever do—I will need to make my own runes.

This is in the tradition of the first rune mother, the goddess Iduna, who in her wisdom carved the first runes on the tongue of a young god who visited her magical apple garden.

Many mornings and many nights I've sat atop our cliff, looking over the coastline and imagining setting sail in my own longboat. I see myself standing on new ground, places where the mud is not a dark purple and steam does not rise from the earth. Places where I can hear the strange sounds of a new language. Places where I can be someone else.

When I reach our hut, I go to my room and find my other dress. This one is thinner and even uglier than my wet one, but at least it's dry. I throw it on and then grab one of my father's old, heavy cloaks out of a trunk.

Núna's cry comes from outside the window, and I open it to greet her, but she isn't there.

I search the sky and spot my raven circling overhead, calling out in shrill alarm. From the village a thick plume of black smoke billows, and when the wind changes direction it carries with it the scent of burning flesh and the screams of my people.

FOUR

My heart clenches hard in my chest before thumping out of control. I take a deep breath and hold it, forcing the air down and bearing into it. Sometimes this helps make the erratic hammering slow back down to a steady rhythm. If I don't get my heart to calm itself, I will pass out. And I cannot lose consciousness. Not while there is such terror unfolding down in my village. I can't have my sickness. *Not now. Please, not now.*

From the window of the hut I cannot really see what is happening. I need to get to my lookout—a place farther up the path that I've built up out of rocks and odd stones and shells. I like to hide out there when I want to do nothing but stare at the sea and escape village life. From there, I will have a better view of the settlement below.

Scrambling through my room and out the door, I fall over the threshold and crack my knee. I rub it as I hobble as fast as I can through the chill of the evening to my lookout.

The air is acrid, filled with the scent of burning. *Don't look back*, I tell myself, hurrying to reach the safety of my rocky barricade. I give a final push of energy as I run up the steep path and throw myself, heaving and shaking, over the low rock wall. I lie there on my belly a moment, ignoring the pain of sharp rocks digging into my ribs, and then raise up on my knees to peek over the other side.

From here I can see everything. The open sea, the hills to the north, the rocky cliff path, and my village, now a scene of mayhem and fire. Jötnar warriors have come, and they are making their way through the village with ruthless speed. Sheep and horses run amok in a confused frenzy, having been released from their pens when the huge warriors invaded the stalls to kill the keepers. The Jötnar stab at animals and people alike with long spears or hack at them with axes as they run past. Sheep run headlong into burning piles, too stupid and scared to understand the danger. Those who escape the flames run instinctively for the high ground. Some scatter up and over the hillsides on the other side of the village, and others careen up the path toward me, only to fall over the perilous cliff edge to their deaths. Their bleating, sickening screams are matched only by the terrified sounds coming from my people.

Sýr. Where is Sýr? Panic flushes through me. I need her. I know I have to fight, but I have no weapons, and my runes and my skills are not strong enough to cast a spell of consequence.

Scanning the chaos, I try to find her among the men, women, and young ones fleeing their burning homes, but the smoke is too thick. And now there's something else obscuring my vision.

A yellow dust floats out over the village, swirling in menacing plumes, and I know right away that it is not a thing of nature. It is not of this realm. As the people of my clan hurl themselves into the throng to fight the invaders and try to protect one another, many of them drop to the ground as soon as they encounter the strange cloud.

I trace the path of the plume to a higher point on the hills and see two men standing together. The larger of the two, a massive Jötnar warrior, is blowing the yellow dust from a long horn. I can't see well through the haze, but then the wind shifts, and for a moment I see the other figure. I can tell by the tall, lean frame that it's Einar Ymirsson, the Jötnar heir, the one the girls were giggling about. He's mixing something in a pot on the ground. As I watch, he scoops a yellow mixture into the horn for the enforcer to blow over my village. It is *his* doing! *His* poison that is felling my people! Einar's expression is unreadable, and the warrior continues to blow.

"Damn you!" I cry, directing all my fury at them. I clutch my runes. I have no confidence that a spell will work, but I will try.

"Einar Ymirsson of the Jötnar," I say, standing to get a better look at him, "I will cast you into the realm of Hel, and even the dead will shun you there."

Einar stops mixing and looks up. I drop back down, my heart once again skipping and the terror clenching my chest. I may die from fear. I have no way of knowing if he saw me, but it feels like he did. Though his eyes are not visible from this distance, something inside of me felt seen. *Don't panic.* I try to calm my heart again, but I feel my grasp on this realm slipping.

No. I have to stay here for Sýr. I cannot fall into my sickness. Not now. The air around me swirls, flashing lights in a sea of white, and I drift into the forgetting dream again.

I wander in a fog-filled graveyard. All around me are the markers of the burial places of my people. I pause in front of a large stone marked with a blue circle. I know Sýr is buried here. I don't know how or why I know, but the knowledge is in my bones. I drop to my knees and place my hands on the smooth rock. I will resurrect her. I will find a way.

Stay with me.

Sýr's voice. She's leading me through the fog. I follow her voice as it beckons. The haze clears a little, and I can see her waiting for me.

Sýr, I call out, but she doesn't answer. She stares at me with a sad look and then opens her cloak to reveal a deep wound in her belly.

I hurry toward her, but as soon as I reach her, she disappears. I jerk back to reality again, my ears filled afresh with the screams of my people.

There aren't as many crying out now. This time, when I peek over the rock wall of my lookout, there are just a few people left standing.

I see Haraldr the Elder being dragged from his dwelling by Ymir, the Jötnar chief. Ymir had earned the name Ymir the Devourer, for both his ferocity in battle and his insatiable appetite. He once consumed an entire sheep in one sitting, including the offal and the marrow. That Ymir was a hulking, powerful man, but this Ymir is smaller and wasted down, as though starving.

I watch in horror as he stomps on Haraldr the Elder until the man is dead, the blows coming with sickening force. The old man cannot defend himself. I struggle to make sense of what I'm seeing. Ymir is known to be a warring man, but not a cruel one. I have not heard tales of him being such a coward as to kill an elder. So why this? Why now?

I get my answer when another figure emerges from the dwelling behind Ymir. It's a woman clad in a golden robe, with yellow hair that flows in serpentine locks around her face. Her demeanor is relaxed, as though this is any other day and the carnage taking place around her is a common thing. But in the next moment, power glows from her, crackling with energy, and I understand that this is all because of her. I blink, trying to get a better look at the woman, but my eyes keep jumping around, making it hard to focus. It's not just my eyes though. There's something about her. Her image keeps bouncing, and I can't fix my gaze on her. It's as if she has shrouded herself with an obscuring spell.

This must be Katla, the mysterious sorceress said to have infiltrated the Jötnar clan. No one knows where she came from, and many think she is hungry for power and intent on taking over the Jötnar. To what end, I cannot imagine.

She is magnificent to look at—and terrifying. She changes even as I am looking at her. At times she resembles a beautiful young woman, and at others her face looks withered and scaly. Her black eyes are unblinking, like a serpent's, and she seems to grow and shrink in size. I must be seeing things.

When she moves, she appears to glide over the ground. I cannot look away, even though it hurts my eyes to look at her, the way staring at the sun makes them burn and water.

Helpless, I watch as Katla directs the Jötnar to kill the last of the fleeing villagers. I see movement on the hillside, as Einar the dust-maker runs toward the violence with the long horn in his hands. He probably wants to murder more of my people. He's making his way to his father and to Katla, arriving as they close in on the last two figures remaining.

Sýr. And Frigg.

My sister and her lover stand together, stoic, clasping one another, their backs against the wall of a dwelling as its roof smolders.

I can see that Frigg is holding Trollbonker out in warning.

Katla and Ymir advance toward them.

There is no time. I must cast a protection spell. I pull my Ýr rune from my pouch. "Give me the power of the yew," I say, unwrapping the bandage on my thumb. I squeeze blood out onto my runestone and then use it to form the

Ægishjálmr, the Helm of Awe, on the dirt in front of me. This is the bindrune we use to overcome enemies.

"Please," I whisper to the rune, begging as my blood drips over the soil of my homeland. "Protect Sýr. Please."

But I know it won't work, for I am too scared, and casting this rune requires confidence.

As I watch, Frigg charges at Katla, but one of the Jötnar guards strides forward, his sword aimed straight at Frigg's heart. Before the blade can pierce her body, Einar blows a plume of dust at Frigg. She freezes and collapses to the ground, a look of surprise and pain on her face.

My sister screams, and the sound is an assault on my heart. Even the stones of my lookout seem to rattle from the force of her anguish. I have never seen Sýr so full of rage. My gentle sister is now aglow with hatred, but for some reason she doesn't act. She doesn't run or fight.

Katla, holding a dagger now, advances on Sýr. The weapon is sharp and menacing, but as Katla draws closer, Einar steps forward and hands her the horn. He says something to her, but from up here I cannot decipher his words.

Sýr chooses this moment to wield the flickering moonstone, holding it high above her head so that its light flashes over her in a frantic rhythm, like a heartbeat close to stopping. I pray to Freyja that Sýr's own heart doesn't fail her. Though the stone seems to be failing, my sister mouths a spell I cannot hear but that I imagine must be one of protection.

In response Katla blows the dust at Sýr.

It has little effect on Sýr, for her spell acts as a shield, and the cloud dissipates as soon as it reaches her.

Now the two witches are locked in a silent battle, hands outstretched, each of them directing all her power at the other. Sýr's blue light extends outward, pulsing at Katla, and Katla responds with her own yellow glow. I don't see a stone or amulet or wand in Katla's possession. The energy with which she's fighting Sýr seems to be coming from her own hands. I've never seen anything like it before. Though Katla and Sýr are standing still, glaring at one another, I know each of them is using everything she has to gain control of the other.

"Sýr," I say. "I believe in you." I rub the protection rune once more, saying its name, and use all of my love to direct its power toward my sister.

It's almost as if my little spell causes a hiccup in the action, because as I intone the words, both Sýr and Katla turn toward me, looking up from the village below to where I am standing, now in full view, on the clifftop.

Sýr smiles at me and says something, but as Katla looks at me, she somehow has two faces. One is staring at me in fury, the other at Sýr with vicious glee.

Sýr holds up the moonstone. For a moment I think she is going to throw it or crack it on the rocks at her feet. Does she mean to destroy the coveted stone? Could she?

Instead Sýr tosses it up into the air. It does not come back down again. In a flash of blue light, the stone disappears.

Katla screams a wail of despair so high-pitched it rings in my ears until it feels like my head will split open. Sýr and

Einar clutch their heads in pain too, and I watch as my sister falls to her knees. Ymir appears unaffected, standing still and expressionless until Katla gives him an order. A witch commanding a chief? He steps forward and searches Sýr for the stone, ripping at her garments. Sýr continues to kneel on the ground and doesn't fight. She ignores Ymir and keeps her gaze, tender and sad, on Frigg's lifeless body.

Sýr glances up at me for one brief moment. As she does, I hear her voice, distinct in my mind. *It will always be the two of us, Runa. Until the end of time.*

Ymir, having no luck finding the moonstone, lifts his sword to strike Sýr, but a small movement from Katla stops him.

Two large Jötnar warriors step forward and grab Sýr. They drag her toward Katla and pull her to standing as the witch takes out a long rope from inside her robe. I can see that it's made of the same kind of silky fabric as her cloak, complete with a yellow-and-white diamond pattern. She uses it to bind Sýr's hands and then confiscates the sack of runes hanging from Sýr's neck. I realize in horror that they intend to take my sister with them as their captive. The only reason they have spared her is because they desire the moonstone.

I long to call out, to chase after them, but I know I am powerless. At least Sýr is not dead. Not yet. But I know they will kill her as soon as Katla can decipher whatever spell Sýr used to make the moonstone disappear.

I am so busy watching my sister being dragged away that at first I don't notice Katla looking up at me from amid the devastation. As bodies burn and my village lies in ruins, the witch smiles a sick smile, her mouth wide and filled with sharp-looking teeth, her eyes flat and unfeeling.

Our eyes meet, and her image finally stops bouncing around and comes into clear focus. For a moment she is locked in my gaze. My hearts feels as though it will stop in my chest, and I gasp for breath.

No. Not now. The edges of my vision blur as Katla reaches into her cloak and pulls out a thin dagger that drips with a glowing substance. Poison? I try to move, to scream, but I cannot.

With a silent spell spitting out between her teeth, Katla hurls the dagger at me, and I watch, paralyzed with fear, as it flies through the air and strikes me in the chest with a thud. It feels like a shard of ice has pierced me through, so cold it feels hot. Once it is embedded in my chest, it seems to disappear. There is no blood, only agony.

I fall backward onto the rocks of my lookout, splayed like a sacrifice to the gods, my eyes open to the darkening red sky. A plaintive cry floats out over the village. Turning my head, I see Sýr. She has seen me take this hit and calls out to me before falling limp in the grasp of the Jötnar guards, her strength sapped.

They drag Sýr along as Katla cackles, Ymir following her. His mindless obedience and stiff way of walking reminds me of a draugr, the undead creatures powered by witchcraft that Amma has told me about. Only Einar seems free from the control spell afflicting the other Jötnar, and he stands staring at me from afar. He stays that way for a long while, and I'm starting to wonder if he's planning on coming back to finish me off. Finally, Katla calls him away. He turns but casts a backward glance at me.

I reach out my hand, trying to will a spell to leave my fingertips and travel on the wind to punish him and make him suffer, but my arm falls limp. The pain in my chest is too great, and the sight of my sister, unconscious and enslaved, has broken my heart.

I struggle to stay in this realm. Perhaps I am trapped in a terrible dream. None of it can be real. I'm not here, this isn't now, and when I wake up, Sýr will be here. The whole world is covered in the blood of my people, and darkness comes to consume me.

FIVE

I am lost in a dark place. The silence is the worst part. I see flashes of the slaughter of my people and the capturing of Sýr, but it's like watching everything unfold from far away and through water. I see Einar, and he looks as if he's trying to tell me something. But I don't want to hear it. I struggle to retreat, move away from him, or fight, but I cannot.

Sýr's face hovers over mine. *Stay with me*. She is gone again too soon, replaced by Katla's laughing face. *No*. I have to find my way back to myself. *Wake up, Runa. Wake up*.

A bright flash of lightning jolts me awake and freezes the night sky in jagged relief. A drenching rain pours over everything. The sea below rages with waves that will destroy the small skiffs left untended on the beach. My lines and traps and nets will all be lost at this rate, but none of that matters. The sky booms and rumbles, as if Thor himself is angry with us.

I search the heavens for a sign of Núna, but she is nowhere. I pray the Jötnar didn't kill her with their yellow dust. I want to call out to her, but my voice won't come. When I open my mouth, sadness sucks my air from me.

And Amma? What of my amma? I did not see her in the turmoil, and I pray to Freyja that she was hiding when that strange cloud blew over our village. If she doesn't know, how will I tell her that Sýr is gone? Frigg is dead, and so many of our clan too. I fear that I have lost all of them. *Please, not Amma.* What will become of us? Of me? And Father? Even if he finds his way back to us, there will be nothing left. We are in ruins.

I sit up, groaning at the pain in my chest. My mind flashes back to the dripping dagger Katla hurled into me. Was it real? Magic? There is a faint mark on my chest. It could be the shape of a crescent moon, or perhaps a fang. I touch it with trembling fingertips, the light graze shooting a deep ache all the way through to my back. I gag and then vomit a thin, yellow fluid.

The dagger must be embedded within me, but how can that be? With my thumb I squeeze a few drops of blood out of the cut and use it to make the sickness rune of Hagall on top of the mark on my chest, shuddering at the sensation. Whatever Katla impaled me with, I must fight against it, for I can feel a cold ache spreading throughout my body now. It could be from the rain that has been soaking me while I lay here unconscious for hours or from the wind that rattles me now, but I know within myself that the ache is from the witch's dagger. The physical pain mixes with my deep fear that everyone I know and love is gone.

I cannot give into the sadness spreading through me like poison. I must get up. I must find Amma. *Get up*, Runa. *Get up*.

My village is blanketed in the black robes of night as I struggle to my feet. The usual torches and tallow candles are unlit. There is no one left to light them.

I stumble over the rocks surrounding my lookout and make my way back to the little dwelling Sýr and I share. Pushing open the door, I see there are still some coals glowing in the hearth, and I stagger toward them to try to warm myself. A stub of tallow candle sits on the stones next to the fire, and I ignite it on the coals and place it in its holder. Shivering, I carry it through my empty home to light the way, stopping to share the flame with other stubs, until I have enough light to see that I am alone in a way I have never been in my life before. When there's no one else around, the world seems an unkind place. Even the beloved objects around me, the tools and trinkets of daily life, take on an air of indifference that is almost sinister. How can an empty bowl feel like a punch to the guts? I don't know, but it can.

I'm so cold, but I have no time to change. I grab the patched sheepskin hanging across the entrance to my room and throw it over my shoulders, its heavy weight and musty smell a welcome reminder of Frigg's wares, and her generosity with them. She always made sure Sýr and I had warm hides if we needed them. I will miss her kindness, her bravery.

I fight back the tears. There is no time to cry. I have to go down to the village, and I have to be strong, for I need to find Amma and check for survivors. I believe the Jötnar have left, but they could have sent assassins to finish off anyone who escaped the first wave of the raid.

We have no real weapons here save for basic hunting and fishing tools, but I remember that Sýr and I once found a long fishing spear on one of our shoreline explorations. I search through our collection of walking sticks and sheep staffs in the back corner until I find it, recognizing its unusual feel in my hand.

The material is unlike any other I've seen. It's pale and shimmering, not at all like wood, and the spear is too long to be made of bone. I've also never seen bone with an iridescent sheen like this. Swirling designs much like waves are carved into its length. On the shaft end there is a fitted stone cap made of a brown translucent rock that suffered a crack at some point. The other end is sharpened into a fine-tipped spear with a curved hook. It's a long spear, much taller than I am, and it looks like something from a distant land. When we found it I begged Sýr to let me keep it, and she relented, even though she was sure we could have gotten a good trade for it in the market. There was something about it that I loved.

It's lightweight but also strong. It's pale and fragile-looking but also deadly. These are the qualities I hoped I'd develop one day, and I dreamed I'd get there with Sýr's guidance. I know now that the future I imagined is gone, and I will be lucky to survive the night. The Jötnar will murder me when I descend to the village, or the magical dagger Katla stabbed me with will freeze my heart, or the deep loneliness I feel now will end me. As I stand in my empty little home without my sister, my truest friend, I feel this with a stark clarity.

A sob builds in my throat, and I clamp my free hand over my mouth. *Be brave, Runa. Amma needs you.* Sýr's voice in my mind, as always, though I must be imagining it now. Sýr is gone and I'm on my own, but of course this is what she would say.

I cannot descend to the village along the cliff path without a light. I would fall to my death, despite my knowledge of the terrain, but I cannot walk out of here with a lit torch in case the killers are waiting. They would never encounter an easier target.

I need to light my way. A rune spell? Yes, of course. I open my pouch of practice runes and pour them out on the table.

With shaking hands, I touch them all, trying to be tender and unhurried so as not to offend or rush them.

"Now," I whisper, "please help me. I need to light my way. I ask you to be a guiding light for me."

I arrange my runes in the shape of Sól, the rune for the sun, and close my eyes to try to imagine the warmth of the summer sun, the heat of a bonfire, the flicker of a candle.

To cast a rune, I must trust my feelings, and I must live in the present moment. A runecaster who wants to cast a vengeance spell must feel the rage within and harness it to achieve their goal. A runecaster who wants to make a marriage spell to join two people together must understand romantic love. The most difficult runes to cast are ones that combine complex emotions and elements from the physical world. Heat and fire and love and passion. Cold and ice and contempt and war. The runes of time and of invisibility and mastery over death have eluded runecasters throughout our history, for these are difficult to experience.

After a few minutes my hands begin to tingle. I open my eyes, and the runes are glowing. I can't believe it worked. "Thank you," I whisper. The last time I tried this spell, I started a fire by accident and destroyed a large pile of moss Sýr had been saving for soup.

I gather the runes and place them back in the pouch hanging around my neck. It glows enough to help me see a few inches in front of me. If I hold the pouch out from my body and walk along in a crouch, this should work, and the light is not so bright that it can be seen from afar. It will have to do.

I creep out the door, holding my spear in front of me to steady me on the path, and I half-crouch, half-walk down the rocky cliff side toward my village, the runes glowing enough to show me where the edge of the path falls into darkness. I can't see the black, raging sea below, but I feel it. The sea goddess Rán beckons, and I wonder if the ocean hungers the way people do. I say the rune of the sea, Lögr, *Please don't kill me this night.*

Going along my path a few feet at a time has a calming effect on me. Any other time, I'd be panicking about what was about to happen next or what I'd find at the village, but being forced to focus on the space in front of me is soothing somehow, and I'm grateful.

The rocky path gives way to wet sand, and the spray from the violent waves hits me in the face. Sneaking up the banks to the village enclave, I listen for any sounds of life, for murderous Jötnar, for the injured, for anything. All I can hear is the wail of the wind over the pounding of my own heart.

Any fires set by the Jötnar have long since burned out or been extinguished by the heavy rains, and I find myself standing in the village center with the dead bodies of my clan piled around me, all life suspended at once, all work and survival and busyness halted.

Each one of my clanspeople awakened this morning with the day stretching out in front of them. They were certain of the time they had, focused on the fish they needed to catch, the goats they needed to slaughter, the people they needed to love. Now that is over, and I am here. Alone. The wind wails. The sea churns. And death doesn't care.

Despair pours over me and chills me more than the rain. I cry out as thunder slams the sky. It is followed by a strike of lightning, too close, and I jump when I see a standing figure briefly illuminated by the light of Thor's bolt. I crouch with my spear raised. If I'm going to die, it will be fighting.

"Say your name," I command over the wind. My voice comes out much stronger than I expected.

The figure does not answer. Thor's great show of rage and power continues to drum and flash overhead, lighting up the shape of the motionless body over and over. It makes no sound, no advance. It is as still as a dead man.

I step toward it, moving closer to where it waits, solid and unyielding as stone, between the remains of the stalls and dwellings of my people.

Closer I edge, and I hold up my glowing runes to give me light between the flashes. Still the dark figure looms unmoving.

I am a spear's length from it now.

"What say you?" I ask. "I demand to know."

It does not answer.

"By the goddess Freyja and her armies, I command you to speak," I say, giving the figure a poke. The sharp tip of my spear squelches into its shoulder. A dagger of lightning, bigger than the rest, sizzles above me, striking the half-burned roof of a nearby dwelling, and the figure's face reveals itself in the firelight.

It's one of the village woodsmiths, Sveinn Sigurdson. My father sought him out whenever he needed quality axe handles. Now here Sveinn stands, still as a tree himself, transfixed by a power I don't understand, and I realize with horror that the tip of my spear is still poking into him. I withdraw it in haste.

"I'm sorry," I say, the wind howling around us, but Sveinn does not react. His eyes are glazed over, and I wonder if the strange dust Einar blew over the clan is to blame. Indeed, I spot smudges of yellow around Sveinn's nostrils.

I place a hand on the man's shoulder, and even though he is one of my own, his countenance is terrifying. I give him a little shake, hoping to wake him, but if a spear to the shoulder did not jostle him, what will a gentle nudge do? I must push a little too hard, because he falls backward, thudding to the wet ground like a tree falling.

"I'm sorry," I say again, crouching next to him. I realize now that the woodsmith is not alone in his strange state. All around me, lit by the flashing night sky, are people I know, stiff and unmoving, as if they have been robbed of their souls. Some are standing, some are lying on the ground. Some are sitting, some still holding their arms and hands out in the pose they were in when the dust hit them.

I rush to each of them in turn, waving my hand in their faces, jostling them, calling their names. I check each one, but none of them respond to me. I am invisible to them.

As far as I can tell, they are alive. I've seen my share of dead people. These villagers aren't bloated or mottled or stinking or stiff, as at least some of them would be by now if they were dead. It doesn't take long for the bugs and the worms to find the dead, but there are none on these bodies. They're as they were in life, but frozen.

Frigg! She was felled by the dust too, and I must find her. I am frantic as I search for her body. So many of my village landmarks have been destroyed, and the flashing sky makes it even harder for me to see than usual. My eyes have never been reliable at night, and now I feel near-blind.

At last I find her, and my heart surges with hope that I can wake her. She is curled on her side in the mud, and she looks much smaller this way. I brush her hair back from her face and see that the rain is falling into her open eyes. Gently I try to close them, but no part of her will move. I try to pull her over to a half-burned shed, but she is too heavy, and I curse my own weakness.

I will not leave her exposed, so I gather as much unburned wood and scraps of fabric as I can find and create a makeshift shelter for her. It's not much, but it keeps the rain from her face.

I kneel next to her under the hastily made canopy and make promises as the storm rages around us. "I will go and find Sýr, and she will help you, Frigg. I swear this to you. I won't let you stay like this forever."

I hold my runes and whisper to them as I weep, begging them to undo the curse, but it doesn't work. I use more of my own blood to make protection marks on Frigg's forehead in hopes that it will keep her safe. After covering her in hides and blankets, I make my way through the village and cast safety spells on all my frozen people.

"Girl." A weak voice in the darkness startles me. I spin around, holding out my glowing runes and my spear.

There, slumped by a swordsmith's hut, is my grandmother.

"Amma," I cry, rushing to her.

Amma is not frozen in time. She is not stiff and cold and petrified in position. Amma is dying the ordinary way, having been run through by a sword. I know this because the large, rough-hewn metal is sticking out of her belly. Dark blood seeps from the wound, and I dare not try to remove the sword.

"Amma, no," I whimper.

She reaches to stroke my cheek. "Don't cry, love. Don't despair. I die as I lived."

"Please," I say. "We can get help." Even as I say the words, I know they are not true. There would be no saving Amma from this wound even if the entire village weren't under a spell.

Amma chuckles. "I tried to get to the swords. To fight them. The bastards were faster than me. But I got in a few chops, my girl. Don't worry."

I can't help but smile. My tough old Amma.

"You'll go to Valhalla," I say. "And live with the gods."

"Pish," Amma scoffs. "Give me a little hut on the hill. Maybe some hákarl," she adds, coughing out the words.

Hákarl. I remember the treat Sýr left for me, and I pull the piece I saved out of my pocket. How long ago this morning seems now. "Here," I say, unwrapping the hákarl from the moss and offering it to her.

Amma sniffs it. "Ah, you are a good girl. The best girl. I always knew that."

I am crying again as Amma takes a tiny nibble of the flesh I put to her lips. She is so fragile it makes my heart hurt.

"I'm sorry," I say.

"Don't," Amma chokes out. "I am dying now, and I cannot leave this realm unless I know you will be all right."

I nod. "I am fine," I lie. "I'm not hurt." I don't tell her about the magical dagger Katla stabbed me with.

"Runa. My Runa."

"Yes, Amma. I am here."

"Please, send me to sea when I am dead. I want to travel to my son, wherever he is. Perhaps I will find him again in the great fog."

I nod, incapable of speaking.

Amma whispers, and I strain to hear. "A true descendant of the gods may wield the moonstone."

"Amma, I don't know what you mean. What do you mean?" I ask.

Her eyes roll back into her head, and she shivers so hard her teeth chatter.

"Amma, don't leave me too."

"You must fight, my girl," she says. "You must travel to moonwater. You must follow the red moon and the stars until you see the great green lights to the north."

I shake my head. "I can't, Amma. I'm all alone. I don't know how."

"Find a way, or the clan is doomed," she says. "We are all doomed."

I look around at the cursed figures of my village. My love for them breeds the tiniest of hopes that maybe, if I can find Katla and if the gods are on my side, I can undo this dark magic.

"Runa," says Amma, "I loved you before you were here."

I hold tightly to her, willing her to die soon and without pain, but that is not what happens.

It takes all night for Amma to leave the realm of the living. It is not quick. It is not painless. She sees things, visions, that make no sense. She wails and cries and calls for her own mother. I have never felt such love and such hatred all at one time.

By morning the storm has subsided and the dark sky gives way to a golden dawn that bathes the horror of my home in a light so beautiful it doesn't seem fair. I carry the wasted body of my grandmother to the shore and rest her on a broken fishing raft I find there.

After giving her a kiss, I use her own blood to write the vegvisir on her chest, and then I set her adrift in the cold waters.

"Farewell, Amma," I whisper. "I love you."

I watch her little raft until it disappears on the horizon. In the bright morning light I think I see something dark fall through the air in the distance. But I tell myself I must be seeing things. My eyes hurt. I'm tired and cold, and I feel like walking into the ocean after my grandmother. Maybe now is the best time to die.

I hear a piercing cry and look up to see Núna flying toward me. She alights on my shoulder, and I sob, sinking down onto the black sand. I stay like that for a long time, my raven a quiet comfort.

I don't know if I pass out from exhaustion or if I have my sickness again, but I enter a dark dream. In it I see Katla, her eyes dead and black. She transforms into a giant serpent that swallows Sýr and Amma and everyone I know. Then the serpent comes for me. *Grabak*. I hear the name in my mind, and at first I am terrified, but then I become angry. I feel myself growing larger, until I am bigger than the serpent. I open my mouth, unhinging my jaw, and swallow the Katla serpent whole. It bites the inside of my throat, and I can feel it wriggling in my chest. I drink buckets of seawater to wash it down, but it hangs on, and I wonder how long it will take to die now that it is in my stomach. I feel it squirm, biting my insides until I can taste the blood in the back of my mouth. All I can do is keep swallowing and hope that it doesn't climb back up.

When I awake, Núna is sitting on my chest, her claws digging into me, and I am flat on my back on the black sand, the cold water lapping at my legs. I am so cold that I can't move well, and if I don't get warm soon, I will die. I pull myself up with great effort, the pain shooting through my chest, and I gather my shining spear, my runes, and my sheepskin.

"Thank you, Núna," I say, the words strangling in my throat. "You brought me back. Now we have work to do."

Núna squawks and flies off ahead of me toward my hut. I head up the cliff path, avoiding the scene of my destroyed village and my cursed clan, and as I walk I grow a little warmer. I feel my anger growing too. Each step I take drives it down into the center of me. I know some things now for certain.

I will honor my amma, and fulfill my promises to my clan, by finding a cure. I will travel to moonwater and bring my sister home. Together we will set things right, and Katla and the Jötnar will regret ever setting foot on our shores. And if I find Einar, mixer of dust, I will make him eat his own poison.

SIX

My home seems smaller in this new light, as does everything I look upon. It's as if the world has shrunk since the Jötnar attacked. I wonder if it is my perception or if it's a result of the strange dust Katla's errand boy made. It has given everything a sickly yellow sheen.

I don't understand why Einar created that dust, for all the talk of him has been about his physical beauty and his smarts and his desirability as heir to a great clan—not tales of violence or betrayal. Despite the Jötnar clan's history as warring giants, they've always been a just people. Ymir the Devourer was feared by many, but not for being a tyrant. Now he is a shadow of himself, made into a slack-faced slave by Katla. How many others is she controlling? In a moment of horror, I imagine the whole island, all the clans and magic folk alike, under her command. What if I'm the only one left unharmed?

I push away the thoughts that threaten to spiral me into a panic. I hurry to light and stoke a fire, my frozen hands struggling to strike the rocks. Finally I am able to make a spark against the dried moss we have stashed in a basket. Once the moss ignites, I feed smaller driftwood into it until the flames lick, and then I place larger birch on top. We don't like to have long-burning fires in our village. We warm our homes as much as is needed to make them comfortable and then conserve the wood, as our forests are dwindling and wood is not plentiful. But I want this fire to be a blaze as big as possible, for the chill inside me is growing.

I strip off my soaked garments and shudder naked next to the flames. My chest is the coldest part of my body. I fear Katla has pierced my heart with a shard of ice. That's what it feels like. I use a piece of scratchy wool cloth to rub my hair as dry as I can while I sit beside the fire. Violent shivers rack my body, as much from fear as the cold.

Once I am pink-skinned again, and I can feel the tingling pains in my fingers and toes that tell me I won't be losing them altogether, I focus on warming my insides. Sýr always says seaweed and island moss are the best healing ingredients, so I place bunches of both in our large pot and add leftover dried fish and water until the mixture is bubbling. I drink down the hot soup until it threatens to come back up.

It feels wrong to eat and to enjoy this warmth while much of my clan lies dead and the rest are frozen outside. Even if I can find Sýr and she can cure them, I don't know if they will die anyway from cold or starvation or who knows what else. And if they perish, what will happen to their souls? Will they be frozen too? Or will their spirits ascend to Valhalla or Freyja's Field?

"I vow that I will return, and if we can't save you, I will give every one of you a proper funeral," I say to the empty room. My heart's pain flows out of me, and I imagine it covering my entire village with a glowing light.

It will take a long time, if I am alone, to build rafts for each person and set them all ablaze on the ocean, but even if it takes months, I will accomplish it. I still have hope that Father will return, but he has been gone for long periods before. Once he left when I was three and didn't return until after my twelfth birthday. I remember how he looked at me when he saw me again. I am sure I was not at all what he'd expected, for he'd left a happy sprite and returned to a gangling freak who caused nothing but problems. It's no wonder he likes to stay away for so long.

The red light of the sky changes its patterns on my floor. The day is getting longer, and if I am going to try to find moonwater and embark on the most dangerous journey of my short life, I must set out soon. I know it is practical to travel during the day, so as to cover as much ground as possible in the light, and leaving at dawn would be best. But I also know that I cannot stand one more night alone here with my near-dead clan.

The wincing pain in my chest has given way to a dull ache. I try to set it aside as I get ready.

I take Sýr's pot of cure-all salve from the shelf and rub some on the crescent mark on my chest before placing the pot in a large pack our family used in the past to transport goods on horseback. We've long since grown too poor to own horses, and the Jötnar made sure to kill all the remaining animals in our village during the raid, so it will be up to me to carry the bag. I will have to be careful when I choose what to bring. First I need to find clothes.

Both of my regular dresses are soaked through, so I put on two pairs of my own woolen leggings and socks and then scour Sýr's sleeping area for a spare. I find an old brown knit dress that is too short but could work as a tunic. I decide to wear that and then find a heavier gray dress I can bring with me. A black lambs-wool cap and rabbit-skin gloves will keep me warm, and I also grab Sýr's spare boots, which are still a couple of sizes too big for me. Another pair of socks will help fill in the space. In a back corner I find a heavy old cloak that is much too large and must have belonged to my father. It smells awful, but it is warm, and placing it over me gives me a small sense of protection.

On to supplies. I pack some small, sharp knives and snares for finding and cleaning game, along with some fishing lines and hooks. Though I will be venturing far from the coastline, I will still have opportunity to fish in the streams I find along the way. I will be sure to bring my special spear stick. Maybe I will use it to impale Katla.

I will bring a small axe for chopping wood—it's too tiny to be a killing instrument—and a fire-rock with a sack of dry moss and fine wood shavings. Some tallow to use as a candle to light the darkness, some rope, and a small cooking pot. I will have no shelter and will need to find or make it each night, but I am hoping the journey will not be too long.

As no one knows exactly where moonwater will be, and I don't know which path Katla has taken with Sýr, it could be many days. All I know is that I must follow the red moon to the green lights in the north, and I must be there before the red moon eclipses, for that is when the competition will start.

I make sure to place my runes around my neck, as they will be my most valuable companions. We don't trust each other yet, me and these runes, because I make so many mistakes, and they don't always seem to listen to me, but they're the best chance I've got.

I will also need food, so I gather grains for porridge, dried fish, moss, seaweed, dried goat, a jug of whey, a jug of mead, some roots and a prized hunk of whale blubber we've been keeping for a long time. Our clan rarely takes in a whale, but when we do, it feeds us for years. This blubber will give me food or fire when I need it.

Next I gather potions. Sýr has so many tiny pots with bits of herbs and powders that I can't take them all, and I don't know enough about her oils or tinctures yet to know which ones would be most useful on my journey. But I do know I should take the angelica in case of illness, and I also take her healing salves.

I open the large wooden trunk in Sýr's room and am surprised to find it empty except for a bit of cloth.

How can this be? I have seen Sýr putting things in here all the time. I know the Jötnar didn't take anything because no one has disturbed our dwelling. Looking closer, I see that the bit of cloth on the bottom of the trunk is a runecloth used for casting.

Maybe Sýr used an obscurity spell? I take out my runes with shaking hands and try to quiet my mind, but it's so hard. I want Sýr. I cast my runes onto the cloth.

"Appear," I command and then wait. Nothing.

Perhaps an unlocking spell?

I try again. "Open to me," I say.

This time there is a glimmer on the cloth. Runes appear, and I read them. "*Say the name my heart cherishes, and I will open to you.*"

The name her heart cherishes? It must be Frigg. I say, "Frigg," but nothing happens.

"Amma," I try. Nothing.

I take a deep breath and then whisper my own name. "Runa."

The cloth bursts into a flash of blue flame, revealing a secret latch near the bottom of the trunk. I pull it open and find Sýr's hidden possessions. Pressed flowers, gifts from Frigg, a vial of shiny powder, a feather, and a ring that I slip onto my first finger. And there is a last item that makes me sit back and cry.

It is a black cloak, magnificent in its craftsmanship, with a bright blue lining that looks like it was hewn from the sky. I know this blue cloth had to have been dyed with pigments from a rare mineral found in the lava fields. Sýr would have had to trade for this mineral, and it explains why she was spending so much time giving readings at the markets. She was saving to get this for me. Sýr must have worked on this in secret, at night as I slept, and it must have taken her a long time to finish it. It is my runecaster cloak, meant for when I successfully ascend from apprentice to accomplished caster. Sýr never got to give it to me.

I long to put it on, to feel its glorious weight and relish in its color, but I cannot bring myself to do it. I have not earned this cloak. As I rub my hand along its soft length, I see a glimmer appear. A bindrune has been sewn into the inside of the hood and on each shoulder. One rune says *future*, one says *past*, and one says *present*. Sýr must have created these special runes for me to calm my nerves during my sickness. When I pass my hand down the edges of the garment, more symbols appear. Each rune we cast is accounted for.

I feel a moment of panic when I realize Sýr will not be with me every night to put me to sleep with her soft spells. What will happen to me without her? I clutch the cloak, breathing in the faint herbal scent that always reminds me of my sister, and then place it in my pack with the rest of my belongings.

I try to hoist the heavy bag onto my back, but I can barely lift it. This will be impossible to carry any great distance. I must put a spell on it to lighten the load. I take out my runes and cast them onto the table, whispering to them about my problem. I ask them to lighten my load, but instead of easing its weight, the runes make my pack glow.

"No," I whisper. "That is not what I need. I need it to be lighter, not so heavy. Like this," I say, pulling out Sýr's feather. "As light as this, please," I tell my runes.

My pack stops glowing, and I test its weight. It feels almost empty. I position it onto my back, take a few steps and then fall when the pack grows heavy again. The heaviness lasts for a brief moment before lightening up again.

"We need to work on consistency," I say to the runes, and I feel another pang for Sýr.

I must track Sýr and liberate her from Katla and the Jötnar, but I don't know what I will do once I find them. I know Sýr can't fight them alone with the stone waning as it is, and I know Katla will be headed to moonwater for the gathering of the clans. All of this is about the moonstone. I know that now. Katla will try to compel Sýr to give her the stone, but it isn't so simple. The moonstone will need to be charged in the sacred waters, and Katla must know that when that has been accomplished, the moonstone will be more powerful than she can imagine. We don't even know whether Sýr can wield a fully charged moonstone, and surely Katla will not be able to hold it herself. Will she? I hope not, for once the moonstone is charged, there will be no more use for Sýr.

I must get to my sister before that happens. I must find a way. I will have to sneak Sýr away or find a warrior loyal to my family line and promise them payment for help. Perhaps the members of the ancient council of runecasters will help me if they know my story. To find out, I have to get to moonwater. The best plan is to find my sister as soon as possible and break her free so that Sýr can fix everything.

I'm going to need help finding her, and to do that I will need a vegvisir. A regular runic compass like the cloak clasp Amma gave me won't work. It has to be a different kind. The living kind.

With my pack on my back, I step through the doorway of my home into the clear midday air. If I didn't know about the horrors down in the village, this would seem like any other day. I never thought pleasant weather and the shining sun could seem cruel, but it's almost too much to bear.

I walk uphill along the cliff side to my lookout so I can see all the way to where the ocean meets the sky. I focus on the horizon, where the gods rest in eternity, and pull out one of my sharp knives.

"Please, goddess Freyja, guide me, protect me through the fog of the future, and lead me to Sýr," I say as I press the tip of the knife into the back of my left hand.

The blade stings as it pierces the skin, and I will myself to draw a design into my flesh. Then I mark the points of the compass, all the intricate lines and curves and dots that will tell me which way to go. As my blood bubbles around the wound and the pain burns my arm, I think of Sýr. As I do, my vision clouds, and right as I am about to panic and fight against the oncoming sickness, I see Sýr's face. She's laughing, smiling, looking into Frigg's eyes, down at the stand in the village. Then a flash and I see Sýr again, walking with me through the crunching snow after a training session. Then another flash, and another, and another. Always Sýr's face, always a memory of the past, until I can see all of her faces in a row, stretching back through time, growing younger with each iteration.

A sound like a door slamming shut echoes in my mind, and I come back to myself. My blood drips off the cliff and into the sea as the red moon dips lower in the sky. I look at my hand and make to cover it with salve, but as I do the vegvisir appears to swivel, pointing me in the other direction. It works. Can I trust my spell to lead me the right way?

"Thank you," I whisper to the compass. "Thank you!" I shout out to the heavens.

Before I move on, I mix the remaining blood from my vegvisir with a lock of my hair that I hacked off with the sharp knife. I rub the two together in my palms and smudge the mixture onto a massive rock that looks over our village and informs travelers which lands they are visiting. This is where our ancestors wrote their runes, and now those marks are almost invisible. I whisper to the runes and ask them to protect my people.

"Sleep well, people of Myrkur Strönd," I say. "I will find Sýr, and she will cure you."

I summon Núna, calling her with a mournful cry that soars over the sleeping village. She appears on the wind and alights on my shoulder, and I take a moment to give her a final meal of dried worms.

"Núna," I say, "I must go, and you cannot follow."

Núna squawks and ruffles her wings. I can tell she is not pleased.

"I need your help, Núna. You must fly. You must go out over the great ocean and find Father. Please, Núna. Fly to Father and bring him back." I take the ring from my finger and slip it onto Núna's foot.

She caws and lifts off, flapping in front of me for a moment before climbing higher into the red sky.

"I love you," I whisper.

She flies off and disappears into the horizon, and I feel the ache in my chest grow deeper as I watch the last of my loved ones disappear.

With every bit of power I have, I turn my back on my home, on the people I've known and loved and disliked and survived with for my entire life. They've tolerated me and cared for me, and now I face the open landscape of this mysterious island alone. It's a world I've never been allowed to discover.

I turn my back on the open sea, on the adventures in far-off lands that I've dreamed of so often and on the father I fear has been lost. I hope Núna finds him, and soon.

I don't know what lies beyond the hills of my home, what lurks in the forests or hides in the great cracks of the glacier beyond, but I must meet it head-on. I cannot return without Sýr, without a cure, without hope.

I am walking in my sister's shoes, and I do not fill them. I wish someone else had survived this attack. Someone stronger, someone better. All my people have now is me. Runa Unnursdóttir, near-child, unprepared apprentice, village freak.

I take a last breath of the fresh sea air and set out on the path north. Fear follows me with every step, my constant companion. I wish we didn't know each other so well.

SEVEN

My vegvisir points north-northeast, and I see the red moon advancing higher in the sky. Soon it will hover over everything, and then it will eclipse the sun. The main road my people take to trade with other villages runs this way, and I can follow it for a time. I know already that when I reach the crossroad and the well-traveled path leads toward the east coast of the island, where the realm of mortal men eke out their survival on the calmer shores, I will have to choose a different way.

Moonwater is not easy to find—and it's not meant to be. As a magical place, surrounded on all sides by a powerful barrier of green light, it takes incredible tenacity and devotion to the runepath to find it. And once found, not all may enter. I'm not trying to get inside, not unless I have to. I'd prefer to find Sýr and escape with her back home while the rest of the island's magical people duel for the runestone in our absence. Even if it means Sýr must relinquish the stone, we need to escape. We'll run, Sýr will save our people with a spell, and we can find a boat to set sail for a new land. At least if we start over somewhere else, I might be able to let go of being our family's great disappointment.

My thoughts seem more negative than usual. In fact, they don't quite feel like my own thoughts. I rub my chest where the ache has returned. My family has never made me feel like a burden. Sýr and Amma and even Father have loved me. So why are my thoughts so much like a poison?

The dagger. Katla has infected me. I stop to root through my pack for a tincture Sýr calls engill water. It cures people when they ingest the wrong kind of fungus or when their green shark hasn't aged long enough. I put a drop on my tongue, and the ache in my chest fades. It's still there but not as intense. I must keep going.

I decide I will walk through the night and sleep in the day. Even though we don't have many predators on this part of the island, I'm not fond of sleeping exposed at night, where any manner of ghost or troll could find me and drive me insane.

I walk the uneven road running out from our village, beyond the shoreline and cliffs and wind-battered hills, toward the flats and forests of the interior. The red-tinted sky casts a warm glow over everything, but the moon is high enough now that there is still a blue edge to the horizon, and the white clouds give the whole picture before me a serene aspect. The road underfoot is a mix of dry dirt so dark it is almost black and mud that has a purplish hue. Moss and lichen and wildflowers grow all around, and wild grasses sway in the wind. I've longed to travel, to journey through our land, but not like this.

I walk, my feet already rubbed raw in the too-large boots, for hours and hours, but the distant forest feels as if it will never grow closer. As darkness falls, the light of the red moon casts eerie shadows along the road.

I have not seen any other travelers and am startled when I see a figure crouched on the road ahead. As I approach, it stands. The shape is that of a slender woman, and she is watching me.

I cast a quick glance around, trying to determine if she is alone, but it's too dark to see far. I clutch my spear a little tighter, and I whisper to my runes, "Protect me now."

"You don't need those, love," the figure says. Her voice is like dripping honey. So sweet and relaxing.

I realize I am at the junction where my path intersects with another that runs west to east. But I must continue north, where the figure stands.

I look at the full moon and curse my own stupidity. Elves have been known to frequent crossroads on nights like this, when their persuasive powers are at a high and unsuspecting people are at risk of falling in love with them. Once a human is enchanted, an elf can do as they wish with that person. Amma told me that elves often seek gold, but she also teased that they like to eat mortals. Right now I hope that was just another wild Amma tale.

"Silly girl, you are too thin to eat," says the woman. How can she hear my thoughts? My chest begins throbbing again.

I am at the spot where the roads meet, and I have no choice but to continue. I have nowhere to run to, and if I must fight, I will fight.

"Who said anything about eating?" I ask, the bold edge in my voice surprising even me.

I hear the woman hiss, and she steps forward into the light. She has a tall frame, dark skin, pointed ears and elegant features. She must be an elf, I think, but as I look at her, her face changes, and her black hair takes on a sickly yellow color.

"Katla," I whisper and then thrust my spear out in front of me. But how can she be here? Has she been waiting for me? And why does she look not quite like herself? A sharp pain makes me clutch my chest, and she begins to laugh, her voice assaulting my mind. The sound echoes around me and feels like it will never end.

I clutch my runes. "Stop!" I shout in a booming voice. I feel the word hurl from my body, carrying with it all the power of my anger.

Katla stumbles backward at the force, which surprises me too, and her image seems to separate from her body, floating out overhead. I see Katla in the sky and the collapsed body of the woman in the road.

"Be gone!" I shout again at Katla. I make the sign of Þurs, the rune to cast out demons, in the air in front of me and blow it away with every ounce of breath I have.

Katla's image quakes, struggling to remain. "Embrace the darkness," her voice hisses, and then the image disappears into the night sky.

The woman on the ground groans. I approach her, careful not to get too close, as I am certain now that she is an elf. She has an irresistible quality and is one of the most beautiful beings I have ever seen.

"Are you all right?" I ask. "Can I help you?"

I know this is dangerous. Though my family is rumored to have a small amount of elven blood in our lineage, the elves are still considered dangerous to all. We humans are the weaker species. Elves are the smartest and deadliest creatures in all the realms.

The elf sits up and then stands with an uncommon grace, regarding me. "Who are you?" she asks.

"Runa Unnursdóttir," I answer her, powerless to lie or resist. Her eyes are like golden beams in the night. I have a strong impulse to reach out and touch her.

"Runa, you have saved me this night. The witch had me in her clutches for a long spell. I thought I would never get my body back. I'm not certain how you did that. Are you a powerful witch too?" she asks, extending a lithe arm to stroke my wild hair.

"No," I whisper. "I'm just Runa."

"Well, Just Runa," she says, "I am Falleg of the Ör people. I am eternally grateful to you," she says, pressing a small golden coin into my palm.

"Thank you," I say.

"It is but a small token of my debt to you," Falleg says. She nods and then turns west and runs off into the dark without another word. It takes a brief moment for her to disappear and leave me on my own again.

I take her lead and set off running too, north, holding my spear out in front of me and whispering to my runes to glow the way. They do, and I'm able to see a few feet ahead. If there are any big holes in the road, I hope to avoid falling into one and breaking both of my legs. And if I come to any more crossroads on this journey, I'll run straight through, spear first, and won't look back.

I alternate between running and walking most of the night, until the darkness starts to lift across the land. I must rest soon, but I need to find shelter. As dawn breaks I can see that the main road is ending. I will need to decide between crossing the flats to the east to meet up with the common path around the great forest or keep going north on a less traveled footpath that goes through the forest and includes harder terrain. If I go around, it will take days, and I must find Sýr sooner than that. But if I continue straight ahead, I'm entering a realm I know nothing about and have been warned against. I cannot find Sýr if I don't survive the journey.

"What to do?" I mutter to myself.

The grasses at my feet ruffle, and I jump backward as a small brown rabbit hops past me on the path. It pauses at the trailhead, looks back at me, and then continues.

"Sýr?" I whisper.

Could she be sending me a sign? Or is this just a rabbit that I should try to catch and eat?

I sigh. My energy is draining from me. This is impossible.

I consult my vegvisir. "Which way?" I ask.

The compass continues to point north-northeast, the same direction the rabbit went.

"Fine," I say. That is the direction I will travel. But first I must find a place to stop for a couple of hours.

I'm not excited about entering the forest, but it does offer some cover and protection. I try not to think of Amma's stories of fairies and sprites and other hiddenfolk.

As I am looking around for a suitable place to rest, I spot an immense rock, almost hidden by brush, right on the edge of the forest. The sight of it strikes fear deep in my belly.

It is a black rock, smooth as glass, big as a boat, and as I get closer, I can see that the ground on the far side of the rock is littered with the skeletons and bones of people and creatures who tried to pass.

I know there is more to this rock than what my eyes can see. I suspect this is a fairy rock, but whatever it is, I cannot advance past it without more information. But I cannot retreat either. Fairies have a phenomenal sense of smell.

I crouch on the ground among the bones. I'll have to try an illumination spell to see if there's a message on the rock.

I whisper to my runes. "Let me see what is hidden," I say, tossing them at my feet. They clatter together and some figures appear on the rock. It's a fairy language, I think, but I cannot read it.

As I speak to my runes again, I feel a slight vibration in the earth. Whatever lives here is coming. "Please," I whisper. "Let me understand what is written." I cast the runes again, and this time the figures on the rock change, and a message written in runes appears.

"All who seek to pass have no fear but to ask. Seek permission and go unharmed," I say, reading the message out loud.

Is it a trick? Fairies are known for such tricks.

I take a breath as the rumbling intensifies. I can hear tiny voices chittering now, building to a frenzy.

"Please," I call out. "May I pass by your rock? I mean no harm."

The voices quiet. I gather my runes and edge closer to the rock.

I have no choice now but to act on faith that I will not be harmed.

"Thank you," I whisper as I make my way around it.

I want to look behind me, as I feel a strong presence at my heels.

But I know I must resist. I know that if I look back, the fairies who own this land might devour me in tiny pieces.

I don't look back, and I do not stop until I am deep into the forest cover.

At last I find a large hollow stump and crawl inside. I stuff a few pieces of dried fish into my mouth and chew, getting them down before I fall into a deep and dreamless sleep, lulled by the sound of the trees swaying overhead, and my own beating heart.

EIGHT

I wake with a start a few hours later, and for a moment I swear I am back in my room at my clifftop dwelling. My vision is hazy, but I can see Sýr moving beyond the sheepskin curtain, and I can smell the faint scent of porridge.

"Sýr?" As I say her name, the image disappears, the world transforming back into the forest, the stump, the damp air. The ground beneath me is so cold that my leg bones ache. I must do a better job of finding sleeping places. And I know I must rethink walking at night. The encounter with Katla and Falleg at the crossroads is reason enough, and who knows what else I will meet in the darkness.

For now it's still day, later in the afternoon from the looks of the sky, though it's hard to tell with the tree cover and the red hue.

I crawl out from the stump, my chest aching with the movement. Slowly, I pull off my boots and unwrap my feet, wincing as the skin on both heels sloughs off where large blisters popped during my night's walk. Sýr's healing salve will help, so I slather it on before lining my boots with thick leaves to try to reduce the space. I clench my teeth as I stuff my stinging feet back inside.

My stomach growls, my body ignoring the urgency of my journey. It wants to eat and to eliminate, and I have to take care of both. Once I've relieved myself, groaning as I finally empty my full bladder, I set about getting something to eat.

Rather than dip into my supplies of dried fish again, I decide to forage in the area around my stump. Before long I find a patch of kale, which I detest, but I rip the greens from the ground anyway and tear off pieces to chew on. The bitter, leathery leaves stick in my throat. A crowberry bush nearby yields a couple handfuls of berries, which I stuff into my mouth. They're not quite ripe yet, and they're so sour they make my eyes water. As I chew I glance around, unnerved by the feeling that this forest may have eyes. Everything is so much scarier when you're alone.

I hear some chirping overhead and see there's a bird's nest in the tree above my stump. I clamber onto the rotting top of the stump and brace myself against the tree. I hoist myself up, shimmy to the next pair of branches, and peek into the nest.

Two baby birds chirp at me, so new they are still sticky with gunk and bits of shell. They're an easy meal, a bit of meat, but as they peer at me from their dark bird eyes, the pupils shining like lava stones, I can't help but think of Núna.

I tell myself the birds would be too much trouble. I'd have to clean and cook them, and I don't have time.

"Sorry to bother you," I say to the birds, being careful now not to disturb the nest any further. I don't want their mother to abandon them.

I'm wasting time here, and I need to find some water. I didn't bring anything to drink other than whey and mead, so I gulp down half the whey before shouldering my pack again. My mouth feels dry, and my lips are flaking.

As I set off into the trees, consulting my vegvisir to ensure I am still going in the right direction, I remind myself of Amma's warnings. She always said the forest is full of mystery. During our long talks, Amma would tell me there is more to the surface world of dirt and bugs and trees and animals. There is another world, one we don't always see, but that a person trained in magic can recognize if they have the gift. I asked her once if I had that gift, but she just smiled at me. For someone people went to for answers, my amma sure liked to make me figure things out for myself.

As I pass beside rings of toadstools, I hear my amma's voice in my mind, warning me never to step inside one lest I be condemned to an eternity in the realm of fairies. Amma said there's no telling what horrors the fairies would subject me to, and I do not want to find out.

"Amma, protect me now," I whisper, touching the vegvisir clasp on my cloak. My fear is getting to me. A forest witch could be concealed behind each dark tree and within each long shadow. These are not the runecasting witches of my ancestors, and they're not even the evil kind that Katla seems to be. No, these are older, darker, indifferent beings. If I attract their curiosity, I could become their slave.

I feel my runes bumping against my chest in their pouch. I cradle them with my free hand. "Guide me. Help me find Sýr."

I reach the boundary of the trees a few hours later, and the sky is beginning to darken. As I step from under the tree cover, the rains hit me. I pull my cloak hood up and wrap it around me until it is tight.

"Sól," I say, invoking the sun rune. "I call upon you for warmth." My runes reward me with a bit of heat.

As I look out onto the open plain, I see a creature poke its head out of the tall grass in the west. It might be a fox. At least, I hope it's a fox. It could be a skoffin, which would be very bad for me. I look away, just in case.

When I was little, some village children wandered too far from home. Their mothers went to find them and discovered the children dead. There were no obvious signs of harm, no evidence that they had eaten poison. Nothing was amiss. A wise woman from the village said it must have been a skoffin.

To look into a skoffin's eyes is to die in an instant. These enchanted cat-foxes are difficult to kill, because you cannot ever look directly at them. Few people have encountered a skoffin and lived, for it is a malevolent servant of evil. If there are skoffins here, then they're Katla's doing.

The creature disappears, and I choose to think it was a fox, as much to quell my own fear as anything. I must focus on the next steps. Which way to go?

"Guide me," I say to my vegvisir, but when I look at it, the compass swirls erratically, not settling on a single direction.

I am unsure whether I should go east or west around the badlands that lie to the direct north of me. The vegvisir is not helping.

I take my runes out and cast them onto the grass at my feet. "Please show me the way."

Half the runes point to the east, and half to the west.

"Andskotinn!" I shout, cursing my predicament, and a flock of birds flies out from the trees behind me.

I close my eyes, picturing Sýr in my mind. Her dark hair, her smooth skin, her kind smile.

"Please help me find my sister," I whisper.

When I open my eyes, my runes are all facing north. My vegvisir is also facing north. Right toward the badlands.

I sigh. No one ventures through the badlands if they can help it, and they don't do it alone. It's the most dangerous area of the island, as so little is known about it. Beyond are glaciers, crevasses, and lava fields, but to reach even those dangerous places, you have to pass through a barren land of rock. It sounds safe enough, but it's like walking through a graveyard. It's where the ghosts of the banished go to live out eternity.

"How? Why?" I ask my runes, but this is not the kind of question they answer.

A beam of sunlight appears through the cloudy sky, and the open face of the land affords a beautiful display of my homeland's strange weather. It can be radically different depending on where you are. Today on the flats, I see sun on my left and a sheet of rain on the right. Two completely different weather conditions, split down the middle by the dangerous path I must take alone.

As I contemplate this, the rain to the east shimmers and I see a body walking through it, parting the water like a curtain. Am I seeing this, or is my perspective skewed by a trick of the light?

The walker is dark and hunched over. Another elf? Katla?

My heart starts to pound in my chest, the pain making me wince, and I gather my runes in haste and ready my spear.

As the figure hobbles closer, I see that it is an old woman. Could it be a forest witch?

"Halt," I call out. The old woman stops and looks at me. She smiles, and I can see there is nothing yellow or Katla-like about her. Yet.

"Hallo," she says.

"What do you want?" I ask.

"I am alone," she answers. "And lost." She looks around in confusion. She does not appear to be carrying any bags, and I do not see any weapons.

"Where do you hail from?" I ask.

"I...I live..." She trails off, lost in thought. "I'm not sure," she says at last. "My mind isn't what it used to be."

A little bird flits from a nearby bush and alights on her head for a second.

"Oh," says the old woman. "Hallo, little friend."

The bird flies off, and the old woman watches it. "I love birds, don't you?" she asks.

I nod, not sure if this is a trick, but I do know that dark witches tend to cause everything around them to rot and die, preferring the company of wicked things. Lovely little birds don't land on the heads of evil, do they?

"Say, I don't mean to be trouble," says the old woman. "But I don't know where I am, or when I last ate, or what I'm going to do next. I'm not even sure of who I am. Or how I got here."

"Well," I begin, "that must be terrible."

"Could you help me?" she asks.

I hesitate. "I'd like to," I say. "I can't take you anywhere, for I am finding my way myself. But you may have some of my food."

I pull a hunk of dried fish from my pouch and reach out to hand it to her with a shaking arm. I wish my nerves didn't betray me so, but the old woman takes it with a grateful smile.

"Bless you, child," she says, munching into the fish. "Mmm. Thank you."

"You're welcome," I say.

"Oh!" exclaims the old woman. "I remember now."

She finishes the last of the fish, throws off her threadbare old cloak, and somehow seems to double in height. She loses the visage of the old woman altogether, revealing a tall figure clad all in black, from flowing garments to thick cloak.

I stagger backward, taking in the massive height and gleaming silver helmet. The face as smooth as white stone. Eyes of an impenetrable black. There is no trace left of the old woman and I am awestruck by the majesty of the entity looming above me.

"I… I…" I cannot speak.

"I am Oski," says the being. "You have released me from a forgetting spell with your kindness." They bow, their long legs folding into sharp angles. I can see now that the helmet they wear is decorated with the marks of wings and wind.

"What are you?" I ask, my voice a whisper.

"I am Oski," they repeat. "What are you?"

"Runa," I say, my voice trembling.

"Everything in nature resembles itself, Runa," Oski says, rising again. "A cloud is a god is a pile of wool is a bank of snow is a swirl of white water is your breath in the air. You are this and that and when."

"When?" I ask. What do they mean?

"Yes. When are you?" Oski asks.

"Um, I am now," I say.

"Are you?" Oski asks. "Hmm."

"Please," I say. "I am confused."

"All is well," says Oski. "You are Runa. I am Oski. I am here to serve you on your journey. You are on a quest, yes?" Oski motions at my pack and my spear.

I nod. There is something about this Oski, something familiar, but I cannot place it. It's like we've met before, but I cannot remember when or how. It's there on the edge of my mind.

Oski nods at me. "Yes, Runa."

Can this strange character hear my thoughts?

Oski nods again. "Don't worry, not every thought. The ones that matter, that pertain to me."

"And you know me?" I ask.

"I do," they say. "And your grandmother. And your grandmother's grandmother."

"How?"

"Oh, I've taken them all to Freyja's Field."

Their statement swirls in my mind. Freyja's Field. The afterlife. I realize, with a sudden and violent clarity, who it is that stands before me.

"Valkyrie," I say, the word rushing from me in a breathless gasp.

Oski grins, standing taller, before faltering a bit. "Former Valkyrie."

"Former?" I ask. But I don't wait for an answer. I have to know about Amma. "You saw my amma? She is safe in the afterlife?"

Oski nods. "For now."

"What does that mean, for now?"

"It means that what happens with your quest matters a great deal. The moonstone cannot be possessed by the witch Katla." Oski stares at me hard with those dark eyes.

"How do you know all this?" I ask.

"That doesn't matter now. We should go. Time is moving around on us."

"We?"

"Yes, Runa, we." Oski cocks their head at me in curiosity.

Can I trust this powerful being? I've never heard of a Valkyrie being present in mortal realms unless they were choosing the slain to be taken to Valhalla.

"Where is your horse?" I ask.

"Gone," says Oski, their voice sad.

"Your wings?" I ask.

"Gone," Oski says again. "Taken."

"By whom?"

Oski smiles, their expression wistful. "A tale for another time," they say.

I take a breath. Something tells me I will not be able to convince this Oski to leave me alone, and there is no way I can defeat a Valkyrie, former or not, wingless and horseless or not, in battle. Oski is huge, and though they seem to be kind and gentle now, the Valkyries are known to be bloodthirsty. This being has a plan, and it includes me. I will have to let them accompany me for now.

"And then?" asks Oski, interrupting my thoughts. "You'll get rid of me?" They laugh, the sound a disturbing echo across the flats.

"If you want to come," I say, "you'll have to stop doing that." I am shocked at how bold I'm acting, but I don't have the time to be polite. I need to find my sister.

Oski puts up their hands. "On my word," they say.

I clasp my runes. "To keep you in truth," I say. I whisper to them and scatter them at Oski's feet. "Show me honesty," I instruct. The runes shimmer for a moment, and then I scoop them back up.

I look at Oski, who is regarding me warily. "What do you want with me?" I ask.

Oski opens their mouth to speak, hesitates, then sighs. "Revenge," they say at last.

"Against whom?" I ask.

"Against the god who betrayed us all." Oski's voice has taken on a dark tone, and I can see the anger radiating from within their body.

"Which god?" I ask, scared to hear the answer.

"Odin himself," Oski says.

I nod. Oski must be insane to want revenge on Odin, but as long as they are willing to help me on my journey, I can stand to trust them a little. I regard them for a moment.

"Will you harm me?" I ask at last.

"Never," says Oski. "I will skin myself alive first."

"I doubt that will be necessary," I say, sounding far more confident than I am, "but as long as you behave, you may come with me."

Oski smiles, their bright white teeth shining like the inside of a shell.

"Which way?" Oski asks.

I point ahead to the badlands, and Oski gasps.

"You are a brave one, runecaster."

"I'm not a real runecaster," I say.

Oski shrugs. "If you say so."

The sky is darker now, and we agree to walk through the night, following the constellations. The red moon is higher in the sky. The days are getting shorter, the nights seemingly endless.

I speak to my runes in a whisper they alone can hear, and I power them with my intentions.

"Help me be worthy of you," I say, as much to them as to Sýr, wherever she is. I hope she can hear me.

NINE

We walk for hours, not saying much. Oski leads the way because it makes me uncomfortable to have them behind me and because they stride forth with such a menacing gait that anything ahead on the path will run away.

We stop at last in a field of large boulders, and Oski wants to talk.

"Tell me about the runes," they say, kicking a long leg out to stoke the small fire we've made.

I want to eat and go to sleep, but the presence of a Valkyrie has me on edge.

"What do you want to know?" I ask between sips of moss soup. The deep night is cold and the ground even colder. It seems as though we are surrounded by stones, and even the sky could be made of rock for all we know. If it were not for the presence of the red moon overhead, I would have thought we were in a tomb. The world is a graveyard.

"Show me how the runes work." Oski moves closer, and I get a better look at their face in the firelight. Their skin is so fine that I'm not sure it even is skin. They have no eyelashes or eyebrows, and no hair on them at all that I can see. When they cast their eyes at me it is unsettling, like looking into a deep crevasse. It isn't menacing or unkind. It's more primitive than that. Like any other powerful force that comes from nature, Oski has an innate indifference in their eyes. Looking into them is not unlike staring into the sea or witnessing a huge wave sweep someone from the shore and drown them. It isn't personal. It just is.

I don't know what I have to fear from Oski, but they are here, so I will talk.

"These are my practice runes," I say. "A caster must carve their own, but these were given to me. Some casters use a cloth to cast upon, but I like to cast them onto the earth. I don't know why, but it helps me. I'm not that good at it, in truth."

"Is that why do you not call yourself runecaster?" Oski asks.

I don't answer. "This is the stave," I say, holding one up and running my finger around its edge. "It's the shape of the rune, or what it's made of. These are wood. But they would be more powerful if they were made from bone or a rare stone."

Oski nods. "How do you read them?"

"Well, when I cast them, they lie in their stead, which refers to the direction they're pointed in. Their position helps me divine their nature and meaning, and whether they are dark or light, up or down, positive or negative. And I feel it."

"Feel it? How?" Oski asks, reaching out to touch one of the runes.

I swat their hand away before I realize what I'm doing. "No," I say and then immediately cower away from them.

Oski recoils, a flash of anger across their face. "You strike me?" they bellow, their voice sending a wave of fear through me.

"I'm sorry," I say. "I shouldn't have done that. But you cannot touch them, you see? They could be drained of their power. And they are fickle enough as it is."

"Fine," Oski mutters. "I just wanted to see what it feels like."

"You could get your own," I say, gathering my runes and securing them in the pouch around my neck.

"At least show me a casting," Oski says.

I sigh. "Very well. But you need to ask a question."

"Tell me about your sister."

"That isn't a question. You must ask something about yourself."

Oski scoffs. "I already know everything about me. Tell me about her."

I hesitate. I don't want to talk about Sýr right now, but at the same time I miss her so much that talking about her makes me feel closer to her.

I give in. "Sýr is the sister everyone wishes they had."

Oski smiles their wide, unsettling smile. "I don't have any sisters. Or brothers. Or parents."

I nod. "Well, it's like having someone who is always on your side. Always on the same quest."

Oski brightens at this. "I like that."

"Then you would love Sýr," I say. "She's smart and strong, and she always knows what to do."

Before I realize it, I am crying. I'm horrified to be showing weakness in front of Oski, but I can't help it. The tears come anyway.

"My heart tells me she is alive," I say through my sobs. "For I believe the world itself would cease to exist if she were gone. It would for me."

"There, there," says Oski. "I will help you find her. Maybe she is in the stars?"

I glance up. "Maybe," I say. I clutch my runes, staring up into the night at all the twinkling stars the gods use to watch over us. Rubbing at the scabbed vegvisir on my hand, I whisper to it, "Help me find Sýr."

My vegvisir doesn't move, but something else does. A flock of white moths flutters from the dark sky like stars come to life.

"Am I seeing this?" Oski says.

The moths cluster together, forming the shape of a person.

"What is this?" I say to Oski, but they seem far away, and my vision starts to rattle and shake. I feel woozy, like I'm going to pass out, and I know I'm having my sickness again.

Everything goes white, and I hear Sýr's voice. *Stay with me.*

"Sýr!" I call out, but I can't see anything through this white fog. It won't clear.

All at once I find myself rushing forward as if the world is falling around me, and I come to a stop on a green hill, surrounded on all sides by a shimmering golden lake.

I turn and see Oski standing before me, but they have long, flowing red hair and massive wings that unfurl behind them. I stretch a shaking hand toward them, but before our fingers can touch, I am yanked backward, tumbling into a cold darkness.

I come to with Oski's concerned face above mine, and their strong, icy hands gripping my shoulders. "Runecaster," they say. "What was that?"

I groan, sitting up. My head is pounding. "My sickness," I manage.

"But why did you take us there?" Oski asks.

I stare at them, and they stare back at me.

"*Us*?" I ask.

"Yes, runecaster. Us," they say.

"Stop calling me that," I mumble. "It was a dream, my sickness. I get them sometimes. But I don't have Sýr to help me with her sleeping spells and her tinctures. So I've been getting worse."

"I don't know what that was," says Oski, "but it was no dream."

"Wait," I say. "You're saying you were there with me?"

Oski nods.

"What did it look like then?" I ask, testing them.

"A golden lake," says Oski. "One I've been to before, a long time ago."

I shake my head. "No. That's impossible. You're reading my thoughts, and you promised you wouldn't."

I stand and begin gathering my belongings. This Valkyrie can't be trusted.

"Stop, Runa, please. I am not lying."

"No?" I ask, incredulous. "A golden lake? I've never been there in my life. Impossible."

Oski shakes their head. "But you were there."

"I don't have time for these games. I have to find Sýr."

"Wait," says Oski, holding up a long arm. "I hear something."

"Now you're stalling," I say.

"Shh," Oski says, standing so fast that I don't have time to react. They grab hold of me and clamp an icy hand across my mouth. This is it. They're going to kill me now.

They whisper in my ear. "Someone approaches."

"Who?" I ask, my voice muffled by Oski's hand.

"I don't know," Oski says, "but they've been following us for some time. And they stink of elf. They're close."

I hold still, my heart hammering in my chest, but I don't hear anything. Oski drops me to the ground and whirls around with blinding speed, emitting a battle shriek. They unsheath a long bright sword from inside their cape, one I didn't even know they had, and it glints through the night as it strikes against a large rock. Sparks fly, and I don't see anything at first, but then I glimpse a shadow dodging Oski's movements with incredible speed.

"Get them!" Oski yells, and I see a large shadow hurtle toward me. I grab my spear, but instead of jabbing the pointed end at the dark figure, I ram the blunt end into its center by accident.

"Oof," a voice bellows, and the shadow falls limp at my feet, gasping for breath.

Oski leans down and rips back the attackers woolen hood, revealing the face underneath. It's Einar Ymirsson. I've knocked the wind from his chest and he is lying there, vulnerable. I spin my spear and jab the pointed end toward his throat, but Oski snatches it back at the last moment, preventing me from exacting my bloody revenge.

"What are you doing?" I shout. "He is the enemy."

"No," says Oski. "He isn't."

"You don't know what you're talking about. He made the dust that cursed my entire clan. He's responsible. He has to die."

I struggle to pull the spear from Oski's grasp, but they are unmovable. They look at me with a quiet pity.

"Aargh!" I yell and then start kicking Einar in the side until Oski lifts me away, holding me under one arm the way an exasperated mother might hold a tot who refuses to listen.

"Release me!" I shriek, but Oski does not let go.

"When you are calm, I will release you. Stop squirming," Oski says.

With my free hand I grab my rune pouch and hold it while I stare at Einar. I summon all my hatred and rage, trying to remember the darker runecasts Sýr warned me against using. I pluck the leather cord around the pouch, and my runes tumble onto the black ground, glowing as red as the moon overhead.

"Pain," I hiss, directing all my power in Einar's direction.

Oski drops me, wailing with a tone I've never heard before in nature. It's so loud that both Einar and I grasp our heads and cover our ears. Though bothered by the noise,

Einar does not seem to be in pain. My runes did not cast onto the correct foe. Instead they attacked Oski.

I turn and see Oski writhing on the ground, their body glowing red-hot, steam rising into the cold night air.

"You're burning them alive!" Einar shouts. "Stop it now."

"I can't," I say, stepping backward. "I don't know why this is happening."

Einar leaps up and tries to grab Oski, but he snatches his hand back. "Ah! It burns."

I look at my runes, still aflame with my anger. I bend to pick them up, but they're so hot I cannot gather them.

"Please," I plead with my runes. "Stop."

"Do something!" Einar shouts as Oski continues to wail.

Think, Runa. Think. I have to interrupt the pattern. But how? My spear. I grab my white spear stick and flip my runes over so they're no longer casting their murk-staves. Turning them so the opposite side, the bright side, is up will help me to cast a new spell. As I flip them, Oski quiets, and their color turns from red to pink.

"Keep going," says Einar. "More."

I bend down and blow on the runes, willing them to cool, but I am still angry, and my runes are connected to me. They're much more connected to me than I realized.

I take a deep breath. I must try to calm myself. I think of Sýr, of her open, kind face, and my heart fills with love.

I say the rune for ice, "Ís," and at last the runes are cool again. Scooping them back into their pouch, I put them away. "Sleep now," I whisper to them.

I turn to see Einar helping Oski drink from a jug.

"What is that?" I ask suspiciously.

"Mead," grunts Oski, revived by the drink and returned to their normal color of bone white.

"Don't drink it," I exclaim. "You don't know what's in it."

Oski waves a lithe hand at me. "I don't care."

"He's a known poisoner," I say, my voice growing vicious again. I struggle to quell the rising anger within me as I advance toward Einar, my spear stick held out.

He places his hands up, relinquishing the jug to Oski, who downs it at once.

"Look, I'm sorry," Einar gasps at my feet, his face lit warm by the fire's glow. "You don't understand. Please don't set me on fire."

"It really hurts," grunts Oski between gulps.

"You. Destroyed. My. People," I say through gritted teeth.

Einar shakes his head. "No. I didn't want to. Katla has my clan under her spell, and my father..." He trails off.

"Is a coward," I finish for him.

"He's not," Einar argues. "He's enchanted. They're all enchanted. It's dark magic."

"You poisoned them." I draw my spear back toward his eye and he leans back, shaking.

"Yes," he says. "But not in the way you think. It's true that I made the dust, but..." He tries again. "Katla wanted to kill everyone. She wanted a dust that would melt everyone to ash. Even the children," he adds.

"Go on," says Oski, tossing the empty mead jug aside.

"I asked her to let your clan live and allow me to use a different kind of dust if..." He doesn't finish.

"If?" I ask, kicking him in the side with my boot.

"Ow!" He recoils. "If I could guarantee your clan would be under her control. Permanently. I told her it would be a waste to kill everyone. That you could be used. She liked that. There's nothing she likes more than absolute control."

Oksi curses and mutters under their breath.

Einar continues. "So I made a sleeping dust, a complex one, but then Katla enchanted it and made it so that no one would ever wake from it."

Einar's amber eyes take on a faraway look. "She's so strong. So strong. She demands sacrifices. She says she needs more power before the competition. She has been stealing people. Even elves."

I think back to the elf I met at the crossroads. Falleg.

"Katla's been burning them in her fires," Einar continues.

"So the runecaster and the witch have something in common," says Oski, giving me a pointed look.

I narrow my eyes at them in return.

"Yes," says Einar, "but you're very different in another way."

"How?" I ask.

"I saw her eat...the flesh of the people she killed," he says, his voice quiet and haunted. "The people we helped her steal."

We all remain in silence for a moment, taking this in.

Then Einar continues in a whisper. "We heard a baby crying in the night. A tiny village in the forest. She wanted me to get the baby for her."

My heart lurches in my chest.

"Did you?" Oski asks what I cannot.

"No!" Einar says. "I could never do such a thing. That's when I knew I had to get away. But I couldn't just run. I didn't want her to kill my father or punish my clan. I had to convince her to let me go."

"How?" I ask. I don't believe a word this Jötnar is saying to me.

"I told Katla I would find you and use you," he says.

"Use me for what?" I ask.

He hesitates.

"For what?" I shout, pressing the spear into his side. This time Oski doesn't stop me.

"Ah," he cries out. "Because if your sister doesn't survive, she will need a substitute."

I don't like where this is going.

He sighs, holding his hands up again. "Please, listen to me."

"Be quick. And if you lie, you die," I say.

"Fair," he says, spitting some blood onto the ground.

"Katla isn't mortal," he says. "She can't enter moonwater. Not like you can. And not in her own body. She can't take the moonstone either or else she will die. She needs to do it through someone else. Through Sýr."

I take a step backward and stumble. Oski reaches for me, but I wave them off. This is as I expected, but it's shocking all the same.

"Go on," I say.

"If Sýr dies, Katla wants you in her stead," he says.

"What do you mean, if Sýr dies?" I ask, my voice a whisper.

Einar's sadness is evident on his face. "I've seen it before. I've seen what happens when Katla takes over a body. The original gets consumed."

I feel sick, and it's all I can do not to vomit all over him. It would serve him right. But his words have a ring of truth.

"Why find me?" I demand. "Why didn't you run? Or find a ship and set sail for another land? Believe me, I would have!"

"Because she's watching," he says. "Always watching. And you wouldn't have run. Not if you'd seen what I have. I cannot leave my clan. I cannot let her continue to hurt my people. She won't stop. You know she won't."

I sit with a sigh, my spear clattering to the rocks. "I know."

"I'm sorry," Einar says. "I wish it was different."

"How do you know all about Katla's plans?" Oski asks. "The witch tells you everything?"

"No," he says, shaking his head. "My mother was her victim too."

I stare at him, at the openness in his eyes and the sadness he wears like a heavy cloak. His voice is choked with pain as he talks. "Katla took my mother's form to entice my father and infiltrate the once-mighty Jötnar. Now my mother is dead, consumed by the witch, and Katla still uses her face. She is doing the same to Sýr, and I cannot abide it."

"And your father?" I ask. "He isn't complicit?"

"No. My father is a proud man. A just man. But he is under a deep spell, as are the entire clan. They can't see her for what she is. When my father looks at Katla, he sees his beloved bride."

"And you can see her for what she is?" I ask.

He nods. "I have been training as a potion mage since I was a boy. Part of that training means ingesting small amounts of poisons and other tinctures that would make others sick. I've been drinking a special tea for years, and as far as I can tell, it keeps me from falling under Katla's spell. But sometimes it's hard. Confusing. Sometimes I see my mother when I look at her, and I wish I was enchanted too."

"Why does the witch not mind?" asks Oski.

"I play along," says Einar. "It's all that seems to matter to her. Once she is finished with me, she will consume me. And," he adds, "I've done terrible things."

"Terrible things," I echo. "Like the dust."

He nods. "And worse. For my people. And I'd do it again."

I understand what he's saying. I'd do anything to stop Katla and save Sýr and my people. Anything. Would I mix a poison dust to curse another clan? If you'd asked me a few days ago, I would have said no. Now I'm not so sure.

"I don't blame you if you hate me," Einar says. "But it doesn't matter."

"No?" I ask. He is bold to say so.

"No," he says. "Go ahead and hate me. Kill me if you must. Just promise me you'll destroy her. She's taken everything from me, and no one wants to see her dead more than me."

"I'd be willing to fight you on that," I say. Can I believe him? "What can I do?" I ask him. "Why me? I'm just trying to find my sister. She's the one you need."

He sighs. "I know Katla's secrets because I've been watching and listening. I know she covets the moonstone. And I know there is something about you that worries her. It unsettles her enough that she let me go. She fears you in some way, and that's reason enough for me to help you get to moonwater to stop her."

"But I'm no one," I say. "I'm not even a real runecaster."

Einar shrugs. "I just know that I need your help. My clan needs your help. And I've got nowhere else to go."

I look at Oski, who nods. "I've seen inside his mind. He tells the truth."

"I'm sorry," Einar says. "I had no other choice but to mix the dust. Nothing else would have worked. And everyone would have been killed. I didn't know *this* would happen."

"About this dust," I ask. "Can my people be restored?"

He looks uneasy. "I've never made it before. It's a complicated potion. If it hadn't been enchanted, then I could have made a cure for it. But now nothing will work unless the witch is defeated. If we kill her maybe we can set everyone free."

We stare at each other in silence before Oksi interjects. "Fine. No cure unless we kill the witch. I am all for killing. Now how do we do it?"

Einar looks at me, his gaze intense and hopeful. "I think a runecaster can kill her. Like you."

"I like him," says Oski in their cheerful way, earning a dark glance from me. "What?" they ask. "I do like him. And he can help."

"If you're so powerful with your potions," I ask Einar, "then why haven't you killed the witch or poisoned her?"

"You don't understand," Einar says, his voice grave. "She isn't mortal. She is immune to my potions. I have tried, even casting henbane seeds into the fire so that the whole clan has visions and nightmares, myself included. But not her. She never breaks. She eats the hearts of the animals we kill. She moves in total silence and fast too, like a fox."

"Or something like a fox," I say, remembering the creature in the field that made me so uneasy.

Einar looks at me. "You've seen it?"

I nod. "I think it was a skoffin."

Oski gasps. "Vile creature. Hard to kill."

I am confused and exhausted, and this information is hard to take in. I have fantasized that I would find Einar Ymirsson and make him suffer on behalf of my people, but now that he's here I cannot do it. I believe him. Damn it.

He turns to me. "I saw you up on the clifftop when Katla took your sister. I saw that you took a dagger to the chest.

And here you are still. I've never seen anyone withstand her magic. I thought if anyone could help me, it's you."

I laugh, and the sound is more bitter than joyful. "You thought wrong."

Einar stares at me, his gaze so intense that I want to look away. "If Katla can harness the power of the moonstone through Sýr, then everything we know will be gone. My people, your people. Everything."

"What can I do?" I ask at last. "I'm not powerful like Katla is."

"But you are a runecaster," Einar says, pointing to my runes. "You'll have to try to beat her."

"I can't do that." I shake my head. "I'm an apprentice. A bad one. I'm not even allowed to battle at moonwater."

"Then we are all doomed," says Oski with finality.

"Maybe someone else," I begin, but I know there is no one else.

"It must be you," says Einar. "Sometimes I have feelings about people. My mother had that gift. She always knew when someone was good. When they could be trusted. And you love your sister enough to risk this journey on your own."

"Not alone," Oski interjects.

"My point is," says Einar, ignoring Oksi, "I think you are brave enough to take her on. It's our one chance."

I stare at the dark sky, the red moon glowing like the red heart of the gods. I feel a surge of anger as I imagine Sýr being being forced to do unspeakable things by the evil Katla.

"This is crazy," I say. "But I will fight her. It will be me. In the name of my sister and my clan, I will have revenge."

I look at Einar, whose face has taken on a hopeful expression, and at Oski, who grins their maniacal grin.

"I will help you avenge your mother and the Jötnar," I say to Einar. "In exchange for your vow to help me defeat Katla and release my people from their cursed sleep."

Einar stands and pulls out a dagger, slicing into the meaty part of his palm. The dark blood runs and sizzles as it drips into the fire. "I swear it," he says. "I pledge myself to you."

I know this to be a significant gesture, for elf blood carries its own magic and is never spilled on purpose without binding consequences. This vow he makes is the best assurance I can have that his allegiance lies with me, although I will never fully trust him. To do so would be foolish.

I look at Oski. "And you?"

Oski stands, pulling up to full height, and lifts their long, shining sword. "I am Oski, and this is Chooser of the Slain. You will have my sword and whatever is left of my soul." They run their hand along its razor-sharp length and black blood springs forth, coating it. Oski holds the sword over the fire, and their blood drips into it.

Einar and Oski look at me. I nod and hold out my hand. Einar presses the hilt of his knife into it, and I don't hesitate. I slice myself as I've done several times since my entire life fell apart, the pain nothing compared to what I will feel if we fail on our quest.

My blood flows out of me, carrying with it all my love, all my hate, all my hopes and dreams and fears. It drops onto the dying embers and unites with Einar's and Oski's. We are bound together now.

I look at them both and then hold up my runes.

"It's us now," I say, my runes aglow in their pouch. "My blood, your blood. You live, I live. I die, you die."

"Then let's get to it," says Einar, holding out his hand.

I place my hand in his, startled by the heat of his skin before I remember that elves run hot. Oski adds their cold hand on top of mine, and we stand together, three unlikely allies under a rising blood-red moon, about to embark on a quest that is destined to kill us all.

I'd be lying if I said it wasn't a little thrilling. I'm looking forward to finding Katla. I'm going to find a way to make her suffer as we have suffered. It's going to be fun.

TEN

We hike all day, pausing to rest among the boulders and rocks of the great stone valley, and then we continue through the afternoon and deep into the night. We don't stop until Einar and I are near exhaustion. It's almost morning, and we've made it to the outer edge of the badlands, where the boulders make way for the barrens. Oski is as chipper as ever. I don't think they ever sleep.

As for me, I haven't been able to sleep much when we stop to rest, despite Oski's assurances that they will keep watch, because I do not trust Einar. Having him with me is like carrying a tincture in my mouth and trying not to swallow it in case it turns out to be poison.

I don't know what to make of him. As we settle to make camp and strike a fire on the border among the last of the large, craggy rocks, I glance at him while I prepare a meager meal of my last supplies of dried fish and moss.

I watch as Einar sparks a fire with some dark granules, getting it stoked and burning hot. I scoot a little closer to take the chill off the early morning. We'll eat a little, sleep a little, and then walk some more.

Einar is tall and broad-shouldered, with eyes that are an odd shade of glittering golden brown. He is difficult to look at without getting lost in staring. While other girls have mentioned his height, his dark hair and honey skin, and the subtle point to his ears, the thing I notice most about him is the downturned curve of his lips. He has the look of someone who hasn't smiled much, who is familiar with sadness, and it makes me want to understand why.

I imagine that if we were friends, I would feel compelled to try to make him smile, to catch a glimpse of the elven fangs that protrude on either side of his grin. So far I have not seen his face lose that sad look. Though our circumstances are grim and we haven't had occasion for happiness yet, Oski is always grinning about one thing or another, and even I have managed a smile or two in this last day—over a comment Oski has made or with delight at discovering a berry bush or a fresh bit of spring water bubbling from a rock face.

But Einar has never smiled, not once. The pain of losing his mother to the witch Katla is to blame, and now his father and his clan have been taken from him too. I don't say anything to him because I don't need to. His pain is my pain.

I see Oski staring at me with their uncomprehending black eyes. I shrug at them. "What?" I ask.

"Hungry." They smack their abdomen.

"We're all hungry," Einar mutters.

"And we're out of supplies," I say with a heavy sigh. I hold out my scraps of moss as proof.

Oski groans. "Hungry."

"Well, we can take some time to set traps," I say, motioning to a brushlike area to our west. "We might find wild hare or perhaps weasels. I don't see any signs of a river yet, so no fish."

"Bah," says Oski. They love fish.

"Maybe there are some more berries nearby," I suggest.

Einar shakes his head. "We still have a long way to go, and we won't make it without a nourishing meal." He doesn't usually speak this much to me. Despite our mutual goal, I've made it clear he's not my favorite person, and he has been keeping his distance.

"Agreed," I say, my voice brisk. "What do you suggest?"

"We need to find supplies, maybe some better gear." He looks pointedly at my boots, which are still causing me no end of agony.

"What can I do about it?" I ask, pulling a boot off in anger. "I left with everything I had."

I toss one of the boots at Einar, and it thumps against him and lands on the ground between us. He grabs it and places it on a nearby rock.

"Let's have it then," he says, motioning to my remaining boot.

I remove it with a grunt and hurl it at him, missing his head by a wisp. He doesn't duck or move at all. Instead he regards me with that same sad and patient look, then retrieves the wayward boot and places it with its mate.

The image of Sýr's broken-down boots, alone on the rock, is enough to make me start crying again, but this time I do not. I take a deep breath and fold my arms across myself, pushing my emotions down as far as they will go.

Einar and Oski are silent.

"Now what?" I ask, my voice betraying none of the unsteady feelings I have inside.

Einar shrugs. "Rest your feet by the fire. I will make soup with what we have."

He sets about mixing moss and herbs together with a deftness I admire. He takes his time warming the soup while Oski and I watch.

Even though he is large and strong, Einar carries himself as if he is shy, often shrugging his shoulders in answer instead of speaking, as though he has the words to say but not the nerve to say them. He does this a lot more with me and seems to prefer speaking to Oski, whom he finds fascinating.

I've heard rumors about elf women marrying warriors of the Jötnar clan, attracted to the giant descendants' size and power, their marriage a perfect union of beauty and skill and strength. I overheard Einar telling Oski that his mother was beautiful beyond comprehension. I believe it.

Oski, in their strange way of saying what I'm thinking, even though they are not supposed to be reading my thoughts, makes mention of it.

"You must look like your mother," they say to Einar, breaking our silence.

Einar stops stirring for a moment and shrugs.

Oski turns to me instead. "Do you look like yours, Runa?"

Einar focuses hard on the soup pot. He has the decency not to act too interested, but I can tell he is listening.

Do I look like my mother? "No," I say at last. "I don't know who I look like."

"Well, how is that?" Oski asks. "You must look like someone. With that hair!" They toss a pebble at me.

"At least I have hair!" I shout at them.

I meant it as an insult, but Oski roars with laughter. Einar pours soup into our cups and brings one to me. I take it without looking at him. He doesn't release it right away, and when I glance up, I see he's looking at my hair. Studying it. I hate it.

I snatch the cup from him, hot soup sloshing onto the back of my hand and making my vegvisir burn. "Ah!" I cry.

"Careful," he whispers. He turns to go back to his spot but looks back at me. "Wherever you get your hair from, I think it's unique." He averts his eyes again and sits with his back to me.

Oski continues to giggle, and it's all I can do not to toss the entire cup of hot soup at them. But I'm starving, and I gulp it down, growing sleepier and warmer by the second. I should be more careful about eating things Einar has prepared, but I'm too hungry for caution. Besides, if Einar wants to kill me, he has already had plenty of opportunity. And Oski would know what he was planning.

"What was her name?" Einar asks me.

I look at him.

"Your mother," he says.

I sigh. "Asta," I say. I don't know why I'm telling him this. "My mother's name was Asta, after the loveliest flower on the whole island."

I lie back on my heavy cloak, my head on my pack, and stare at the sky. The red moon is higher now, and a flock of birds flies overhead.

"Take me to Sýr," I whisper to them, and I imagine myself as a bird, flying over everything, far above all this pain and confusion, flying free wherever I wish.

I'm on the verge of sleep, lulled by this daydream, when Einar asks Oski a question I've been dying to know the answer to.

"What *did* happen to your hair, Oski?" he asks.

Oski drains their soup cup and lets out a long belch. "Ah. Boring story."

"No," I say. "You ask us everything. Time for you to tell, mindreader."

"Mindreader?" Einar asks, a startled look on his face.

I wave my hand at him. "Don't worry. They promised not to, right, Oski?"

Oski shoots me a sharp glance.

"Oh, well, if they *promised*," says Einar, slurping his soup.

"The hair, Oski," I say. "The story."

Oski sits back against a craggy rock, their black cloak pulled around them. They look like a huge bald bird perched high atop a cliff.

Oski runs a bony hand across the top of their head. "I used to have hair. I used to have a horse. I used to have wings. Now I do not."

"Why?" asks Einar in his gentle voice.

Oski doesn't say anything for a long time, and when they do, it's as if they're speaking to us from far away. "My own warriors were forced to carry out the punishment on me."

They snicker, pointing a finger at the sky. "Because I betrayed a god," Oski says, drawing out the last word as if it were dipped in poison. "I did it to protect a mortal. A mortal I loved."

I am heartened by this. "Loved?" I ask, noting how Einar, too, seems to be hanging on the Valkyrie's words.

"One of the Fates," says Oski. "A Norn named Wyrd. She was gifted with the ability to weave the future, but longed for a simpler life. A mortal life. She chose that over the wishes of a god, who wanted her to create destinies that favored him. He was not pleased."

"My mother used to tell me tales of the Norns," Einar says. "Their weavings contain all of our stories."

Oski chuckles. "Já. Yours. Mine." Oski looks at me. "And yours, runecaster."

The memory of standing by the golden lake flashes in my mind, and for a moment it feels as if I am there again. It's so real I can smell the clover growing on the green hill I stand on. Then the memory is gone, and I am back among the stones with Einar and Oski.

"What was that?" Einar asks.

"What was what? What do you mean?" I ask.

"You both flickered. Like flames on the fire," he says, blinking his eyes, an edge of fear in his voice.

I shrug. "I don't know."

Oski continues speaking, raging at the sky with a quiet anger that chills me.

"Now I quest, and I search for Wyrd in this realm, and I scheme against the very god who punished her and then me. But I will triumph. I managed to keep my closest friend—my sword," they say, brandishing it in the gleaming daylight. "I snatched Chooser back right before I fell to earth."

Oski shakes their sword. "Oh, it made him so mad!" they shout, their voice echoing into the sky.

With their weapon held high and their voice raging, I can clearly see Oski destroying enemies on a battlefield. Their true nature is stunning.

Oski looks at me. "I have not been honest with you, runecaster," they say.

My heart pounds, not knowing what will come next. Einar shifts as though he's getting ready to stand, and I see one of his hands reaching behind him for his pack. I watch as his long fingers find the handle of his dagger.

"I spoke the truth when I said I will help you on your journey," Oski says. "But I am also searching for my true love." Oski sheathes their blade and slumps back.

"Wyrd?" Einar asks, releasing his own dagger. "You can't find her?"

Oski shakes their head. "I think she is hidden in Alfheim. But I have not found a path to it yet. The elves are secretive."

Einar looks uneasy. "The elf realm? I know a way," he says.

Oski stands, a flash of white and black. "You must take me there at once."

Einar shakes his head. "I'm not supposed to. And I don't know where Wyrd is, but I know where to find someone who does," he says and then looks at me. "And I think they can help you too."

"Enough," I say. "I'm too tired for all of this. I need to rest, and then I need to find my sister. I can't waste time looking for lost loves."

"You must," says Oski.

"Give me one good reason," I say, trying to get comfortable on the cold, hard ground that is to be my bed tonight.

"Because Wyrd knows where to find the entrance to the great library," says Oski.

"I've always wanted to see that," says Einar, awestruck.

"The great library is a myth," I say. "And besides, why do we want to go there?"

Einar answers for Oski. "Because there we may find information about how to get rid of Katla once and for all."

I sigh. "Okay, so let me see if I've got this. Now you want to go on a quest to find someone to help us find Oski's lover so she can help us find a mythical library that might give us some answers. Thanks, but I have all the answers I need," I say, pointing to the red moon. "*That* is my journey."

Einar's eyes flash brilliant gold in anger. "This is bigger than your journey," he says, shocking me by raising his voice for the first time.

"This could help everyone," he continues. "Even if we make it to moonwater, how will we defeat Katla when we get there?"

I'm so tired, and all I want in the world is to be with Sýr. "How far out of our way will we have to go?" I ask. "Or maybe that's what you want, eh? To delay me?"

Einar glances toward the east, where I know a dark forest lies. "Look, it's not far. The place we seek is beyond the trees. And no, I'm not delaying you."

I am filled with a sense of foreboding. "What is in there, Einar?"

"Elves, yes," says Oski, their voice reverent. "They will know where to find Wyrd, for they are the keepers of secrets. My Wyrd. She angered the wrong god, made him lose in battle, humiliated him."

"What if she's dead?" I ask, and Einar gives me a sharp look.

Oski turns to me and smiles. "No, not dead. I would know. I'd feel it in my soul. Wyrd is not dead. But it might be easier if she were."

"What does that mean?"

"Shush," says Oski. "Rest now. Sleep. We will see the elves this night."

I look at Einar, who gives me his usual shrug.

I wonder if Sýr is all right. *I'm coming*, I say to her with my mind's voice. *I will find a way to save you.*

I sleep a black, dreamless sleep, and when I wake I see Einar's face above mine. He's close, and I should be afraid, but I'm not.

"Shh," he says. I can smell the sweet scent of his breath. "There are night creatures approaching us, and we don't know if they're under Katla's command. We must move, and quietly, to the distant tree line of the dark forest."

Groggy, I stagger to my feet and shoulder my pack. Einar hands me my spear stick, giving it a quizzical look when he touches it. "Odd thing," he whispers.

I nod in return, trying to stifle a yawn, and he frowns at me. Why do I feel like the disappointing kid sister on this quest? When did Oski and Einar take control of my path? I'm too tired to act on my irritation though. I hear an undulating howl in the darkness and hurry behind Oski, who stamps out the fire and leads the way.

We hug the line of rocks bordering the open land of the barrens, where nothing grows and there is no shelter. We try to keep the natural wall of the badlands to our backs, but we are exposed.

I cannot see anything out here, and my eyes hurt from straining, but I know we're being stalked. More than once I hear the huff of animal breath behind me. Einar draws closer, his large form a comforting presence. Even if he and Oski are taking this journey on a tangent, I am grateful I am not alone.

It isn't far to the trees, and we reach the first spindling outliers soon enough. Once we are within the forest's boundaries, we turn and face the open field to see our pursuers. There is nothing there, save for the glinting eyes of creatures shrouded in darkness. We hear growls coming from the barrens.

"So the witch sends her beasts," Oski growls.

"What do we do?" I ask. I feel overcome with worry.

"This way," says Einar. "Hurry. We will be safe in here."

I turn to follow him, but it is so dark that I have to grab hold of his flowing cloak. He reaches back and hooks his arm through mine, and I reach out on my other side and link arms with Oski. We are like a chain in the darkness, forging ahead into the unknown.

We come to a place where several large trunks have intertwined and created a braided archway overhead. It's dark, but the moon casts a glow through an opening in the treetops.

"We need more light, Runa," Einar says to me.

I gather my runes in my palm, being careful not to drop them on the forest floor, and whisper to them. "By the rune of day, Dagaz, please light our way," I say. They flicker at first, and I'm worried I have imbued them too much with my fear, but after a moment they glow bright again.

"Hold your runes up," says Einar.

I lift them over my head, and strange markings appear on the tree trunks.

"Elf speak," says Oski.

Einar steps forward to run his hands along the markings. He shakes his head. "Not speak," he says. "Touch." As his lithe hand traces the markings, they illuminate with a sparkling light. It's as if the wood is alive with light bugs.

"Starlight in the wood," I say, my voice breathless in the cold night.

Einar reaches the end of the markings, and there is a creaking sound in the wood as a heavy trunk pushes inward.

Einar turns to me. "This place may not be safe for you."

"I am not staying out here," I say.

He nods. "I knew you would say that, but it's..." He trails off.

"What?" I ask.

"The elves can smell you," he says, shifting a little on his feet.

Oski giggles. "Right, your elf nose has been smelling her this whole time."

I feel like the forest floor is going to split open and engulf me, and my skin flushes. If it wasn't so dark, I'm sure they'd both see how red I am.

Oski jabs me in the ribs. "If you run hot like that, you will stink to Valhalla."

"Oski," Einar admonishes them. He turns to me. "It's okay, but you should put this on your skin." He hands me a salve that he pulls from his collection of little traveling jars. He's like a walking apothecary.

"What is it?" I ask.

He hesitates. "It will make you stink."

Oski continues snickering.

I have the urge to kick a Valkyrie, but I refrain. "I'm amazed you've ever had any friends."

Oksi just laughs harder.

I take the salve from Einar. "Why does it matter?" I ask him. "Are they going to eat me?" I struggle to swallow, my throat dry.

"No," says Einar, offended. "Elves don't eat people. Usually. But we want to go as unnoticed as possible. So please put it on."

"Fine," I say, taking a whiff of it. "Phew! That is rank."

Einar grins. "Yes. Put a little on your wrists and behind your neck. There," he says, directing me. "Yes, better." He places the salve back in his pack.

Oski takes a step backward. "Runecaster," they say, "you stink."

"Thanks, Oski," I say.

"You're welcome."

"Ready?" asks Einar.

"Ready," I answer.

He reaches out and takes my hand, his warmth calming my fear even if his hand is shaking a little. "Remember, you're with me. And I'll do my best to protect you."

"Okay," I say, following him into the darkness. Oski covers my back. I don't know what we will find on the other side.

ELEVEN

The darkness of the entrance to the elf realm gives way to a long corridor of lined-up birch trees, all aglow with the sparkling elven writing. At first the place seems uninhabited, but I notice candle flames and hidden doorways and windows as we walk farther in. Faint music floats through the night, and when I look up I cannot see the sky. The red moon is gone, and in its stead is a different pattern of stars.

"What gods are those?" I ask, pointing at the stars.

"This way," says Einar, ignoring me.

Oski and I follow him to a door ringed with warm light, and when he pushes it inward, I'm hit with a flurry of sounds and smells. We step through into a bustling tavern and sit at a table against the wall.

All around us are the most beautiful creatures I've ever seen, and my heart pounds with fear. I'm grateful for the salve Einar gave me, for every now and then an elegant elf glides past us in fine clothing and wrinkles their nose. They can smell me but aren't interested at all. There are some non-elf creatures here, including a group of trolls that occupies the rowdiest table in the tavern.

We sit, Oski and I agape at the sights, while Einar scans the room.

"What's next?" I whisper.

"Drink," says Oski, eyeing the jugs at the bar.

"No," Einar whispers urgently. "Do not eat or drink anything. You could be enchanted and stay here forever. It will be the best-tasting drink you've ever had, and it will be a lie."

I stare at him. He's scared too, even though he's half elf, and I realize he's never been here before.

"I hope you know what you're doing," I say.

He looks at me and opens his mouth to say something, but I suddenly find myself transfixed by a scene playing out across the tavern.

Two elves are throwing darts, but that isn't what is remarkable. What *is* remarkable is that the darts travel so fast I don't even see them leave the elves' hands. I watch as they pick up the bolts, and then the darts instantly appear in the target on the far wall, embedded as if they've always been there. But then, on another throw, the darts seem to move much slower, taking a long time to reach the target. So long, in fact, that it seems like I would have enough time to cross the tavern and pluck them from the air myself. My eyes feel aching and strange, and I worry that I'm going to have my sickness again. It has been a while since I've had a full episode. I've thought the urgency of my journey might be keeping it at bay.

As I look around the room, things seem to be speeding up and slowing down. Oski and Einar are humming with a kinetic vibration. Maybe I'm reacting to the stuff Einar rubbed on me. I feel so weird. My eyes.

"Oh no," I say. "Einar. My eyes hurt. It's the salve."

Einar looks stricken. He leans in. "Oh, Runa, I'm sorry. The herb I used sometimes helps people with eye problems but can have side effects. Can you see?"

"Yes, but everything is moving in an odd way," I answer. I watch a dart leave an elf's hand and slow to the point of standing still in the air.

"Oski, Einar," I say. "Do you see…?" I trail off when I see their faces. They are frozen.

I look around, and everything and everyone around me has slowed to a standstill. The mead and wine pouring from cups, the elves talking and dancing and kissing and eating, the candles flickering, the tallow dripping, perspiration beading, breath coming out in puffs—everything except for me. And someone else.

Two golden eyes flicker across the room. A dark, elegant elf in the far corner lights a pipe, his face shrouded in darkness, and the embers glow in the haze of smoke.

The elf is dressed in fine garments, and his long legs are crossed. He wears pointed boots made of buttery leather, and a hat tilted at a stylish angle. As he uncrosses his legs and stands, emerging from the darkness, I am entranced by his glowing eyes. They pierce through the shadows around him. He is handsome beyond imagination, far more beautiful than any of Amma's tales could give him credit for, and he gleams in the candlelight.

He walks toward me, smelling the air, and when he reaches our table he sits. As he does, I glance at my companions, my heart in my throat.

I try to whisper to them. "*Oski. Einar.*" They don't move, but I see something flicker in Einar's eyes.

"You smell strange," says the elf, taking a long puff on his pipe. "What are you hiding?" He extends one long, sharp-nailed finger and touches my cheek.

My heart is pounding. His eyes are hypnotic, and even though he radiates danger, I long for him to plant his lips on mine. He's enchanting me, and I'm powerless to stop it. I see his mouth turn up—he knows what I am feeling. He stares into my eyes, then casts a furtive look around the room.

"The herb you stink of won't hide what you are," he says at last.

"What do you mean?" My voice quakes. "Please don't eat me," I say, and then regret it.

He laughs, the sound assaulting me like little shocks to the skin.

"Why are you doing this?" I ask. "Make it stop."

"Me?" he says. "I'm not doing anything. You are the one who has pulled us out of time."

"What?" I don't even get the word out before the room returns to its normal pace with such a violent burst of sound and sight that it makes me jump.

As soon as Einar and Oski are able to move again, Einar has his arm in front of me and Oski has the tip of their sword at the elf's throat.

"Now, now," says the elf. "I'm no foe. In fact, I think I may be family," he says, looking at Einar.

They stare at each other, and I at them. The resemblance is strong. All elves are beautiful, but both Einar and this older elf have the same notched eyebrows and constellation of freckles across their cheeks, not to mention the same gold-flecked eyes.

Oski withdraws their sword from the elf's neck, but keeps it trained on their target.

"Thank you," says the elf, before returning his attention to Einar. "Are you of the Svartálfar people?" he asks.

"I am the son of Renna. From the Jötnar clan," says Einar. "She was born Renna Ör."

"Ah," says the older elf. "She was my cousin's cousin. I am Píla Ör. This is my tavern, and my store, and I have influence here."

He reaches out and touches Einar's shoulder. "I was sorry to hear of your mother's death. It was far too soon. I am sad to say this is the risk an elf takes when living in the realm of mortals. I see it often."

Einar nods, seeming lost for words.

"How I would love to show you the cities of Alfheim," Píla says to Einar. "It is the most magical of the nine worlds. You'd never want to leave."

"Isn't this Alfheim?" I ask.

Píla laughs. "No. This is just an outpost. You would never get inside the deeper levels of the realm on your own."

"Please, can you help us?" Einar asks. "We need information."

"Of course, we are family," says Píla. "But you will have to make alfablot. On that I insist."

"Alfablot? What is that?" I ask.

"Elf sacrifice," says Einar.

"Sacrifice?" I ask, my body going cold.

"Blood," says Oski, drawing a curious look from Píla.

"You are far from home, Valkyrie," Píla says.

Oski says nothing in response, but gives their sword a little twitch in warning. I wonder how frightened I should be of this sacrifice.

"Whose blood do you want?" I ask, dreading the answer.

"Human, of course," says Píla. "It can be valuable to an elf. Oh, don't worry, you don't have to spill it all. Just a few drops." Píla takes my left hand, and before I can protest, he pokes all my fingers with a dart.

Oski snarls and tries to intervene, but Einar stops them.

"Wait," he says. "This is necessary."

Píla pulls a cloth from his pocket, fine and silken and white, like a woven spiderweb, and presses my fingers into it. Then he studies it.

"Hmm. You all seek someone," he says.

"Yes," I say. "A Norn named Wyrd." I do not want to mention Sýr.

Píla nods. "You will find what you seek beyond the valley of the rock, beyond the crags, beyond the glacier. You must find the place where the island shoots its anger into the sky."

"The geyser," says Oski.

Píla nods. "And you must go before the yellow witch finds you."

"You know of Katla?" I ask, noticing as he slips the bloodied cloth into his pocket.

He looks at me. "Yes. We know of the witch. She has poisoned and enslaved our people, taken our essence. She impersonates our kind."

"Like my mother," says Einar. The sadness in his voice makes me ache.

"An abomination," says Píla, his rage humming under the surface of his words. "It is a capital offense. The sorceress Katla must die. She carries a great serpent inside her. Some say it is Grabak, one of the serpents that guards the roots of the world tree. And it eats power with an appetite that cannot be quelled."

Píla's words strike fear in my heart, for I know every word to be true. "I've seen it," I whisper. "The serpent."

Oski and Einar look at me.

"When?" Einar asks.

"In my dreams," I say.

"Are you certain they were dreams?" asks Píla.

We all sit in silence for a moment, considering this.

"Whatever protection the elves can afford you on your journey, you will have," says Píla. "I pledge this. On one condition."

"Anything," I say.

"Runa, be careful what you agree to," says Einar.

"Fear not, I will not bind her or take her sanity," says Píla. "I want her to destroy the witch, and if she's able to bring me a little piece of her, I should like to eat it." He chuckles a chilling laugh, his eyes flashing.

"I will destroy her," I say.

"You must go, and soon, for she commands all the vilest creatures of the land, and she knows you are coming. That you can trust."

"There's something else," Einar says. "More common, but still important."

"Name it," Píla says.

Einar tells him we need supplies. "But we don't have much to trade," he says.

"Wait," I say, digging into my cloak pocket. I pull out the small coin I received at the crossroads and hand it to Píla. "Here."

"Where did you get this?" Píla asks. He seems impressed.

"An elf named Falleg gave it to me," I say. "After I helped her escape from Katla."

Einar stares at me. He's impressed too.

"This is elven gold," says Píla. "And it will pay for whatever you wish."

"Good," says Einar. "Because I have quite a list."

After Einar fills him in, Píla bids us to wait while he gathers the items.

After a time the elf returns with some small bundles for

each of us. He then puts a larger one in front of me. Atop that bundle he places a pair of leather boots so fine and new that I want to cry.

Einar crouches next to me as I stare at them. "I know you're fond of your boots," he says. "But they're hurting your feet. Let me carry the old ones for you. That way you don't have to throw them away."

I nod, overcome by this kindness. I peel off my sister's boots, wincing at the pain, and hand them to Einar, who packs them away with care. The new boots fit me as if they were made to measure, and they are so soft that if my feet could sigh with relief, they would.

I slip into a back storeroom and put on the rest of the clothing Píla brought for me. He's provided me with fresh leggings, in a thicker weave and much warmer than my others, and, instead of an impractical dress, a tunic the color of an evening sky. It's so warm and easy to move in that it feels like it was made just for me. A new cap hides my hair and warms my head. I start to put on the dark gray cloak he's given me and then decide not to.

"Ah," says Píla when I come out of the storeroom. "Better. But the cloak—do you not like it?"

"I do," I say. "And I am so grateful. But I already have a good cloak."

Píla glances at the heavy, dirty cloak that sits in a pile with my other worn garb. He is too polite to say anything.

"Not that one," I say, opening my pack. I pull out my runecaster cloak, the one Sýr made for me. Black as the ocean at night, soft as an embrace, and lined with the most gorgeous blue I've ever seen.

I unfurl it and drape it around myself and then take my vegvisir clasp from the old cloak and fasten it at the neck. I feel like I'm wearing an embrace from Sýr. I know I shouldn't wear the cloak until I am an anointed runecaster, but if I don't start behaving as one, how can I become one?

I look down at myself, at all the runes Sýr stitched onto my cloak. They glow before becoming invisible again.

Einar gasps. "What is that?" he asks, reaching out to touch the edge of my cloak.

"It is Runa," says Oski, answering for me. "The runecaster."

Einar stands and looks at me as if seeing me for the first time.

I tend to shy away when people stare at me, but not this time. Perhaps it's the elegant new elf-fashioned clothes, or the flush of Sýr's love I feel from donning the cloak she made specifically for me, but I find myself meeting his gaze. Our eyes lock, and I will mine to stay steady.

Píla speaks at last. "This cloak is better."

"Do you like it?" I ask Einar, hoping the shyness in my voice isn't too obvious.

He nods. "Yes, it's...it's...you," he says finally. "It seems right."

I smile at him. "It is right."

Píla steps forward and embraces Einar, the two of them touching heads together for a moment.

"Thank you for your help," Einar says.

"Take this," says Píla, pressing something into his palm. "If you are captured. It will reunite you with your mother in the afterlife."

Einar lets out a deep breath, as if he's been holding it in for a long time. "I won't let the witch steal another elf body."

I watch as Einar places a tiny jar into his vest pocket. His eyes flick over to me, and this time I look away. The moment is too intimate, and as much as the jar strikes fear into me for Einar's sake, it is not my concern how he wishes to die. Leaving this realm by his own hand seems a far sight better than existing as a tool for Katla's evil.

Katla. Even her name in my mind causes me to rage inside. I am coming for you, witch, I think.

"Ow!" I exclaim, lurching into a nearby table. For the first time in days, the spot where Katla stabbed me is burning. I have to grab a chair to pull myself back up, and both Einar and Oski are at my side at once.

"Runecaster," says Oski, "what is it?"

I rub my chest, but I'm gasping for breath. The pain is so bad that I cannot answer. I'm growing dizzy, and it feels like someone is squeezing my neck. I don't want to perish in this elven tavern. Sýr will never know what became of me.

"I'm sorry. I'm sorry, Sýr," I say, my voice strangled from pain.

Píla pushes Einar aside and opens my cloak, yanking down the front of my new tunic.

"Hey," says Einar.

"Hush," Píla admonishes, holding up a hand. I try to focus on him, on his handsome face and elegant features, but he seems to be floating away from me as if he's underwater.

"Here," he says, touching my chest. He brushes my skin with his fingertip in the place where Katla's yellow dagger pierced me, but the pain is the same as if he stabbed me too.

I scream, and any sense of privacy or indifference we had enjoyed in the tavern to this point is now gone. All the patrons and workers stop to stare at us, at the freakish mortal with the red-rimmed eyes, the bad stink, and the wild hair poking out from under her hat. At the odd, bald, wingless Valkyrie staring down everyone in the place. At the gorgeous half elf who is now scooping me into his arms.

I have no strength left to be annoyed by this move, no ability to fight or protest. I feel like I am disappearing—and fast.

"Quickly!" a voice calls out.

Píla spins around, and behind him I can see an elf staring at us. I recognize her. It is Falleg, the elf from the crossroads. I fear for a moment that she is Katla, returned to finish me, but she walks forward and presses her hand against my cheek. I want to cry at how smooth and cool and gentle it is, like Sýr's when she tended to me when I was ill.

"Follow me. I have something in my dwelling that can help me get it out of her," she says to Einar, making for the door.

"Wait. Get what out of her?" Einar asks.

"The witch has wounded her," says Píla. "If anyone can help, Falleg can."

Oski looks at us in irritation. "Then we must hurry."

"My home is this way," Falleg calls.

Einar, holding me to him, rushes out of the warm tavern and into the cold night, following Falleg, with Oski and Píla behind us.

The black air around me is a blur of twinkling lights and odd smells. I'm carried through another doorway into a small room. This must be Falleg's home. I can't see well, but I still feel Einar holding me close as he sits down in a chair, his warm body behind me.

I am losing my hold on this realm, and I struggle to focus on my friends. Their voices come to me, in and out of the darkness, like torchlights marking the path back to them.

Falleg's face appears, and I think she's holding a large ram's horn. But why?

"I don't have much time," she says. "It must come out now."

"What is it?" Oski sounds panicked. I didn't know they could get so upset.

I sink further back into Einar. Further into a sleep I didn't know I wanted so much. Yes, rest. I want to rest. I want to sleep. Forever.

"Help," I hear Einar say. "She's fading. I don't want to lose—"

I feel the tip of something cold pierce the skin on my chest, and I shiver away from it.

Runa. Sýr's voice cuts through the darkness, and the light of the world comes rushing back to me.

"Sýr!" I scream, lurching forward so fast that I break through Einar's hold on me. He clutches me back to him again so that I don't fall face-first onto the floor. The room is bright now, and my heart beats so hard I'm sure everyone can hear it.

"Do you hear that?" I shout. "My heart!" It's deafening.

Oski, Falleg, and Píla stare at me, their faces awash with concern. Einar keeps his arms around me and his face pressed into my hair.

I look around, frantic, trying to make sense of where I am. It's a little kitchen, and it's filled with odd objects and tools.

"What did you give her?" Píla asks Falleg.

"A little kick," says Falleg. "Now for the hard part." She places the ram's horn over the sore spot on my chest. At first I think she's going to use it to listen to my heart, because it is beating with such erratic thumps, but instead she places her mouth on the pointed end of the horn and begins to inhale.

"What are you doing?" Oski asks, horrified.

Falleg pauses and then spits out a vile yellow fluid that sizzles on the stone floor.

"The witch has impaled her," says Falleg. "I must remove it. Or she will turn."

"T-t-turn?" I ask, my teeth chattering. I'm so cold.

Falleg sucks on the horn again and spits out more yellow gunk. "Into the witch's slave."

There is silence while everyone takes this in, the only sound being Falleg's rhythmic inhaling and spitting. She removes the yellow stuff bit by bit.

"Is it poison?" asks Einar, his voice shaking. "Can I give her something? I might be able to—"

"No," says Falleg. "Not poison. Venom. The most potent venom I've encountered. No antidote." She spits again, and now she seems to grow very tired.

"Venom," says Oski. "Yes, of course. The witch is not what she seems."

"Nothing is what it seems," says Falleg, stumbling back from me. "Not anymore. Not for me, not for you, and not for her."

Falleg takes one last great breath inward, and when she does she stretches her arms out toward me.

"Runa," she groans, falling backward. "*Fight*."

Píla catches her, his movements so quick I hardly perceive them.

"Falleg," I cry, pushing against Einar's arms. I want to get to her, but I'm still weak and cold.

Píla holds her close and caresses her face, speaking in a whispered language I don't understand.

"What can we do?" asks Oski, their voice grave.

Píla shakes his head. "It is futile. She is already gone." He looks down at the limp body of his friend, his face a mixture of devastation and love. "She took it into herself."

"But why?" Oski asks. "Why would she?"

Einar whispers, "Because she knew it was Runa's one hope, that no one else would have a chance of withstanding the venom."

"She wanted you to survive," Píla says. He continues gently stroking Falleg's skin.

I know what he says is true, and I wish I could take it back into me.

"Runa," Einar says, trying to calm me. "Shh, it will be okay."

"No," I sob. "When I met her, Katla had possessed her. I set her free. Now she is dead because of me. She should never have met me."

"No, Runa," says Píla. "She would still be in Katla's clutches if it weren't for you."

"No. No, she didn't deserve to die." I can't take this. I push away from Einar. I'm a little stronger now, and he lets me go.

I stand on wobbling legs and turn to face him. Then I look at Oski. "You'll both be killed if you stay with me. I'm cursed. I'm a freak."

Einar stares at the floor where Falleg lies, and I am horrified to realize that this radiant dead elf reminds him of his mother. It's too much, and I turn to walk away.

"You will be better off without me," I say.

"No," Oski says, "Don't move one more step." Their voice is cold and hard, unlike anything I've heard from them before. I turn toward them, and they rise above me in all their menacing height and physical power.

"You made an oath to me. A blood oath. You will continue on with me at your side. You will help me find Wyrd. Together we will find the great library and a way to defeat this witch once and for all. You will fulfill your destiny."

I am shaking with fear, with cold, and from exhaustion. I don't know how much more I can endure.

"I don't know if I can," I say, my voice small.

"Maybe you can't," says Einar, gathering his pack and mine. "But we're going to try. Together."

He walks over to me and refastens the clasp on my cloak. "Put your hood up," he says. "The night is cold."

I allow my friends to guide me back out into the forest of the mortal realm. As we leave, I look back at Píla, still holding Falleg. He watches us leave with a kind resignation. He blows me a kiss, and I feel it travel on the wind and land against my cheek with the softness of silk.

"Thank you," I whisper to them both, as much with my heart as with my voice.

I know they hear me.

TWELVE

When we emerge, night has turned to day. After a while we stop to rest and eat, though I do not feel like consuming anything.

Einar gathers moss, roots, and herbs and cooks them into a stew, and Oski runs their sword through a weasel and roasts it over the fire. It's heartening to have meat again after such a long time, and Einar watches me until I have chewed every last bit of my portion. Every bite imbues me with strength, and I feel my old self returning. Einar prepares tea for me and offers a salve to rub on my chest. I notice he is most content when he is caring for someone and looking after them in this way.

We must leave the relative protection of the trees now and pass back across the barrens, retracing our steps toward the rocky badlands. Then we will have to pass the steep rocks that jut from the earth and will have to bypass the glacial fields to find the great geyser.

We set off walking, me struggling to keep up, and by afternoon we are at the edge of a volcanic field dotted with scalding jets of steam and lava. Somewhere out there is the geyser. And Wyrd.

"It is no wonder she was banished here," says Oski, their anger apparent in their voice. "This place is like the realm of Hel."

"Which way?" Einar asks, and it takes me a moment to realize he is asking me.

"Oh," I say, glancing at my vegvisir. It isn't moving. I pull out my runes and cast them onto the black earth, among the lava stones and strange green flowers growing between.

"Show us the way to Wyrd," I say. My runes spark, and an image of a bindrune appears in the air before me. It's a new vegvisir, this one made from burning light, and it rotates beyond my reach. I try to touch it, but it moves farther away, as if wanting me to follow it. I have never seen such a thing before. Sýr has never spoken of this.

"Runecaster," Oski says. "What are you doing?"

"Do you see it?" I ask them, and they look around, everywhere but at the vegvisir.

I gather my runes and walk forward in the direction of the burning vegvisir. "This way. Follow me."

We walk on as the sky grows darker and the blood-colored moon hangs ever higher in the sky. We don't have many days before it eclipses and the competition at moonwater commences.

We spot a small hot spring along our path that is so enticing we all agree to take a moment to soothe our aching muscles. I'm reluctant to break our momentum yet again, and it's a little odd that Oski doesn't want to press on, but the steaming water is too inviting.

I'm not fond of the idea of Einar seeing me without my clothes on, given how skinny this journey is making me, but I can't wait to slip into the warm waters. I peel off my gear and hurry to join Oski, who is already reclining in the pool. I try not to look at them, for they seem sensitive about the scars across their back and the strange lumps on their shoulder blades where their wings used to be.

Einar, for his part, does not stare at me. Nakedness is not something he should ever be ashamed of, for his form as it slips from the spring's edge and into the water is very impressive. I don't let my gaze linger, but I see enough to be sure of that.

We mean to have a quick warm-up, clean off some of the grime, and bolster ourselves with the healing minerals, but the water is so calming, so inviting…

Runa. I hear a whisper. *Wake*. Sýr's voice? I look to the sky to see if I can find her face in the stars, but I notice that night has given way to day again, and the moon is even higher now. I stare at my fingers. The flesh is wrinkled and pale. How long have we been in the hot spring?

"Oski! Einar!" I say, but neither of them answers. They both float in contentment, oblivious to me.

"No," I say, looking around. "This spring is enchanted!"

I turn to see if I can reach my runes, but they're too far away, and every time I try to crawl from the spring, I grow so weary that I'm sucked back in. My spear. If I can just grab the tip of my spear, I can get free. I reach for it, and I'm so close. The tip of my longest finger makes contact with the cracked brown stone on the blunt end, and I inch it closer to me. Once I've got it in hand, I use it to hook my rune pouch and pull it toward me. I need to hurry before we're bones and hanging flesh.

I shout to my runes, "Help us! Give me strength!"

They glow and begin to chatter, and I keep hold of the pouch as I feel a surge of power rush through me. Please work, I think as I drive the edge of my spear into the surrounding rocks. I pull with everything I have until I gain enough edge to pull myself free of the spring.

"Einar!" I shout, but he does not appear to hear me.

I place my runes around my neck and hold my spear out to him to grab onto. "Wake!" I shout, and I feel my runes clatter.

Both Oski and Einar blink as if waking from a long sleep. They look around in confusion and stare at me. I must be a sight. Naked, withered from the hot water, with wild hair and glowing runes and my spear pointed at them both.

"Hurry," I urge.

Einar grasps my spear and I haul with all my strength until he is able to find purchase. He pulls himself up next to me, dripping and steaming in the cold night. Together we pull Oski from the water, and when they emerge, some of the skin on their back sloughs off, including one lone black feather.

They watch it fall to the ground, wet and matted, and then pick it up with so much sadness that I have to look away.

We all dress with haste, keeping our backs to the hot spring, as it still calls to us, its waters as alluring as ever. As we leave I glance back at it, and I swear it looks more like a mouth than a pool. I shudder.

"Are you okay?" Einar asks. "Don't look back."

I nod and lead on.

The day brightens as we walk, and we begin to see smaller geysers springing up around us. Before long we come to a large crater in the earth. A deep rumble forms, and then a huge column of water shoots skyward, reflecting the red hue of the sky.

As it rages I see a reflection, an image, in the water. It looks like a statue. When the water recedes back into the earth, so does the image.

"There," I say, pointing beyond the geyser.

"Where?" asks Oski. "I don't see anything."

I walk over to a barren spot in the land. It looks as if nothing is here, but the ground in this spot is smooth while the rest of it is craggy with volcanic rock. Whatever lies in this spot, it's invisible.

"What are you doing?" Einar asks. "What do you see?"

"Her," I say. "A woman made of stone."

THIRTEEN

I cast my runes onto the barren spot in the ground. "Show yourself," I command.

The earth rumbles again as if the geyser will spew, but instead a large stone woman appears from the ground. She is beautiful. Her carved robes are flowing, and her hair curves away from her face in gentle swirls. Her gaze is cast toward the sky, and she has a wide-open face and a full mouth.

Oski falls to their knees at the statue's feet, kissing it.

"My love," they say. "Oh, my love."

I feel an odd sensation in my head, like something crumbling. I have flashes of glaciers moving, of great eruptions, of the slow passing of time. More than that, I feel the stone lady's aching loneliness.

Tell me this, says a sweet voice in my mind. *What do I desire?*

I have a flash of Oski's face, gazing in love at the statue. Then a flash of Frigg's face, the way she looked at Sýr.

"To be seen," I answer.

Einar casts a quick look at me, surprised by my words.

Oski stares at the stone lady, tears in their eyes.

"To be loved as if you're not made from stone but of flesh," I say, echoing the thoughts of the statue as they appear in my mind.

"To be mortal," says Oski. They must be reading my thoughts. In this case, I don't mind them listening in. I think about that single, sad feather.

Can you release me? the lady asks.

I see ancient runes appear in the rock, some older than what I can understand. Bindrunes.

"I don't have anything powerful enough to open these," I say to Oski.

"What do you need?" they ask.

"I need...love," I say.

"Then you're in luck," says Oski, "because I have loved her all this time."

"Then a sacrifice from you," I say.

Oski takes the feather from their cloak and touches it to the stone lady's hand. "I gave up my wings for her. I knew the consequences of my defiance, but I did it anyway."

The stone lady begins to crack and split and crumble, shaking, and then a woman of flesh appears.

"Wyrd!" Oski exclaims, wrapping the woman in their long arms.

"My Valkyrie," says Wyrd. She tries to embrace Oski, but her arms are still made of rock.

"Your arms," says Oski.

Wyrd tries again to lift them, but they fall heavily at her sides. She shakes her head.

"Runecaster," Oski says. "She isn't whole."

"I'm so sorry," I say. "I don't know what else to do."

I look at Einar, and he takes one of Wyrd's stone hands in his, turning it over. "I wish I could help," he says, "but I don't have a potion for this. Maybe we can find something at moonwater?"

"No," Wyrd says. "I'm grateful to you all the same." She looks at Oski. "You gave up your wings. It's fair that I give up my weavers."

"I will find you a cure," says Oski. "We will travel to moonwater together."

Wyrd looks sad. She nods at her feet. They also are still made of stone and are melded together in one solid block held fast to the earth. "I will remain here, as I always have."

"Then I will too," says Oski.

"No, love," says Wyrd. "I have seen that you have important work yet to do. After all, I spent much of my existence weaving destinies. When you are done with this part of your journey, then you can come to me. We've waited this long. We can wait a little longer."

Oski is crying, and it's hard to watch.

"Einar," I say. "Can we make a fire? Give them some time?"

"We don't have much time, Runa," he says, nodding at the red moon overhead.

"I know," I whisper. "But if we can't stop for love..." I don't complete the thought. I don't even know what I was going to say. *Is* it all worthwhile? Would Sýr want to be saved at any cost? Or would she stop? I think she would stop.

Einar looks at me for a long moment and then nods.

"Okay," he says and sets about making camp for the evening. "We will stay until Oski is ready to say goodbye." His last word is almost inaudible. He's afraid Oski won't be able to leave, but I know they will. If there's one thing a Valkyrie takes to heart, it's a quest bound by a blood oath. They have reminded me of it often enough.

We give the two lovers some privacy to get reacquainted, building them a small fire and then one for ourselves that's a little farther away and out of the path of any geysers that want to shoot us skyward.

It is both maddening and comforting to spend the evening resting and eating soup. I want to run on into the night, toward the moon, toward Sýr, toward whatever bloody destiny awaits. And I want to stay here, with my friends, in the warmth of this moment.

"Is Sýr like you?" Einar asks, breaking my thoughts.

"Like me? How do you mean?"

"Strong," he says. "Kind."

I don't answer at first. No one has ever called me strong before. I don't know if I'm kind. I've never had much in the way of friends. I don't say any of this to Einar because I doubt he can relate. He is one of those people that everyone loves. Beautiful, an heir to the leadership of a great clan, powerful in every sense. And even though this journey is changing me with every step, I am still me. Freaky Runa with the broken mind.

"No," I say at last. "Not like me. Better. Much better."

"Impossible," Einar says with a smile, one of the first I've seen. It's slight, and it disappears as fast as it came. I place the image away in my mind. I will try to remember it.

"Well," I say, "if you want to talk about strength, then we can talk about how Sýr raised me from a babe when she was a child herself. She's taught me, cared for me, kept me alive, despite my weaknesses. And my sickness."

Einar nods, listening in silence.

"I have problems with my eyes, as you've seen, and sometimes I lose my grip on this realm. I...see things that aren't there, and I get confused. It happens a lot when I'm scared."

"You seem okay now," he says.

I shake my head. "I'm not. I miss my sister. Sýr has never made me feel like a freak."

"How could she?" he asks. "You're..."

"What?" I glance at him, and he looks away.

"You," he says at last.

We are quiet for a moment, enjoying the crackle of the fire, the murmurings of Oski and Wyrd's conversation and the occasional whoosh of geysers going off around us.

"Everyone thinks I missed out, not having my mother," I say. "But Sýr has been a mother to me."

Einar stokes the fire and offers me another cup of soup. I wave it off, not sure I can fit any more into my belly.

"I didn't know my mother at all, because she died when I was born. But it's odd. Sometimes I feel like I remember her. I know that's impossible. If anything, I know her because of Sýr. She always told me stories about her. And everyone says that Sýr is the very image of our mother. Still...I wish I had something of her."

"I can't help with that," says Einar. "But I understand it. I keep my mother's pin with me always." He unclasps a golden pin from inside his cloak and holds it up. It glints in the firelight.

"Wow," I whisper. "Elven gold is the prettiest gold."

He chuckles. "Yes, it is."

"What is the design?" I ask.

"It's an arrow" he says, "named after my family line." He turns it over and over in his hands, the sharp end glinting dangerous as any weapon I've seen. He puts it back with care, making sure it is attached and secure.

"Lucky," I say. "To have that." I feel myself flush. "I didn't mean..."

He nods. "I know," he says.

Einar stokes the fire and then opens his pack, pulling out a small bundle. Wordlessly he holds it out to me.

"What is it?" I ask, thinking it's more medicinal herbs. He's always pushing them on me.

"I found it in the forest. After we left the elf realm. It's not much. "

I unwrap it, and the scent hits me first. Then the soft purple color. It's an asta flower. My mother's namesake. I can't speak. I stare at it and then at him.

He doesn't look at me and keeps stoking the fire.

I inhale its scent and hold the flower close to me, closing my eyes. I wonder if I try hard enough whether I can conjure my mother's image. But nothing comes. When I open my eyes, Einar is gazing at me. A slight smile appears across his sad mouth.

We sleep for a few hours, snuggled in our cloaks, back-to-back. Our heads rest on our packs, and we dream next to the glowing embers of the fire.

Oski wakes us, jostling our shoulders.

The cold morning rushes across my face like a rude slap. I groan.

"We must go now," Oski says. "Before I lose all nerve."

I nod, gathering my supplies. Einar hurries off to relieve himself and is almost blasted into the sky by a large geyser. He lets out a whoop, and I can't help but chuckle. I look at Oski, whose face is a mixture of sadness and something else. Anger? It's so hard to tell.

"What is it?" I ask.

"Wyrd knows the entrance to a root of Yggdrasil," they say.

"The world tree?" I ask. I've never thought of it as a literal place. Amma used to tell me tales of Yggdrasil, and how its branches hold all the realms of the world. I could never understand how a tree can hold such a vast area, heavens and earth and underworld, within its roots and branches.

We walk over to Wyrd, still stuck to the ground. It seems as if she could walk away at any moment, but there she rests, a permanent outcropping.

"Runa," Wyrd says, "when you find the root, you will find the library. And in the library, you will find answers."

"But how do I find the root?" I ask. I feel a glint of hope again. If we can get to this library, perhaps we can find something with which to defeat Katla. Perhaps I can learn more about how to battle her with runes. My education is still so incomplete.

"I know the way," says Wyrd.

"Okay," says Einar, walking up behind us. "Tell us."

Wyrd shakes her head. "I know it in my body, not in my mind. If I walk, I will be led there. But I cannot describe the way."

"How will that help us?" Einar asks, frustrated. "You cannot walk."

I put a hand on his shoulder.

Oski holds out their hand, and Wyrd places her heavy one in it.

"She means to send a piece of herself with us," says Oski.

"I don't understand," I say.

Oski takes a step back. "Watch."

Wyrd lifts her left arm, and with a great yell brings the heavy stone down onto her outstretched right arm, cracking it in half. The stone hand and forearm tumble to the ground, and Oski scoops it up and kisses it.

"Wyrd!" I exclaim. "What have you done?"

"It will point the way," she says, smiling. She looks at Oski. "Bring it back, my love. And bring yourself too."

"My wings, your weavers," says Oski. "I will return."

I step forward and embrace Wyrd as best I can. "Thank you," I say.

"Go, child," says Wyrd. "For all my hope rests with you."

I swallow. "And if I fail?" My voice is thick with dread.

"Don't," she says. "I have but one other arm."

Oski laughs before taking a last long moment to bid Wyrd farewell.

I pull Einar along with me to give them privacy.

At last Oski manages to tear themselves from their love and rejoin us, wielding Wyrd's severed arm in front of them like a demented compass. "Onward!"

Einar and I follow, with Oski blowing kisses on the wind as we walk away from Wyrd. As we retreat the ground rumbles, and Wyrd disappears back into the earth once again.

I say a quiet spell of protection. Not for us, but for Wyrd. I ask the runes, and the earth, to watch over her until we can return. One day we will set her free.

FOURTEEN

The stone hand waves in a macabre arc as Oski holds it out in front of them. It settles on a direction, and Oski leads us away from the geyser fields, past crags of lava flow and into a fertile valley. A small stream, verdant bushes, and a sense of eerie calm are all that exist here. That and a massive ash tree rising in the center of everything.

We descend into the valley, and I note that there are no other trees here. The tall tree ahead has a strange allure. I've never seen one like it before. Ash trees are not supposed to grow as thick as this one is, and it has the quality of something that's been woven in fabric—a picture of a tree rather than the tree itself. But I can see as we near it that its upper branches are swaying, so it must be a real tree.

"Is this the root we're looking for?" asks Oski, pointing at the tree. "Wyrd's hand is pulling stronger. And there's something about this tree…something off."

"Yes," I say. "I feel it too."

"It doesn't seem like much to me," says Einar. "I thought a root of Yggdrasil would be more magnificent."

"Hmm," I say. "Perhaps not. It wouldn't be very well disguised then."

He looks around at the valley. "Too…nice…here," he says, echoing my thoughts.

"Yes," I say. "It feels odd. Perfect. Maybe dangerous."

"A spell?" Einar asks. "Do you think this place is enchanted, Runa?"

Oski scans the landscape. "And eyes in the fields?" they ask, pointing to the tall grasses to the east of the tree.

"I don't know. I don't see anything," I say. And yet I know we are being watched.

"I feel the presence of Katla," Oski says.

"Me too," says Einar. He is shaking. I place a hand on his arm to steady him. He lets out a breath.

"Then let's not waste any more time," I say.

"How do we enter?" Oski says as we approach the tree. "There is no door. All I see is this mark."

It's a phrase in runes. I read it out loud. "It says, 'Make the sound to enter.'"

"What sound?" Einar asks.

"I don't know. What sound do you make to open a tree? A knock?"

Oski knocks. Nothing.

I knock. Nothing.

Einar shrugs. He knocks. Nothing. "What now?" he asks.

"I don't know," I say. But then I get an idea. I turn to Oski. "May I have Wyrd's hand?"

Oski passes it to me, and I use the stone appendage to knock. After a moment the wood groans, and a door appears and opens inward.

I can see that it's very dark inside the tree. I have no desire to enter without knowing what's there, but Wyrd's hand pulls me forward with a jolt.

"Runa!" Einar shouts. I hear them lumbering in behind me.

The door shuts, and we find ourselves in a small chamber. It's too dark to see, so I glow my runes.

"There," Einar whispers, pointing. The room narrows to a small stairwell that has a faint light coming from it.

We go down the small staircase, which opens up into a great hall. It's wider and taller than any hall I've seen—bigger even than the huge gathering places my people use for celebrations. Everything is covered in a twinkling dust. The floor and the walls all shine, and I think this place must be enchanted, but I don't feel any of the uneasiness I did in the exposed valley outside. No, this place is warm despite its loftiness, and it smells like my amma's hut.

I realize why when I see that there are scrolls and books and parchments all over the room. They line the walls, rest on ladders and are scattered all over the tables. They're spilling open, large and small, a jumble of ancient knowledge. Some of the books are shelved so close to the ceiling that I wonder how anyone could reach them. As far as I can tell, the hall goes up to the heavens and continues down into the depths of the earth.

"The great library," I whisper. I feel a terrible pang of sadness. "Amma will never get to see this. She would have loved it."

Einar places a hand on my shoulder.

"I have seen only one book in my lifetime," says Oski. "And I didn't read it."

Einar chuckles. "I've read lots."

"You have?" I ask. I've seen some old spellbooks that Sýr has, and Amma used to let me peek at her scrolls from time to time, but not much more than that.

"Yes," says Einar. "I was training to be a potion mage, remember? A lot of it is reading the old wisdom. And my mother loved to read." He runs a finger across the worn spine of a thick green book. Then he picks up a large brown one and gently turns its pages. As he does so, the gold lettering flakes off a bit and falls glittering to the floor. This must be where all the twinkling dust is from. I realize now that the books and scrolls in this library are a special kind.

"Magic books," I say.

We hear a sound, a frantic scurrying across the floor, from somewhere in the room. We look around but don't see anything. The sound echoes in the great hall.

"Oski, did Wyrd say anything about a keeper?" I ask.

"No," says Oski. "Nothing."

"We're not alone," says Einar, pulling a dagger from his belt.

"That is obvious," Oski says. They unsheath their sword.

I ready my spear. *What is it?*

"You won't be needing those," says a croaking voice. "Words are all that exist here."

Suspended high above the floor, hanging from a rope, is a strange creature. As it lowers itself, the rope squeaking and groaning, I see that it is a man who looks more like a tortoise than a mortal. He is short, with a curved, shell-like back and greenish skin.

"Hello," I say, my voice wavering.

"What *is* that?" Einar hisses.

"Should I kill it?" Oski asks.

"No!" I plead. "Don't!"

The man laughs. His feet now on the floor, he limps toward us, and I can see that he is very, very old. Groaning, he pushes some books aside and leans a weary arm across the table.

"Messy in here. My apologies. I am always trying to get the books in order, but they never seem to stay put!" He peers at me.

I note that his eyes are like slits in his head, and when they open and close they bulge out at me. It's unsettling.

"What are you then?" he asks me.

"What is *she*?" Oski scoffs. "What are *you*?"

"I'm the Keeper of the Books," he says. "Name's Orð. Who are you?"

I clear my throat. "I'm Runa. This is Einar and Oski. We were directed here by, well, by our friend." I hold out Wyrd's hand, and Orð gasps.

"Don't worry," I say. "We didn't do this to her. It was a gift."

"Funny gift," says Orð.

"Our friend Wyrd," Einar says, stepping forward. "She said we could find the knowledge we seek here."

Orð appraises Einar. "Haven't had too many elven folk here. So what kind of knowledge is it that you seek? Potions? Cures?"

Einar nods. "Yes."

"Of what sort?" Orð asks. He regards us with suspicion.

"The kind needed to kill a bad witch," says Einar.

"A bad one, eh?" asks Orð.

"The worst," says Einar. "And you have so many wonderful things..." Einar trails off, enchanted again by the books and scrolls and endless reams of parchment. He can't help touching them.

"Well," says Orð after a long pause, "they *are* wonderful. Do have a look around. See what you can find."

Einar starts combing through the stacks. Somehow he seems to know what he's looking for and approximately where to find it. Oski plonks down on a pile of books, looking bored.

"I could use some help," I say.

"Go on," says Orð. "If we don't have it, no one does."

"I need a book on rune magic. A spellbook of old. I must take my training to the next step."

"Ah, a runecaster you are. I thought so. With those eyes."

"What do you mean?" I ask, feeling defensive. I hate it when people notice how strange my eyes are.

Orð doesn't answer. He scuttles across the floor, weaving with grace through the piles of books. He clambers up a rickety ladder and retrieves one for me from a high shelf. He tosses it into the air, and I catch it. The cover has a strange bindrune on it that I've never seen.

"What is this?" I ask.

"Don't know, can't read it," says Orð. "I've tried many times, and I cannot."

I turn it over in my hands and notice that the strange bindrune disappears and then reappears. I open the cover and see that the first page is blank. And the next. And the next.

"No wonder you can't read it," I say. "There's nothing here."

"No?" Orð asks. "Touch it and see."

I run a finger across the page. A series of silver-colored illustrations of runes appears. They are old, but I can decipher most of them. They appear to be instructions for various spells and rituals, including a method for making runestones for casting.

"I guess only a runecaster can read that book," says Orð. "Take it. It seems you were meant for each other."

"Thank you," I say, opening my pack to place it inside.

"Oh say, what have you got in there?" Orð scoots over and pulls open my bag.

"Hey!" I protest.

"What? You want the book, yes?" he asks.

"Yes, and you said I could take it," I answer.

"But we must trade for it," Orð says, rummaging in my pack.

He finds the tiny vial I took from the hidden compartment in Sýr's wooden trunk.

"Oh...reflecting powder," says Orð, examining the little container with awe.

"Is that what it is? You know what it does?" I ask.

"Oh yes," he says. "Whatever you sprinkle it on will see itself. But be careful. It's very powerful. Not always wise to see yourself."

I nod.

Orð continues rummaging through my bag. He finds my father's old dirty cloak. "Oh," he says. "Warm." He looks at me.

"You want *that*?" I ask.

"Please," he says.

"Go ahead," I say.

Orð grunts in delight as he pulls out the cloak and wraps it around his curved frame.

I look around for Einar, who is now emerging from the stacks with a small book. It's deep blue and thin, and it bears an elven mark.

"How much for this?" Einar asks.

"Bah!" says Orð. "Not much use for it myself. Elf potions. If you want it, maybe you trade for a drink of mead?"

Einar shakes his head. "I'm sorry, I don't have any."

Orð grumbles. "My back. Oh, it is so sore from climbing and hoisting. Books, books, books. A drink of mead would be the thing."

"Wait," Einar says. He opens his pack and pulls out a small jar. "Put this in your tea tonight, and it will help with your sore back."

Orð takes it and sniffs. "Blech! Smells like troll!"

Einar smiles. "That's because it's made from crushed troll bone." He glances at me. "I didn't kill one! I just found the bones. They're very valuable. Trolls are strong, and their bones, hair, and even toenails are wonderful cures."

"That's disgusting," Oski says.

I look at Orð. "Will you accept the trade?"

"Yes," he says. He leans in to speak to Einar in a low tone. "Say, will this make me younger?"

Einar grins. "No, but you will feel like it does."

"Oh!" Orð whoops.

Oski sighs. "Are we done here?"

"I am," says Einar.

I have another question. "Orð?"

"Hmm?" He is busy admiring his troll potion and snuggling into his new cloak. He doesn't seem to care that it's so long it billows around his feet.

"You've read everything in here, yes?"

"Most," he says with false modesty.

"This book says that if I want to be a real runecaster, I have to forge my own runes. And I definitely need to do that. Because I will have to fight a powerful witch at moonwater."

Orð stares at me. "Then you will need very powerful runes indeed," he says, nodding.

"Yes, but I don't have the right kind of materials. Where can I find something powerful enough?"

"Well," he says, pausing for a moment to think. "You could kill the elf and use his bones." Orð looks at Einar, very seriously. He laughs, an infectious, chortling sound that makes Oski look up from their perch and smile.

Einar frowns.

"No," I say, fighting to suppress my own laughter. "We need him."

"The Valkyrie?" the turtle man whispers.

"Mm-mm." I shake my head.

Oski hisses at him and waves Wyrd's hand.

I hold up my own hand. "Stop."

Orð rubs his fleshy chin. "Hmm. There is something that could work," he says. "But it is very powerful. Too much power for most runecasters. But a special one like you, with eyes like yours...perhaps you can benefit."

"What is it?" I ask. "Please tell me."

"Oh..." says Orð. "Time stones."

Einar lets out a funny sound. I'm not sure if it means he's excited or worried. Knowing Einar, he's probably worried.

"You might as well say we need pieces of the moon," says Oski with a dismissive wave of Wyrd's hand. "There *are* no time stones, lunatic. No one has seen them for generations, if they ever existed at all."

"They exist!" Orð shouts. "I have seen them myself. Granted, it was a long time ago, when I lived a different life outside the great tree's root. But I saw them. Before I was chosen to keep the knowledge."

"Where did you see them? Please, I have to know," I say.

Orð leans toward me and grasps my shoulders. His voice is quiet but intense. "I saw them at the bottom of the ocean."

I groan. He *is* a lunatic. "That won't help us," I say. I feel despair wash over me, sapping my strength. I'm so tired. How can I possibly find something at the bottom of the ocean?

"Ah, but there is a place to get help," he says. "A keeper I know."

"One like you?" Einar asks.

"No, not like me at all," says Orð. "He is very mistrustful of mortals. Doesn't like to trade. It could be suicide."

"Great," mutters Einar.

"Exciting," Oski says.

"But, runecaster," says Orð. "If you can get the time stones and forge the runes, you will be unstoppable. Especially with those eyes."

"Why do you keep saying that?" I ask.

"Oh..." says Orð. "Your eyes are very unusual. Special. Didn't you know?"

"I-I..." I trail off, speechless. "No. My eyes have always been my weak point."

Orð laughs at this.

I look at Oski, who smiles at me.

"The crazy little man is right about one thing," they say. "Time stones will change everything."

I look at Einar. "What do you think? Did you find the poison recipe you need?"

Einar nods. "But it's not going to be enough. If I can get to Katla, and if I can deliver the poison, it could weaken her," he says. "But you're the one who will have to defeat her. I think we need to try to get the stones."

I sigh. "This keeper you speak of," I say to Orð. "Where can I find him?"

"Oh, it's not far," says Orð. "Go to where the ice breaks apart into the sea. You will have to go into the water to access his cave. Very cold. It will be dangerous."

"Of course it will," says Einar.

"How will I know where his cave is?" I ask.

"Oh, the spear you carry will help," Orð says, pointing to it.

"What? Why?" I ask.

"Because it belongs to him," he says.

I stare at my spear, illuminated in the glow of my rune pouch and the candlelight of the great library.

"See the runes along its length?" Orð says.

I realize with a shock that the elaborate swirling designs along the spear are not decorations at all. They are indeed runic staves devoted to the sea goddess Rán.

"Speak the runes, and the spear will take you to the cave you seek," says Orð.

"Thank you," I say. "I don't know how to repay you for your kindness."

Orð grasps my hands in his, and when he speaks his tone is grave. "You can thank me in the next life."

FIFTEEN

Once we are safely outside the tree, the door closes and then disappears. I clutch the spellbook Orð gave me. I can't stop thinking about what he said about my eyes. *Special* eyes. What did he mean? I should have asked more questions.

Special gifts are for other people. People like Sýr, who have always been beautiful and loved, and who have steady hearts and strong bodies. I've always been weaker than the others, prone to sickness, and my goals have always been selfish, not altruistic. My dream is to sail away, not to stay and serve.

"Are you okay?" Einar touches me on the wrist. The sensation travels up my arm in an electric flush.

I shiver. "Yes," I say. "That turtle man gave me a lot to think about."

"I know," he says, gazing into the sky. The red moon is overhead, growing bigger and darker every hour. "Listen." He turns to me, leaning in so I can feel his warm breath on my cheek. "If you want to go find moonwater now and forget about this time-stone thing, I'm with you. And if you don't want to face Katla, want to just run away…" He trails off.

"I know," I say, meeting his steady gaze. But we both know that quitting isn't a choice either of us can make. Our clans and families and futures are at risk.

"Thank you," I say. "For being on my side. And for everything else."

He continues looking at me. Being this close to him isn't awkward like it used to be, but it's not comfortable either. I'm trying to get used to meeting the intensity of his gaze. I feel like there's not much stopping one of us from kissing the other, and I wish I had more time to dwell in this moment. But the red moon won't wait. Sýr cannot wait.

"We need to continue northeast toward the ice," I say, breaking the soft tension between us. "It shouldn't be far. Just beyond the valley toward the coast. My spear will help us find our way, I suppose. But we need some replenishment first." Píla had given us some food, but we've run out.

"I agree," he says. "We should take a bit of time to gather food and then go." He pauses. "I don't like what Orð said about it being so dangerous." Einar touches my spear, a frown on his face. I think he wishes I had never found this thing.

"I'll be fine," I say. "I have you."

Oski interrupts with complaints of their ever-growling stomach, so I pull my hook and line from my pack to see if I can catch some fish in the stream we saw on the way into the valley. Einar sets about gathering moss and scavenges the grassy fields surrounding us for herbs and roots. Oski, as usual, does nothing.

Once I'm beside the stream, I dig grubs near the soft earth along the water's edge. It reminds me of Núna. Where is she now? I pierce the worms' fat bodies and toss my line into the water. It isn't long before I catch a few smallfish.

As I am cleaning them, I see something in the shallow water. It's a rune, one made of whalebone. I recognize it as one of Sýr's collection.

I dive forward, splashing, and Einar hurries over. "What is it?"

I scoop the rune and cradle it in my hands. "It's Uruz," I say. "The rune for strength and will. It's a message from Sýr!" She wants me to stay strong. The world is alive with Sýr, and Sýr is alive! I am so full of glee that I embrace Einar in a sudden hug.

I let go of him just as quickly and hold out the rune in explanation. "She must have left this for me."

"A positive sign," says Einar, still standing close to me.

We roast the fish over the fire and gobble them down, all of us silent. I wonder if they're worrying about the next step in our journey. Orð said it would be dangerous to seek the time stones, but I have to try. Sýr's rune has given me new hope.

"Runa?" Einar's voice startles me. I look up to see him standing over me. "Everything okay?"

"Thinking," I say. I move over so he can sit next to me on the damp trunk of a fallen tree. He sits close enough for our shoulders to brush against each other, his soft gray cloak rustling against mine.

His cloak fits his broad shoulders so well. It has a fuzzy softness to it that makes me want to bury my head in his neck, though I dare not do such a thing.

Einar is looking at me with a curious expression, as if trying to read my thoughts. I often catch him looking at me this way. It used to make me feel like I was a problem for him to solve, him looking at me the way he studies his plants and potions, but not anymore. Now I long to have him look at me this way.

"Here," he says, offering me a handful of plump just-picked winterberries, smooth and black. I know they must have been very hard to find.

"Thank you," I say, "but maybe someone else needs them more than I do." I nod at Oski, who sits cradling Wyrd's severed hand.

"You'll need your energy if you're going to swim in the ice water," Einar says, a quaver in his voice. It alarms me.

"Do you think I can really do this?" I ask.

"Well, if you had asked me that when I first met you, I would have said no, I don't think you can," he says. "But now I believe you will succeed."

"If I don't, then promise me you will continue. Find my sister," I say. I try to push down my fear, but I feel it taking over.

"I will," he says. "But I won't need to. I'm just sorry..." He doesn't finish his thought.

"For what?" I ask.

"For being a part of what led you here," he says. "For this being your life. I wish it was different for you."

I take this in. "And your life," I say. "I wish it was better."

I am beginning to wonder if anyone has the life they want. "Maybe existence is a long dream. Maybe we fight against our fate until it's over," I say, "and it all keeps happening, over and over."

Einar gives me an odd look. "Then we don't have much choice but to keep moving forward," he says.

"Do you want to get married?" I blurt.

"W-what?" Einar chokes on a berry and then recovers.

"No!" I exclaim. "I'm not asking. I mean, do you ever. Want to get married. To anyone. Ever. In the future." My face is burning hot and must be red as the moon.

"Oh," he says, regaining his composure. "Yes, I think so. Do you?"

"No," I say.

"Why not?"

I point at Oski. "Loving people means you can lose them. Why get married and have children just to watch them die?"

"That's the saddest thing I've ever heard," says Einar.

I shrug. "It's the truth."

"For you maybe. Not for me," he says.

"There's so much suffering," I argue.

"Runa, there has always been suffering. Our ancestors suffered, and now we are here. That is life. But what is the point of living if we don't have anyone to love?"

He stares at me, and he's so close and the fire is warm and the words coming from his soft lips are a salve on my fearful heart.

"Ah, love," Oski interrupts with their usual expert timing. "The thing worth living for."

Einar chuckles and tosses Oski some berries, which they catch in their mouth like a giant trout gulping flies.

"You are both insane," I grumble as I get up from the fire.

"You know, I was following you for days," Einar blurts. "Before we joined up."

I whirl around and stare at him—hard. "What?"

"I saw you in the forest. When you chose not to take the baby birds from their nest."

I can feel my heart pounding. "You were there?" I *knew* I was being watched. What else did he see? My mind flashes back to relieving myself in the woods. He wouldn't have watched that, would he? And when I was sleeping, did he watch me then?

He nods, fiddling with the clasp on his cloak. "I was."

All that time he was there, and I never knew. I want to be angry, but given everything we've been through, and everything we must still do, it doesn't seem like the right emotion anymore.

"Would *you* have eaten them?" I ask. "The little birds?"

"No," he whispers. "I wouldn't have."

"And so?" asks Oski. "What is the point of all this? Birds are tasty."

"The point is, Runa," says Einar, "I know you to be someone who doesn't eat baby birds even when she is starving. And yet you pretend not to care about love."

I take in a deep breath and stare up into the reddening sky, ignoring his comments about love. "Maybe one day I will discover the invisibility rune, the real Aki rune, or maybe I'll meet Freyja herself and pass through the nine worlds and learn the secrets of our existence. Maybe I will be in charge. Maybe I will punish the gods for what they're doing to us right now. For what they did to Oski and Wyrd."

Einar looks uneasy. "You sound like you desire power above all else, Runa. That is the path of darkness."

"No," I say. "Right now, all I desire are time stones. And if I'm going to die getting them, then I'd like to get to it." I pick up my spear and my pack. "Are you with me? Or do you both want to sit here forever, talking about love?"

"Whoop!" Oski yelps, jumping. They place Wyrd's hand inside their cloak and brandish their sword. Chooser's shining metal glints in the red of the moonlight. "I must say, runecaster, you know how to get a Valkyrie's blood moving."

I look at Einar. He stands, unfurling his tall frame and gathering his supplies. "Lead on," he says. "Let's get this done."

I run my fingertips along the swirls on my spear. "Rán," I say, intoning the name of the sea goddess, "show me the way." As I recite the names of her nine daughters, the goddesses of the waves—"Blóðughadda, Bylgja, Dröfn, Dúfa, Hefring, Himinglæva, Hrönn, Kólga, Uðr"—I think how pleased Sýr would be that I have remembered my studies.

The wave formations carved into the staff glow green and then fade, and I see an image in my mind. An ice floe, larger than the others, right off shore. I turn in the direction of the sea. I know where to go.

We make haste, our bellies full and our camp struck. I lead the way, my spear pointing iceward. Enough with distractions. My destiny awaits.

We pass through the valley, leaving behind our sense of unease at the unnatural perfection of the place. The surrounding hills are not at a high elevation, but the slopes are steep, and though we are going as fast as we can, I have to stop several times to catch my breath.

Einar makes me sit and drink water he brought from the stream, and I feel it bolster me with renewed strength. Oski complains about not having any mead, I accuse them of being a drunk, and they tease that I will need to be carried like a lamb the rest of the way. Einar has to intervene before we begin fighting like a pair of siblings. We're all weary and on edge.

As we are about to make it over the top of the hill, a surprise valley-sneak fog rolls in, surrounding us with white mist. It obstructs our vision, and I panic, reaching out for Einar and Oski.

"Runa, I'm here," Einar says, grabbing my arm.

"You can always climb on my back," Oski says. They are trying to ease my fear with humor, but it isn't working. This is exactly what my sickness is like. Lost in fog with no way out.

But I am not alone this time, and I know how to find my way. I have my friends and my runes.

"Protect me," I say, holding my rune pouch. "Clear the path."

My runes chatter and the fog begins to lift, until we can see our way over the hill.

My spear, tingling in my hand, takes us the rest of the way. The terrain is steep on the other side, filled with crumbling rock that slides out from under our feet and threatens to send us tumbling. It seems to take forever, but eventually we get all the way to the bottom and to the shores of the icy sea.

We can't help but stop and stare at the wonder before us. The ocean is vast, bluer than a summer sky, and dotted with white ice floes sailing along like ghost ships. In the eerie red light of the moon, they appear to be ablaze, like funeral boats carrying the dead to Valhalla.

My spear pulls me, and I have to fight to keep my balance. It's pointing to a large iceberg floating in the water. I will have to cross over these disconnected ice floes to get to it.

"There," I say, pointing it out. "I'm going to have to hop over the gaps."

Einar looks skeptical. "If you fall, you'll freeze to death," he says. "And who knows what's in this water."

"Yes. Could be big fish," says Oski, nodding. "Very big."

I nod. "But I have to get the time stones. I cannot defeat Katla without them."

I start taking off all my clothes except for my boots. I don't want to slip on the ice. "What are you doing?" Einar asks, averting his eyes.

"I'm going to have to swim under to find the keeper of the spear, remember?"

"You can't survive a swim that cold!"

"Then I'll do a warming spell. Besides, I don't want my clothes to be wet when I return." I bundle my belongings and toss them over to him. "Make a strong fire here and wait for me. I will be back."

"We will be here," says Oski. "Waiting around. As usual."

I hesitate for a moment. The cold air is biting into my skin, and I know the water will feel like a thousand knives. "Promise me you will be here when I come out," I say.

Einar looks into my eyes, trying very hard not to look elsewhere. "I will not leave here without you. I'm definitely going to want to see you again," he adds with a smile.

I grin back at him, pick up my spear, and give him a little jab in the side.

"Hey, ow!" he exclaims. "What was that for?"

"For looking," I say.

I touch the pouch around my neck. "Warm," I whisper to the runes, and immediately my core begins to heat up. I'll have to move fast. This warming spell won't last forever.

"Bring me back to the land," I say. "Let me not die in the water."

With that, I hop onto the first ice floe. It is small and tippy, and I almost tumble into the water. I gain my balance and hop to a larger one. I'm doing well so far. I make it to the main iceberg, victorious. But my spear starts pulling me toward the water. I fight against it, backing away from the edge and regaining my balance.

I am going to have to swim now. As I gaze into the clear blue depths, trying to work up my nerve, I see a large shape swim past. It circles around, and as it comes closer I can see it is the biggest green shark I've ever seen.

I look back to the shore where Oski and Einar stand.

"Shark!" I shout, hoping they can hear me.

They can, because Einar starts waving his arms, frantic. He's telling me not to do it, but I have no choice.

I get my spear ready and wait for the shark to circle as far away from me as possible, and then I dive down into the icy water.

SIXTEEN

The cold slices into me. I was right when I thought it would feel as sharp as knife blades. The pain of it makes me lose some of the breath I'm holding, but I fight against the urge to surface. I have to keep swimming deeper.

To my right, on the underside of the iceberg, I see a glowing light coming from a hole that looks like it could be the entrance to the cave. I kick forward, and as I do, I feel something rough and immense brush across my legs.

I whirl around in the water, my spear out in front of me, my lungs burning, and see the shark swimming back and forth in a tight circle. Its flat black eye reminds me of Katla's deadly gaze. It's the eye of a killer who feels nothing but their own thirst for death.

My mind flashes back to the visions I had on the beach at home. Of something in the water circling me. Was it a premonition? Does this mean I am about to die?

I look back at the hole. I'm so close. I have to get there before the shark gets to me. It's watching me, waiting for me to act. I have to move, or I will drown. With a frantic push, I kick fast, stabbing my spear at the huge shark as it surges at me on my left side.

I manage to jab it in the mouth, the deep blackness of its gaping jaws threatening to close down around my arm. I yank back on my spear, and the water around me fills with blood. I don't know if it is my own or the shark's, and for a moment I am sure this is the end of me. But then I feel the slippery contours of the opening in the ice, and I reach with my free arm and grab on, pulling myself through. At any moment I expect the shark to bite off my legs, but it doesn't. I look up and see that I am near the surface. I break through with a gasping, pained breath. I have found the cave at the center of the iceberg.

I hear a voice in my mind. *Do not be afraid.* Is it Sýr's? It sounds similar but different somehow. Regardless, it brings me a touch of comfort.

Shivering and weakened by the cold and the fear and the lack of air, I pull myself up onto a smooth lip of ice.

"W-warm," I chatter. My runes glow, and I clutch myself, willing my body not to freeze solid. My hair hangs in icy ropes around me.

The ice cave is empty, with slick walls that look as though they have been eroded for thousands of years by the seawater. I can't see well, due to the low light in the cave, but I feel my way along, moving toward the glowing green light that attracted me in the first place.

As I crawl farther in, I imagine I am traveling down a long, deep gullet. The sides of the cave, wet and rippled as they are, will soon close in on me and swallow me forever. I put my hands out in front of me and feel nothing but cold air. The emptiness is overwhelming, and it's getting hard to breathe. I don't want to have my sickness here. I might freeze to death. I have to do this fast.

Focus on the light, Runa. That voice again. It must be Sýr's. It's so familiar.

I squint as I move forward. The green light in the distance glows brighter and brighter as I advance. Soon I come to a bigger opening in the cave wall. A soothing pale green light flows from the hole, spilling over the shimmering white cave walls and rippled mounds of ice.

"After you," I joke, my voice weak. "No, after you."

I take a deep breath. I don't know what lies beyond the entrance to this glowing chamber, but I know things can't get much weirder than they already are. Sýr flashes in my mind, then Einar and Oski. I can do this. I have to.

I crouch and crawl through the tunnel headfirst. It takes me to a larger, domed chamber, also white and empty. I walk to the center of the chamber and note its iridescent walls. It's like being inside a giant shell.

I turn around, admiring the room, and spot a few more small tunnels leading into and out of the domed room. I look for the source of light and see that there is a narrow, chimney-like flue in the top of the dome that goes out the top of the iceberg. Daylight shines through the hole and fills the room. There is also a hole in the bottom of the cave, like a well opening, and it glows with the most beautiful shade of green, like jewels or new spring grass.

I hear a deep growl behind me, and I spin with my spear outstretched.

A small man stands in the cave, naked save for a leather loin cover. He is no ordinary man, though, and I understand at once why Orð has sent me here. The man's shimmering face is framed by patches of long black hair hanging in shiny sheets like kelp from a rock. His neck has dark slits on the sides, and his hands and feet have wedges of skin webbed between the fingers and toes. I smell the pungent odor of rotting fish and notice that the man's teeth are pointed like a shark's and protrude slightly from his mouth. He carries a net full of fish and a spear identical to mine.

"A marbendill!" I gasp. Amma told me of these creatures. She even had a scroll with drawings of one. I never believed they were real. Who would? A marbendill is a kind of half man, half fish. Amma said no one has ever seen a marbendill above the surface of the water. She told me about sailors and fishermen falling into the water only to be terrorized by such creatures beneath the waves.

Like Orð said, they have an intense hatred of mortals. I know enough to be terrified, for marbendills can see a person's inner emotions, and they can plant ideas and images in the mortal's mind.

I also remember that marbendills can dive deep, to the ocean floor, and are miners of precious stones. If that's true, then perhaps this marbendill can help me find some time stones.

The marbendill doesn't acknowledge my outburst, but stares at me with a scowl on his wide, flat face.

"Where did you get my spear?" he asks at last. His voice sounds like seashells clacking together.

"I found it," I say with a touch of defiance. I don't know where this boldness is coming from.

"Give it back," he says.

"You have another," I say, pointing to the one he's carrying. It is the same gleaming white color as the one I carry and is also inlaid with elaborate swirls.

"Give it," he says again in a low growl, ignoring my reply.

I hesitate. "On one condition—" Suddenly I feel the sensation of something creeping through the edges of my thoughts. A clacking sound.

Give it, give it.

I shake my head and grasp my runes. "OUT!" I shout, forcing the voice from my mind.

The marbendill recoils and then begins to laugh. "Runecaster. What are you doing in my lair?"

He begins to pace back and forth, like he's getting ready to strike.

"Orð sent me," I say, keeping my spear out in front of me.

"Orð! That old sea turtle?" The marbendill stops pacing and stares me down. I can feel him trying to wheedle his way into my thoughts again. "Humph," he grunts when he is unable to gain entry. "Strong runecaster. Stronger than usual."

"Orð said you could help me," I say. "That you're the one." I don't have time to be terrified. I need the stones.

The marbendill scoffs. "Orð is not smart. He leaves the beauty and bounty of the great sea to wither away in an old tree. He is the keeper of death. *I* am the keeper of life." He widens his arms, gesturing to his cave.

"Imagine," he continues, "choosing to spend eternity in such a place instead of free in the sea where you can hunt and fish and swim with the great sharks and eat delicious things."

"Well," I say, "perhaps he doesn't like the cold."

"What?" he shouts. "Not like the cold? Cold gives a long life! Cold can give many lives!" He peers into the green circle between us. "You should learn this."

I can't figure out this creature. I don't know if I will gain his help or not.

"I ask you, runecaster," he says in his growling tone. "What do you seek?"

"I seek time stones," I blurt, and the statement hangs between us in the cold air.

"You have one, runecaster," he says, pointing at my spear.

"Huh?" I raise my spear and examine it.

"Pity," he says. "Cracked. Useless."

"This? *This* is a time stone?" I touch the cracked brown stone on the blunt end of my spear.

"Indeed," he says. "Was. Now broken."

"I can't believe that all along there was a time stone on this thing," I say.

"Not a thing!" the marbendill shouts.

I step backward, startled by his anger.

He points to my spear. "The great weapon of the horned whale. Carved by my own hands."

A whale horn? "How did you manage to kill one by yourself?" I ask and then immediately regret it.

The marbendill hurtles his own spear into the wall, where it sticks with a dangerous finality. He steps forward. "I did not kill her. I am Kálfur, Watcher of the Deep. The great horned whale leaves me her weapon as a token of respect when she passes from this life into the next. It was a gift. Now give it back!"

"I'm sorry," I say. "I found it. And I need it. This spear has saved me more than once. I love it."

The marbendill, all signs of his rage suddenly gone, regards me with curiosity. After a time he nods. "If you love it, then you keep it," he says.

"Thank you," I say. "You are very kind."

"Bah!" he says, squatting to pull fish from his net and nibble on it. He appears to be eating it raw. He offers me some, but I decline.

"The time stones...?" I begin.

Kálfur throws part of a fish carcass at me. "Time stones, time stones, all you ever say. Every time I see you. Time stones, time stones."

"Every time?" I ask.

The marbendill grunts and wipes his mouth. He walks over to the green, glowing hole and pulls a long line from his belt. He holds out his hand, palm up. "Come," he says.

"What?" I ask, edging closer with caution.

"Your rune," he says. "Give it to me."

"Why?" I ask. How do I know there are any time stones left? I can't give this creature one of my runes. "What are you going to do with it?"

"Give it." He wiggles his fingers.

I sigh and pull a rune from my pouch. It is Nauð, the rune for need. I hold it out. "But if you touch it..." I say, hesitating.

"Give it," he says again.

I place the wooden piece in his palm, noting how cold and clammy his skin is.

"Are you going to tell me—?" But I have no time to finish, for he drops my rune into the green hole.

"Hey!" I shout. "I need that."

"No, runecaster," he says. "We will make more. Another," he says, holding his hand out again.

"No," I protest. "I came here to get time stones to make more runes, not lose the ones I have."

"Yes, yes," the marbendill says. "You say this each time. You need more runes, time stones, time stones. You need to trust Kálfur."

"Trust you? You want me to give you my runes so you can dump them in this hole?"

He stares at me. "Yes," he says.

Looking into his deep green eyes, I know I am not going to be able to reason with him. I don't know what he means when he says we've done this before, and I'm certain he is confused. Still, I remove my pouch from around my neck and dump the remaining runes into my hand.

"Thank you," I whisper to them. "I'm sorry, but I believe this is what I have to do."

Shaking, I hand them over to the marbendill.

He takes them, nods at me, and tosses them all into the hole.

"The time stones live in here," he says, pointing at the green hole. "They demand a trade. You want a stone, you offer a stone. You want a rune, you offer a rune."

I nod. Finally he's explaining something. "How do they work?" I ask.

Kálfur shrugs. "Ancient brown water stone holds within it water from the deepest ocean. The first waters. From the time of creation."

"The first waters?" I ask. Amma never told me about this.

Kálfur looks at me. "You call them back now."

"Call them? My runes?"

He nods. "Hurry," he says. "Before they forget."

"Okay." I clear my throat. I close my eyes and call out the name of my runes. "Fé, Úr, Þurs, Óss, Reið, Kaun, Hagall, Nauð, Ís, Ár, Sól, Týr, Bjarkan, Maðr, Lögr, Ýr."

The green hole emits a bubbling noise and then small brown pebbles start popping out onto the smooth cave floor between us.

The marbendill motions for me to pick them up.

I gather them. They look like simple stones and nothing more.

"These are the runes?" I ask.

"Speak to them," he says. "They are listening."

I touch the stones one by one, and as I do, I notice a faint glow as the water within them shimmers. "I call upon you," I say. "I need your help on my journey."

The stones begin to rattle in my palm, and the design of each rune appears in glowing relief before fading to look again like common stones.

"A disguise," I say, delighted.

The marbendill looks at me and grunts. "New runes have memory like water. Hold time like water. Change like water. And they are constant like stone. Strong like stone. You must be both. You must yield and never break. You must move forward and stay here." The marbendill's voice seems to grow farther away.

My vision blurs, and the white of the cave becomes a swirl of confusion and fog. *No*. I thought I was growing beyond these fits. I can't get lost here. I have to get out to find Sýr. *Sýr!*

I feel a hand grasp my shoulder, and I spin to see Sýr standing behind me. Her face appears as if underwater, like there is another face floating on top of it. I see a faint smirk flash across her mouth and then disappear again.

"Sýr," I call. "I'm coming."

She reaches toward me with her hand, so close we could

touch, and as I feel her fingers graze mine, I feel another sensation—a hard blow—across my back.

"Oof!" I grunt, stumbling forward, almost falling face first into the green hole of the cave. When I roll over, the fog has cleared, Sýr is gone, and the marbendill is standing over me, brandishing the blunt end of his spear.

"Are you crazy?" I shriek. "I was trying to get to my sister."

"No," he says. "Not your sister. The witch. She wants your stones."

I look down and see that I've dropped my new runes. I gather them and put them into my pouch. "I'm sorry," I say. "I'm so sorry. I won't drop you again."

Sitting here in the marbendill's cave, clutching my runes, I am struck by the eerie sensation that I *have* been here before. I *have* done this before. But the icy walls seem as foreign as any place I've been.

"I have been here before, as you say." My voice comes out in a whisper.

"Many times, yes," he says.

"For the same reason?" I ask. How can this be happening?

"Yes," he says.

"But I failed?" I ask, afraid of the answer.

"Yes," he says.

"Why?" I am not sure I want to know.

"You did not trust yourself," he says.

How am I any different now than I was before? None of this makes sense.

"In my heart I know I will fail again," I whisper.

"Then I will see you in another turn of the universe," he says.

I am crying now. "I'm tired," I say, wiping at my face.

"You fight yourself," he says. "Very hard to make your journey with a binding spell on your spirit."

"What? What do you mean?" I ask. What binding spell? How can he see my spirit?

"There is spell keeps you here," he says. "It keeps you now."

Stay with me. Stay here. Stay now. Sýr's voice in my mind. The sleeping spell she would say to me every night. But why would Sýr bind me? She was trying to help me expand my abilities, not limit them. Wasn't she?

"Take it off," I say. "The binding spell. Can you?"

"I cannot. I am no runecaster," he says. "The one who can take it off is the one who placed it there."

If it was Sýr, then I will never get it off unless I find her.

"I need to find my sister. I need you to tell me what I should do," I plead.

"You must let me in," he says.

"In? Where?" I ask.

"Into your mind. I will see what has not happened yet."

I hesitate. He has helped me with the stones. But can I really trust him? I must. I have to know. "Fine," I say. "But when I want you to go, you go."

His eyes grow darker. The pupils dilate, and a thin, filmlike third eyelid retracts so that his eyes protrude from his face.

I recoil from the intensity radiating from his eyes. I have a crawling feeling, like a cold hand is reaching under my skin and grabbing hold of my guts. I can feel the marbendill's mental grip on me and am powerless to stop the invasion.

"Why me?" I ask. I hear my own voice as if from far away. "I'm not special."

"No, you're not," says the marbendill. "But you have the burning heart of a seeker. That is all you need."

"I'm scared."

"Yes, yes," he says. His voice is soothing. "Don't be afraid. Everything will work out as it should."

"Tell me," I plead. "Tell me how I can save my sister."

"The answer is always the same. Use the time stones. Enter moonwater. Cast them in the circle. Draw the witch out. Entice her. Her desire for power will be her undoing."

The marbendill releases my mind, and I am left with a feeling like someone left a door open in my head. It takes me a moment to compose myself.

The marbendill leans closer to me, a grave expression on his face. "If you choose to go through time, you may risk your immortality."

"What do you mean, go through time?" I ask. "How is that possible?"

"Your soul," he says, not answering my question. "You might lose it."

"How?" I ask.

He shakes his head. "It is a risk you take. When you live more lives than you have been given. Same warning I always give."

Now more than ever I feel like I am not going to come back from this journey alive. But it doesn't matter. Sýr matters, and the mission. They are more important. I cannot let her die.

"Why are you helping me?" I ask.

"Because you helped me once, a long time ago," he says.

"I wish I remember," I say.

"No, you don't," he says, turning his back on me.

I thank him, but he does not speak to me again. It's as if I have ceased to exist.

I leave him, crawl back through the tunnel, and regard the hole that leads to the icy water. I take a big breath and slip through, the cold penetrating me to the core. The huge green shark is still patrolling the waters, and I swim away from it as fast as I can. I reach the edge of the ice floe, use my spear to climb out of the water, and land on the ice like a sputtering, pale fish.

"Runa!" I hear Einar shout. I watch him make his way to me. Suddenly he's there, draping me in his own cloak. It smells like honey and sweat—and Einar. I shiver and turn back to look at the water. The sharp tip of the green shark's fin disappears back into the depths.

Einar lifts me up and helps me back across the tipping ice floes to the shore, where he deposits me on solid ground, safe but half-frozen.

"We thought you'd been eaten," says Oski cheerfully.

"No we didn't," Einar says, rubbing my arms through the cloak.

I look at him, my teeth chattering so hard I fear they will crack. "You weren't worried?"

"I didn't say that. But I knew you hadn't been eaten," he says, continuing to rub the life back into my frozen limbs.

"How?" I ask, leaning into the warmth of him.

"Because I could still feel you," he says.

"Feel me," I say. "Is that an elf thing?"

"No," he says. "It's a Runa and Einar thing." He grabs a corner of the cloak and rubs my soaking hair with it. "Now stop talking. You need a fire. And soup. And tea."

"We have weird tales to tell you, runecaster," says Oski.

"You have no idea," I say.

SEVENTEEN

Einar prepares me soup and tea, and both he and Oski cuddle next to me to give me as much warmth as possible. Next to them and the fire, I grow sleepy, but we have so much to tell each other.

"I have the time stones," I say between sips of soup. "My new runes." I hold up my pouch, and the runes emit a soft glow, tinkling together like soft music.

"Já," says Oski. "Now you are a proper runecaster."

"I knew you'd get them," Einar whispers.

"Now I have to figure out how to use them," I say.

Oski laughs.

"You think I'm joking, but I'm not."

We sit in silence for a bit, until I feel warmer. I lean back to look at the sky and feel a jolt of surprise when I see that the red moon is close to the sun.

"How long have I been gone?" I ask, panic rising in my throat.

I start gathering my things in a frantic rush.

"Runa, calm down," Einar says, trying to help me.

"How long?" I demand.

"Days," says Oski. "Many days."

I pause. Days. "How can that be?" I glance at Einar and see that he looks very tired and drawn, as if he hasn't slept or eaten in a long time.

"So long that the elf starved me," Oski complains.

Einar packs our things in silence, ignoring Oski.

"What do you mean?" I ask, remembering the large portion of soup Einar forced into me after I got out of the water.

"He saved it all for you," Oski says, picking up their sword and marching off.

I turn to Einar. "Is that true?"

He shrugs, back to his shy way of communicating without words.

"You must be starving," I exclaim, scrambling to find any scraps of food in our pots or in my pack that I can give him. I find a tiny pinch of fish in the pot.

"Runa," Einar says. "I'm fine."

"No," I say. "I need to do a spell, find a way to make this into more."

"We don't have time," Einar says. "We had to make sure you were warm and fed, but now we must go. We've heard stirrings in the trees. Katla is watching us. There are signs. Scorched earth, carcasses, bits of yellow dust everywhere. Screams in the night, Runa. Terrible screams. She knows you have the stones."

I nod. “Yes. I saw her when the marbendill forged the runes for me.”

“The what?” Einar asks, shocked. “You saw a marbendill?”

“It’s a story for another time,” I say. “But Katla was there—in my vision, at least. She tried to get my stones. She wants them.”

“Of course,” Einar says, pacing. “Of course she would want them. They’d be almost as valuable as the moonstone itself.”

“What is our plan?” Oski calls, walking back to us. They are carrying a dead bird on the end of their sword. Not game for us to eat, but a dried-out husk, yellowed and stinking, more evidence that something came through here and left death in its wake.

“We must continue,” I say. “Onward to moonwater.”

“But which way?” Einar asks.

“My new runes will help us find the way. But I need to do one final thing to get ready. I need to charge them. Now that the red moon is constant in the sky, and full, it should be even more powerful than a regular moon charge. At least, I hope so.”

“Red moons, regular moons, what’s next?” Oski says. “Perhaps the moon will vanish one day. And all of us with it!” They laugh their bellowing laugh. “Ah, that would be a delight.”

Einar shakes his head at them. “What do you need?” he asks me.

“Well,” I say, “according to the spellbook’s instructions, the ritual involves laying my new runes onto the bare earth with their steads pointing in all the directions of the compass. I need dirt."

Einar sets to work, clearing rocks from the ground to uncover the dark, rich soil of the island. There is a lot of volcanic ash here, being so close to the sea and the fissures beyond the shore, and I remember Amma telling me that this type of dirt is excellent for growing things. I hope it helps my runes grow in power.

Carefully I spill the newborn runes out onto the cleared area and arrange them with their symbols facing every point of the earth. I place a cup before me to hold the elements of the ritual and add a pinch of dirt inside it.

"I will need you both to place your hands on me," I say. Einar and Oski stand behind me as I kneel in the dirt. Their hands are a comforting presence on my shoulders. "Don't be afraid if you feel...something."

"What?" asks Einar.

"You are not going to set me on fire again, are you, runecaster?" Oski asks.

I shake my head. "Shush. Be quiet for once, and whatever happens, *don't move*."

I hear Oski mutter to Einar, "Do you have a bad feeling about this?"

I want these runes to be as powerful and as connected to me as possible. I am going to be drawing the energy of the red moon into them, as well as the power of a Valkyrie and an elf. But I need more. If I could stand to sacrifice a part of my body, that would ensure the connection, but I worry that too much violence would corrupt my runes. I want them to remain pure. I don't wish to use them for evil. Sýr warned me long ago to never use the runes for nefarious deeds, for once corrupted, they will steal my soul. A power-hungry runecaster is a dangerous force. I'd be no better than Katla.

"Knife," I say to Einar. He gives it to me without hesitation.

I saw off a chunk of my hair and place it in the cup.

"Humph," Oski grumbles. "I have none, and you cut yours off willingly. Ah, what I would do for that wild mane."

"Oski," Einar hisses. "You must be quiet."

Blood is essential when charging runes. I pierce the tip of my left little finger with Einar's blade and squeeze several drops into the cup. To this I add some spit and a piece of chewed-off fingernail. I pull free a few eyelashes from each eye and drop them in as well.

Now for a tear. This is the easiest to produce, because all I have to do is think of my amma giving me the vegvisir clasp, and of my beloved Sýr lulling me to sleep each night. How I miss them, their faces, their smells, their comforting presence. Once I start crying, it's difficult to stop, and I feel both Oski and Einar give me gentle squeezes with their hands. I wonder if they can feel what I feel.

"Flame," I say. "Einar, do you have a fire-rock?"

He pulls a well-used one from his cloak, and I strike the flinty rock with his knife, showering the cup with sparks until the hair singes and the blood sizzles.

I blow the smoke over my runes, pledging myself to them.

"I am yours, and you are mine," I intone. "My will is yours, and yours is mine." I touch each rune, then bring them all to my heart and hold them there as I gaze at the moon. "By the light of the red moon we are bound through time. Even death will not break this bond of mine."

When I finish saying the words, it's as if the world falls away under my feet. Oski and Einar's hands disappear, and I spin around to find them gone. I am alone in a barren land, and I do not recognize it. I spin in circles, seeing nothing but desolation and a gray sky with no sun and no moon. I gather my runes from the ground and place them back in my pouch.

"Sýr!" I call out, hoping she will hear me.

"Yessss," I hear a voice hiss in the distance.

When I turn to look, I see a figure approaching. Katla.

Her yellow cloak floats behind her as she advances on me, wielding her dripping daggers in each hand like a pair of fangs.

I won't let her strike me again. "Do your worst, witch," I challenge. "For I am not the child you met before."

Katla cackles, throwing her head back. As she does, a serpent's head appears in its place, snapping and hissing at me. She is Grabak. I know it.

"Vile creature!" I shout. I clasp my runes. "DIE!" I project the image of Kaun, the rune of death, in my mind's eye.

The snake head disappears, and instead of Katla standing before me, it's now Sýr. She looks at me with an unreadable sadness.

"Why have you failed me?" Sýr asks.

I know this must be a trick. But it's so real. Too real.

"Lies!" I cry out, but Sýr's image remains.

"I waited so long," Sýr says. "And you never came." She reaches her hands out to me, but her fingers begin to crumble into dust, and then her hands and arms, and soon she falls apart in front of me. My beloved sister, now a pile of yellow dust.

"No, Sýr!" I shout.

"Forget her," says a familiar, soft voice.

I turn and see Einar and Oski standing behind me. Einar offers his hand.

"Come with us," he says. "We can leave, run away, forget all of this."

"We can find a new land," says Oski. "One across the sea. A new home."

I shake my head. "No," I say. "You're not real. None of this is real."

I clutch my runes and close my eyes. "Stop this," I say. I open my eyes and Katla is there again, walking in a slow circle around me. Her eyes are dead black, and she reminds me of the green shark that patrolled the water around the marbendill's lair.

"What is real?" asks Katla. "Who can you trust, Runa? How do you know the half elf and the Valkyrie are not in my command, hmm?"

I shake my head. "No. Not Einar. Not Oski. Never."

"How do you know they're not wasting your time? You will never make it to moonwater."

I reach into my pouch and pull out a rune, knowing that any one of the them should be powerful enough to get me away from this vision. I receive Hagall, the rune of transformation. "Take me far away," I whisper to it.

The rune is too strong, for I am not transported back to my present. Once again I find myself in a barren land. I stand on an immense glacier, and this time there is a dead body lying prone before me. It wears a black cloak with brilliant blue lining. It has wild, white hair, frozen solid in a halo around the face. It's me.

"No," I say, backing away.

I don't look behind me, and I trip on a ridge of ice, causing me to stumble over the edge of a crevasse. I struggle to regain my footing, but I'm falling. I know I'm falling, and I know I will never be found.

I scream, "Bjarkan!" The name escapes my lips as I fall into blackness. This rune of secrets is also the rune of new life, and it is by pure instinct that I call its name.

I land on my back, hard, and it feels like every one of my bones has shattered.

I blink and I return to my friends. I'm lying on the ground staring up at the red moon. Oski is looking down at me with concern, and Einar is holding me. He pushes my hair back from my face.

"Runa!" he exclaims. "Are you okay?"

I struggle to sit, my whole body aching. "No, but I will be."

"Runecaster," Oski says. "Your eyes."

"W-what?" I ask.

I look at Einar. "What is it?"

"One of your eyes has changed," he says. "One that was blue is now brown."

"*What*? It must be from my rune," I say, trying to stand up. "I used Hagall, and the changes can be permanent. We must go. I had a vision of Katla. I feel that she is close."

I gather my runes once again and clutch them to my chest.

"Show me the way," I command. A vision floods my mind. I see crumbling ruins next to a wild sea.

"The troll castle," I say. "That is the way we must go."

"Troll castle!" Oski exclaims. "Have you gone mad, runecaster?"

"I don't know this place," says Einar. He casts an uneasy look between us.

"My amma said the troll castle is a region of great walls and outcroppings of rock next to the shoreline," I explain. "It was abandoned after the great massacre of the trolls in ancient times. It is nothing but ruins now. Nothing to fear," I add, with a pointed look at Oski.

"Runecaster," Oski says in a warning tone. "If there is even one troll..."

"My runes want me to go this way," I say. "So I will go."

Oski sighs. "I do admire your taste for danger," they say. "Still, the troll ruins are unprotected. If we are ambushed, there is nowhere to run. There is the sea on one side, and if you get too close you will be washed away forever, for this is the wildest part of the ocean. There's nothing but impenetrable rock on the other side. The way to go is forward."

"Forward is the only direction we need," I say, giving Einar a look.

"I agree," says Einar. "And it's Runa's choice. She leads us, so she decides."

Oski shrugs. "I will follow her anywhere."

"Good," I say. "Now let's go. The witch doesn't rest, and we can't either."

EIGHTEEN

We press on along the coastline, day turning to afternoon and afternoon to night. It's getting harder to tell the difference, with the red moon hanging so low overhead. It's a constant reminder of the threat we're under. We are running out of time to save my sister. Despite our need for haste, we are walking slower than ever. I feel weak, and Einar and Oski carry everything but my spear and my runes for me. The farther northward we walk, the more bitter the cold is, and we are blasted on one side by the giant waves and spray of the ocean.

Einar throws a heavy arm across my shoulders and sidles in closer to me as we walk. "Don't go near the water," he says. "As Oksi warned us, the ocean here has been known to steal people. And I'm not going to let it steal you."

We go as far as we can before I have to stop. I am near collapse and Einar is exhausted. I think Oski could walk for eternity, if they weren't always hungry. We stop to make camp in the dark, the three of us settling in among the ruins.

I'm so tired. I can feel Katla in everything I do, as if she is connected to me, but I cannot feel Sýr. I fear she may be gone. No, I can't think like that. If Sýr were dead, I would know it. I think about how, when I was in the marbendill's cave for so long, Einar said he knew that I was okay. He *felt* it. In my soul I know that Sýr still lives.

The ruins are a barren, desolate place. A place where hope would come to perish. There is nothing alive to be found here, only snow and ice and rock.

"Runecaster," Oski says, breaking through my dark mood. "Look at the sky."

Undulating bands of green light shimmer across the night sky. The great lights of moonwater. They have appeared at last. We are heading in the right direction.

"Thank you," I whisper to my runes.

Our camp for the night is on a bed of stone with a crumbling high wall for shelter. We don't bother trying to get comfortable. There is no point. We simply curl up in our cloaks and try to sleep. But it doesn't come easy for me.

I look over at Einar's dark figure leaning against the rock. My chest tightens. If Katla comes for us here, it may be the end of us. I care less about my own survival than I do about my friends making it through this alive.

I sleep for a little while and then jolt awake when I hear Oski and Einar talking.

"If you're a Valkyrie, why can't you decide who lives and who dies?" Einar asks, an edge of irritation in his voice. "Why can't you choose to save her?"

"I have no more power over who lives and dies than you do," says Oski. "I am here because Runa is the future. This I know. I am no longer a Valkyrie. I gave that up when I turned my back on Odin. And I will not return."

"You gave it all up for Wyrd. And now you are helping Runa on her quest? Why?" Einar asks.

"Listen, boy. I don't need to tell all of my secrets to you. Just know that I will continue protecting the runecaster as long as I have to."

"But—" Einar begins.

"Stop," I say. "I can hear you."

"Sorry," Einar says. "Try to sleep."

"Wait. Do you hear that too?" Oski asks.

"No," I say. "I can't hear anything over your bickering. What is it?"

"A howling," Oski says. "Wait for it."

We listen, and all the night's sounds ring in my ears. The wind and the surf pounding, the water dripping from the ruins. A plaintive wail cuts through the night, a sound like an animal in pain or hungry or disturbed.

We creep on our bellies to the edge of the wall, keeping the largest part of the broken castle to our backs, and look out into the dark night. The moon illuminates the ground below in red relief, the fog glowing red as blood.

"Is that a valley-sneak, or is it some other kind of magic?" Einar asks.

My runes chatter, and I place a hand on my pouch to quiet them. They are so much more sensitive than my old set.

"Magic," I say. "Dark magic."

"She comes," says Einar. "The witch."

The night is alight with scores of glowing eyes in the fog. They draw nearer.

"Skoffins," Oski says. "What do we do?"

"We cannot get close to them without risking looking into their eyes," says Einar. "I can try to hold them off with poison darts." He dips several sliver-like darts into the small jar of green liquid Píla gave him at the tavern. Then he pulls out a tube that he loads the darts into.

"Wait," I say. "Have you had this the whole time?"

He nods. "I don't like to use it unless I have to."

"The elf doesn't have the stomach for killing things," Oski mutters. "I do." They unsheath their glinting sword.

Einar places the blow pipe to his lips. He takes a breath and shoots a dart out into the night.

There is a yelp, and one pair of eyes extinguishes. More appear.

"There are too many," I say, standing.

"What are you doing?" Einar hisses, trying to tug me back down.

"It's me they want," I say.

"It's you we need," he counters.

"If anyone should go, it's me," says Oski. "I'm useless."

"No," I say. "Stay here and be safe. I know what I need to do." I search my pack for what I'm looking for and grab it.

"Guide me," I whisper to my runes.

I close my eyes, my runes creating a path before me in

my mind. I can see where to step, for it's as if night has turned to day.

There are the skoffins, at least a dozen of them, all slavering and yipping, nasty things with Katla's yellow eyes. They draw nearer to me as I advance.

I want them close enough to tear my flesh. Close enough to try to kill me should I open my eyes. But I will not. My runes are my eyes.

I will not let them kill my friends.

I move beyond the protection of the ruins and into the open ground. The skoffins draw closer to me, and closer still, until they are a few arms' lengths away and ready to strike.

"SEE YOURSELF, WITCH!" I scream.

I pop open the vial of reflecting powder and spray it in an arc in front of me. It's the substance Orð warned me about back at the great library. It feels like I've lived several lives since I filled my bag with Sýr's tinctures and potions, and I am full of glee at knowing my beloved sister has had a part in the undoing of Katla's vile creatures.

The shiny powder plumes outward and upward in a shimmering rainbow. The skoffins all freeze, transfixed by their own despicable images. They squeal and wither one by one.

"Thank you, Sýr," I whisper, opening my eyes. We are rid of the skoffins and safe once more.

I return to the ruins, and when I climb back to the crumbling wall where my friends wait, Einar grabs me and crushes me in an embrace.

"Crazy runecaster!" Oski scolds.

"You could have been killed," Einar says before releasing me.

I place the empty vial in his hand. "A little help from my sister."

"Did she give you anything else to help us?" Oski asks. "Because we will need it. Look."

This time there are no eyes. No skoffins. This time the field below us creeps with ghosts. There are so many that it's hard to distinguish between them and the fog around them. Some are large, the ghosts of giants past. Some look as if they are fresh from the grave, with bits of flesh hanging from them and their intestines spilling out. Some wail in a tone that feels like a thorn working its way into my mind.

"They'll drive us insane." Oski sounds panicked.

"It's okay. We need to stay calm," I say.

"I don't like ghosts," says Oski. "I had a friend once. A ghost took a liking to him. That ghost has haunted his children, and his children's children, and his children's children's—"

"Enough," says Einar. "We have to think. What can we offer them?"

"These aren't regular ghosts," I say. "These are Katla's servants. Daylight will destroy a ghost, but it's at least two hours until dawn."

"We won't last that long," Einar says.

I have an idea. "Maybe, with your help, I can create some false light, enough to keep them at bay and to use as a shield so we can flee to safety."

We gather our weapons and begin sneaking to the far side of the ruins, where we can slip through to the ground once the ghosts are distracted.

When we are in position, I whisper to my runes, "Give me the power of Sól." They glow in response, ready to do my bidding.

I look at Oski and Einar. "Now I need you both to concentrate. You need to think of something happy or something that reminds you of the best day of your life. The essence of your positive energy will help brighten the dark."

"How can I do that when I'm afraid?" asks Einar.

"All I can think of are those ghosts," says Oski.

"Ignore them," I say. "Close your eyes. Reach down deep inside your feelings. Uncover who you are. Your dreams. Your desires. Hold those thoughts and do not stop."

"The ghosts will find us," Oski says. "They are attracted to our life energy."

"So then why are we making the energy if they are trying to find it?" Einar asks.

"It's also the way we protect ourselves," I say.

Einar laughs, but it sounds sad. "The way my life is going," he says, "it seems like the thing I need is the thing that will be my undoing."

I take his hand and he lets out a shaking breath. "All you have to do is trust me," I say. "I will get you through this."

Einar nods and squeezes my hand.

"And me as well, já?" asks Oski. "You're not planning on sacrificing me, are you?"

I look at Oski and take their hand too. "Try not to worry so much, Valkyrie. I'd never leave you."

"Then hurry up, runecaster," they say. "I haven't lived this long just to be slain by a ghost."

"Sól," I say. My runes radiate like stars. Oski and Einar are concentrating hard, and I can feel their energies flowing through me. Oski's is cool and old and furious. Einar's is warm and young and loving.

I see Sýr in my mind. I see her helping me sleep at night. I see Amma, and Núna, and my father somewhere out on the open sea. I see Oski, and the light my runes cast brightens.

I think of Einar, and it bursts upward in a wave. It's dazzling. The sky goes blue and bright, as bright as true daylight. I can feel the heat of a midday sun radiating through me. It's the light that brings life, that grows everything green and new and pure, and that cuts through all darkness. I am life and nothing dead can harm me. The ghosts scream as the intensity of our combined light snuffs them out into wisps of yellow smoke.

We hurry on in the false daylight we've created, following the great green lights in the sky as they dance. We draw closer, and the lights grow brighter and taller. At last the real sun rises, and we reach the boundary of what we've been looking for.

Moonwater. We made it.

NINETEEN

The great wall of green light shimmers pale in the daylight. We seek shelter in a grove of nearby birch trees to rest, to eat, to prepare.

We don't talk, not even Oski, and instead focus on building a little camp on a soft bed of fallen leaves among the dense trees. Oski disappears for a short time and returns with a rabbit. Einar gathers weeds to make a tea. I strike a fire using my runes as spark. My runes are so strong now that it takes only one tap to make a flame. Will I ever be able to do it with just a thought?

We go about our camp rituals as we've done so many times before, aware that this may be the last, and we peer out from our tree cover into the silence to be sure Katla or some other undesirables aren't coming upon us.

The day stretches into the afternoon, the green wall shimmering a deeper green, and then into evening, when the vibrating bands of paneled light illuminate the sky in the beautiful show Amma told me about in her tales. Sýr had paid close attention to these descriptions too, for she knew that one day she'd have to make the journey. Little did I know that I would follow her.

After we finish eating our evening meal, I lie back and stare at the sky and its competing green and red lights. Everything is aglow. The red moon is almost in perfect position. Once I get through moonwater's walls—if I get through—it won't be long until the eclipse. I wonder how many runecasters, how many young women like me, have looked at a sky like this. Are they as scared as I am? Do they wish their destinies were different, as I do?

Einar crouches next to me and passes me a steaming cup of tea.

"Here," he says. "Warm yourself."

"Thanks," I say.

Oski pokes the fire with their sword and picks the last scraps of meat off one of the rabbit's legs. The grease from the meat makes their thin lips shine.

"How did you get us out of the troll ruins, Runa?" Einar asks. "I really thought the ghosts would murder us."

"Bah. I knew we would be fine," says Oski, drawing a disbelieving look from Einar.

"My runes," I say to Einar. "They are very powerful now. I hope I can be worthy of them."

Einar is regarding me with an odd expression. Almost like he doesn't recognize me. I'm not sure I like it.

"Are you sure it's the runes?" he asks. "And not you?"

I shake my head. "It was your energy too. Yours and Oski's."

"Já," says Oski. "I felt it."

"What did you think of?" I ask them both. "During the light spell."

"I thought of Wyrd," Oski says. "And mead. And not going crazy from ghosts. And my horse. And running my enemies through with *this*." They brandish their sword.

I nod and look at Einar. "And you?"

"My mother," he says, his voice quiet.

"Of course," I say and return to sipping my tea.

"What about you, Runa?" Einar asks. "What did you focus on?"

I take a sip, and Oski stands, pretending to patrol the perimeter of the camp.

"I thought of a lot of things," I say, trying to avoid the awkwardness of the question I myself asked.

"Like what?" he asks.

"Like Sýr. And my amma. And you." I can't look at him, because if I do, and I meet his gaze, I'm not sure what will happen next. I keep my eyes on my tea. Despite all the dangers I've overcome on this journey, I still have the heart of a coward.

Einar reaches out and places his large hand over mine, covering it. "I know," he says. "It was like your voice was inside my mind. Like your breath was in my body."

His eyes flicker with gold sparks. No matter how many times I look at them, I will never get used to their beauty.

"I hope—" I begin but then falter.

"Yes?" he prompts.

"I hope that when we are apart, you will carry a part of me with you. In case we never see each other again."

He shifts uneasily and pulls his hand away.

"Runa, please don't speak like that," he says.

"Einar—"

"No," he says, cutting me off. "I don't want to hear—"

"Einar, I have seen my own death," I blurt.

He stares at me, his expression a mixture of pain and confusion. I feel awful telling him this, and I hadn't planned on it. I regret it immediately, because he looks as if I've abandoned him like everyone else in his life has.

Oski clears their throat. "I have seen it too."

Einar is angry now. "What?" He spits out the word.

"This is bigger than me, Einar," I say.

"I don't care!" He throws down his cup, and its contents sizzle on the embers of the fire. It's unusual to see him this angry.

"We all die and become dirt," Oski says. "And our ancestors walk on us."

Einar is livid. "Quiet!" he shouts at Oski. "I don't need your crazy Valkyrie talk right now." He paces next to the fire. "What are we doing here? Why are we doing this if it's going to bring more death? If it's going to hurt Runa?" He looks at me, and the pain on his face is too much to bear.

"You know why," I say, avoiding his gaze. "Because of Sýr. And your father. And your clan. And my clan. And because we cannot let Katla get away with it. We must avenge your mother. We must stop the witch before she kills us all. Before we have nothing left to live for."

Einar sits, leaning his solid back against a birch tree. He sighs. "I know," he says quietly. He looks at me. "But I've only just found you."

We sit in silence for a moment, and then I gather every bit of courage I have and walk over to nestle beside him. He drapes a heavy arm around my shoulders, and I lean my head into him, breathing in his honey scent and feeling the warmth of his chin resting against my forehead.

"Look," I whisper. "I will see this through. I will battle Katla. I will do my best to help your people."

"You think that's all I care about?" he asks, but he isn't angry. He just seems tired.

"No," I say, my voice quiet.

Oski crouches before us. "We made a blood oath," they say. "Us three. We will always be together."

"But," I say, "you cannot pass beyond the boundary of moonwater. You're not mortal. And Einar—"

"It's not certain if I can," he finishes for me.

"Then I will wait here in the trees," says Oski. "And so will Einar, if he must."

It is what we agreed to, but after all this time we have spent together, I know now that standing out here waiting for me, not knowing what is happening beyond the green border of light, will be excruciating for them. If there were some way to disguise Oski and Einar as mortals, to mask Oski's Valkyrie blood and Einar's elf heritage, maybe it would be possible for them to cross over too.

"There may be something we can do," I say. "To protect us and to help you get across."

I tell them my idea. Einar gathers ash and uses his oils to mix together an ink. We all add drops of our blood to it. My plan is that we tattoo ourselves with a special bindrune, one that will connect us, protect us, and perhaps allow the two of them to walk where I walk.

I whisper to my runes and cast them to the ground. The stones come together to form a pattern I've never seen before, a complex bindrune displaying the values of friendship, identity, fate, and will. I recreate it in the dirt with my finger.

"That's it," I say. "This is the mark we will use."

"Do you really think it will work?" Einar asks.

"We will have to see," I say. "Each of us will have to try to enter moonwater on our own. If we succeed, we succeed. If we don't, then we wait for each other."

Oski pulls out the lone wing feather they have been carrying with them all this time. They hand it to Einar, who sharpens the quill into a fine point. He dips it into the ink and uses it to poke a rough sketch of the rune into my upper right arm. It stings, but in a good way. Einar works fast, concentrating on getting the shape right.

Once he's done, I tattoo Einar in the same place, dipping the feather in the ink and pressing it into Einar's skin. Then we both go to work tattooing Oski, because, we discover, Valkyrie skin is thick and tough. It takes several tries to puncture their white flesh, but we manage it in the end.

"There," I say. "This will help us find each other."

By this time the fire has ebbed, and dawn will be here soon.

"Sleep now, Runa," Einar says, drawing me back against him. "For a little while."

I close my eyes, resting in the warmth of him.

I dream of Oski.

The Valkyrie is standing beside that shimmering golden lake.

"Oski, am I crazy?" I ask. "Is this happening?"

"It has already happened, Runa," they say. "And will again."

"I don't understand why. I'm just me," I say.

"Yes. And that is enough."

"Are we dead?" I ask.

"I used to think dying was the loneliest thing a soul could experience," says Oski. "But now I know that living beyond the edge of time all alone is worse. For so long my eternity remained a desolate and beautiful place that people passed through, inhabited by my small crew of Valkyries. No one else stayed. Such long lives, if you can call them that.

"We were important, busy, but I began to believe that I was not real after all. In the darkest place of my heart, I feared

I was a whim dreamed up by the limited imagination of mortals. I watched you all live and love, and I watched you all die. Nothing was lonelier than watching human life from afar and wishing I had a small piece of it for myself. How I longed to jump into the mad rage of the world. I imagined time crumbling like rocky cliffs."

"And now?" I ask.

But Oski doesn't answer. They stare into the golden lake, and I feel myself tearing away, floating farther and farther, until I see my old home.

There it is, along the edge of the cliff and overlooking the black sands. From my little dwelling Sýr emerges.

She waves to me, and I draw closer, floating to her as if on wings.

"Sýr," I call out. "Sýr, is this real?"

"Yes," she says, and her voice sounds far away, as if spoken in another time. "This is real, Runa. Come in. Come stay. Stay with me."

Stay with me.

Her voice is soothing. I follow her into our hut, and I find myself in my little bed with Sýr next to me. She is smoothing my hair, and it's comforting.

"Sýr," I whisper. "I missed you so much."

She reaches out and wipes away the tears on my cheeks, and as she does, her eyes flash yellow. It's fast. So fast I'm not sure I even saw it. But I know it happened.

"Katla," I say, and her name comes out like a whispered threat.

She hisses, and her eyes turn bright yellow, her face switching between Sýr's beautiful visage and Katla's sickening scowl.

I recoil and try to escape, but Katla leaps onto me, pinning down my arms and legs, her face inches from mine. She hisses again, and a long, slimy, yellow tongue protrudes from her mouth.

"No!" I struggle.

"Jusssst giiiive iiiin," she hisses.

"Give in," I echo.

"Come with meeeee."

"With you," I repeat. She is hypnotic.

"Ruuuna."

"Runa," I say. Then, "Runes! My runes! Protect me!"

I feel my runes clatter, and I look down as they begin to glow, hot and red. They're angry. Katla reaches out a clawed hand and tries to grab them but screams in agony as if burned. She retreats to a corner of the room.

"Stupid child!" she shrieks.

I rise, my runes giving off intense heat. "I call on Tyr to punish you," I say, and with that my runes send off bolts of red fire that blaze across the room at Katla with a fury equal to my hatred of her.

Katla wails, dodging the fire, and then bursts out of the roof, flooding the hut with daylight.

"Runa!" Einar shouts, shaking me awake. "Runa," he says again, hushed, when I open my eyes. "Was it Katla again?"

I sit, shaking. "Yes." I reach for my runes. They're hot to the touch.

"Are you frightened?" Oski asks.

I remember the fire my runes shot at Katla and how she ran from me. I shake my head. "No," I say. "Not anymore."

"Good," says Oski. "Because destiny awaits."

I stand and look at the green light of the moonwater border. It wavers, perhaps allowing for areas of entry. The red moon is above us.

I look at my friends. "Let's go. I've got a witch to kill."

We gather our packs, stomp down our fire, and walk toward the green light. We find a spot where a space has formed. It's foggy inside, and I cannot see through.

I turn to Oski. "I'll meet you at the golden lake," I say.

They nod. "I will be waiting. I've always been waiting."

We embrace. "Thank you," I say.

I look at Einar, and this time I meet his eyes, staring into the golden flecks that remind me so much of the night's stars. Eyes like that could guide a hundred ships. Eyes like that could guide me home.

"I won't say goodbye," he says.

I nod and force a smile, even though I feel as if the world could be ending. He strokes my hair, pushing it back from my face so it isn't covering my eyes. "That's better," he says. "Now I can see your magic eyes."

My eyes that I've always thought of as strange and ugly. Freaky eyes. My problem eyes. Now they're magic eyes.

My mind flashes to Frigg, how she looked at Sýr with such love and how I wished someone would look at me that way.

Einar is looking at me like that now.

I move to press my mouth to his. As our lips graze, the ground starts to rumble.

"It's time!" Oski shouts. "Hurry!"

The green barrier glows bright. It's our moment to try to pass through.

Oski hurries through the opening. I can't see if they make it to the other side.

I pause at the entrance, Einar right behind me. I turn and reach my hand to him.

He reaches too, and our fingers touch. "Will there ever be a time for us?" he calls out.

But I don't get to answer, for the white fog swirls around me and blocks him from view.

I hope there is a time for us. If there isn't, I will make it.

TWENTY

The white fog is so disorienting that I don't know which way to go. Oski and Einar are nowhere. I stretch out my arms and feel nothing but cool, misty air. There is no sound, save for the pounding of my own heart and the clacking of my runes as they chatter in their pouch.

Which way? What if I can't get into moonwater? What if I'm not worthy? How will I free Sýr then? I push down my rising panic. I have to say calm.

I still myself and place my hands on my runes, holding them close to my chest. I breathe in, then out, and I focus on the sensation of being in this moment, right now.

"I'm here, Sýr," I say. "Help me find my way."

Runa. I hear Sýr's voice in the fog. I turn in its direction, and I see a faint flicker. Drawing closer, I see that it is a lone moth, aflame and flitting around in a frenzy.

I reach out and cup it in my hands, snuffing the flames. When I open them, there is nothing but a smear of ash.

Runa. Her voice again. Farther along is another flaming moth. I follow this trail of burning moths, catching each one, until I reach an area where the fog clears.

The moths are gone now.

"Sýr?" I call out.

Runa. I'm here. Her voice comes to me again, and when I step forward I see a shining, reflective surface in front of me. It's like a door made from thin ice, surrounded on all sides by brilliant light. I don't see any handle, and when I approach and touch it, the surface is so cold that I draw back my hand in pain.

I look at my palm, and the flesh is burned from cold. I breathe on it and try to warm it, but the cold is sinking deeper into my flesh, traveling to my wrist and threatening to claim my arm.

"Sýr!" I call out again.

The reflective ice door ripples and emits a warbling sound. A faint image appears, clothed in a hooded cloak. It looks like Sýr and sounds like her. The image moves toward me, and as it draws closer my heart almost stops in my chest.

It's my mother.

The cold in my wrist is now in my forearm, and I struggle to reach my hand out to the image.

"Mother?" I ask. Is this one of Katla's tricks?

But it can't be. Because the figure in the ice door before me has warm eyes, like Sýr's, and beautiful tanned skin and black hair that is so familiar I feel like I am home.

"Runa," she says. I realize it must have been her voice I heard when I was in the marbendill's cave. "I've been waiting so long, my love."

"Mother, how can this be?" I choke out through my tears.

"You must pass the test, child of mine." She opens her cloak to reveal a bright blue stone. It's the moonstone.

"What test? How?" I ask.

She takes the stone and whispers to it, and it glows a more brilliant blue.

"What will you do with the power, Runa? Such incredible power."

The stone floats beyond the ice door and toward me, then stops and hovers in the air.

"All you must do is take it," my mother says. "And it will be yours."

"Mine?" The blue moonstone has me transfixed. It's as if I can see in it everything I've ever wanted. I would be beautiful and strong and free to roam wherever I wished. I could make anyone love me.

"Yes, Runa. Yours. To make yourself into what you've always dreamed."

My mother's image dissolves and my own takes its place. My wild white hair, my strange eyes, made even stranger by being different colors now, my weak, shaking body. That image fades and a more powerful image of myself appears. Taller, more muscular, with dark hair and green eyes like Sýr's. Like my mother's.

My mother's face comes back again. "Take it," says Mother, "and you will have everything you've dreamed of."

The blue stone pulses. The coldness in my arm has reached my chest, and it feels like soon I won't be able to breathe.

"Yes," I say, my voice weak.

I want to be rid of my old self. To be new and to be special. To have unlimited power.

"Choose," Mother says, and her image fades for a moment. Behind her I see the faces of my sister and my friends. I see Oski and Einar, frozen in place.

Choose. Power for myself. Or power to help the ones I love. Me or them.

I feel the cold clutch around my heart. *No*. I don't want anything if I can't have it with them. I choose Sýr. I choose Oski. I choose Einar.

I step back from the stone, and it stops pulsing.

"I choose love," I say, and the stone disappears.

Mother smiles, tears falling from her eyes. "My child," she says. "My Runa."

"Mother!" I reach for her, but her image fades, and cracks appear in the ice door. "No! Wait!"

"You are the dream I had for myself," she says.

"Mother, please! Don't leave me again," I beg.

"We'll meet again," she says, her voice far away now. "In your dreams."

The ice shatters, and she is gone.

The door is open now, and I can see a dim corridor on the other side that leads, no doubt, to moonwater.

I stifle a sob and wipe my face. I made my choice. Now I have to see it through.

I step over the threshold, and the terrible cold that had permeated my body disappears. I look behind me, and the doorway has disappeared. All that remains is a stone wall. I move along the corridor, noting that the walls look like they've been here for hundreds of years, though moonwater is not a permanent place.

I come to the end, to a simple, unassuming wooden door, and push it open.

I'm here, at last, in the bustling center of moonwater. I step inside, and all around me are the sights and smells of the marketplace.

Tents and stalls. Sword makers. Magic-tool makers. Animals. Food. Entertainment. Drink. Candle shops. Oils. Herbs. Trinkets. Fortunes being told. Fights breaking out. Lovers. No children, as they aren't allowed. No elves or other supernatural creatures. No Oski or Einar that I can see, but I don't know if they got in. I don't know how Katla can get in here, but if she's possessing mortals, and possessing Sýr as we suspect, then maybe she will find a way.

My body tells me Sýr is here. And the moths I saw do too. It's not a huge place, so I'll have to be careful, but maybe I'll find Sýr without too much trouble. I see that the green lights form a dome over moonwater, and the temporary city itself is a big circle. Around the perimeter of the marketplace are makeshift taverns and boardinghouses. The casting circle where the competition takes place will be in the center, as will the sacred moonwater reflecting pool. I walk that way, weaving through the crowd of people buying and selling.

When I arrive, the casting circle is empty. It's much smaller than I imagined it to be. In my mind I had envisioned a huge battleground and a large, majestic pool of water. What I find is a simple dirt arena, surrounded on all sides by stone seats where the spectators and other casters will watch and wait. There is a row of elevated seats on one side, which is where the council of elders will watch. In front of their seats is a small basin about as big as a large cooking pot, forged from stone and rising from the earth. It shines with a reflecting water as still as the ice door that I entered through to get here. The sacred waters.

"Enchanting, isn't it?" says a voice.

I whirl around.

"New arrival?" a haggard woman asks me. "Need food? Board? I have a place."

"Uh, y-yes," I stammer. "Please."

"Good, good. I'm Vilný," she says, reaching out a gnarled hand.

I grasp it. "Uh, hello. I'm...Gudrun," I say, using my formal birth name. No one calls me this, and it's a very common name on the island.

Vilný grunts. "This way," she says and leads me from the casting circle to the outskirts of the marketplace. We arrive at a little shack that looks more like a stable for animals, but I'm so tired I don't care.

"Competition begins tonight," she says, "after the eclipse." She points up, and I see the moon edging next to the sun. "I will bring some stew."

"Thank you," I say and then stare at her when she doesn't leave.

"Oh!" I say. "Of course." She wants to be paid. "How much?" I ask. "Wait. I don't have any money."

She grumbles to herself, then says, "Well, what have you got? I take trade. That spear is acceptable."

I move it aside and place it down with my pack. "Not for trade," I say. "I have jewels though."

Vilný's eyes light up. "Jewels I like."

"One minute."

I crouch by my pack and scoop a few pebbles from the floor. I feel bad for duping the woman, but I don't have much choice.

I whisper to my runes, "Turn stone to gem, by the bounty of Freyja." My runes clatter and glow, and the pebbles in my hand turn into sparkling, clear gems.

Standing, I turn back to Vilný. "Here," I say. "Will this suffice?"

"Oh yes," she says, grabbing the gems with shaking hands. "Pretty. I will bring a big bowl of stew."

"Thank you," I say as she retreats. I hope she trades them before they turn back to rocks.

As I settle onto a mound of dried grasses and blankets, I hear lumbering footsteps outside. I scuttle over to the shuttered window and peer out. Jötnar warriors. Several of them. Huge sentinels that would strike fear into the heart of anyone, but these Jötnar ones have a glazed look in their eyes, like walking puppets. Even so, if they are close by, that means Katla is too. And Sýr.

I must disguise myself. I gather my runes and cast them onto the dirt floor.

"Make me unrecognizable," I say, invoking the rune of Hagall.

I watch as my hands wrinkle and wither and my skin turns a mottled color. The ends of my hair turn a dull gray, and I watch in awe as my belly protrudes. I hope this will be enough.

"What in Odin's name!" Vilný walks back in and almost drops her stew. "Why do you look so different? You are the odd girl I rented the room to, yes? You have the same fancy cloak. And strange eyes."

I look down. My clothes are not different. "Change," I whisper, rubbing my hands on my cloak. It turns from its shiny black to a dull brown.

Vilný gasps. "Magic before the competition is not permitted."

"Well," I say, "won't those gems, and the promise of more tomorrow, keep you quiet?"

"Oh," she says, setting the stew beside me. "I think so, yes."

The smell of it makes my mouth water, and I grab the bowl and start slurping.

"Hmm. Tasty, yes?" she asks. "Are you casting?"

"No," I lie. "I'm watching. Learning."

"Ah," says Vilný. "Be careful."

I look at her.

"Between you and me, I have heard tales of a witch," she says.

I finish chewing a piece of meat before I respond. "A witch?" I ask.

"Nasty one," says Vilný. "Snatching babies. Has the heart of a monster."

"Well," I say. "Perhaps she won't get in?"

Vilný grunts. "There are already whispers of people going missing. Some say the witch changes her face." She looks at me with suspicion.

"And you think that could be me?"

Vilný stammers. "N-no, I did not say so."

I stand and walk over to her. I hold my hand out, offering another tiny jewel.

"Would a nasty witch give such lovely gifts?" I ask with a smile.

Vilný takes the gem. "Ah, I knew you were a good one."

She collects my empty stew bowl and makes to leave.

"Vilný," I say, and she turns back. "If you don't disturb me, and you keep people from my door, I will give you three more tomorrow."

"Three?" she asks.

I nod.

"Sleep well, good one. I will have porridge tomorrow."

She leaves, and I lie on my sleeping pile. I must rest for a little bit, and then, when it is dark, I will look for Sýr. I will need to be careful, for it sounds like Katla is afoot. As much as I want to kill her, I need to get Sýr out first. If Oski and Einar got through and are here in moonwater, I hope they are safe.

I run my hand along my upper arm, gingerly touching our tattoo, and fall asleep with Einar's golden eyes floating in my dreams.

TWENTY-ONE

I sleep without dreaming. A soft fluttering against my cheek wakes me, and as I open my eyes to the darkened shed, I see a cluster of moths. They hover over me, each one in turn sparking aflame, passing the firelight back and forth in a kind of frenzied dance.

"Sýr?" I whisper.

As if in answer, the moths move as a group toward the door. I grab my spear and tighten my cloak around me. The moths want to go, and I am sure they want me to follow.

I ease open the door, letting a loud creak escape into the cold night air, and the moths fly out, sparking as if to beckon me. The alleyway in front of the tavern is empty save for a sleeping man propped against a barrel. He's drunk on mead and doesn't stir when I step out into the night.

The moths move quicker now, and I hurry to keep up, my boots squishing in the mud-caked footsteps of so many others.

The moths lead me to a locked shed that looks like it's used to store dry goods or tools. There is no sign of the Jötnar sentinels, and for that I am grateful. No indications of Katla. To be sure, I consult my runes.

"Reveal the witch to me," I whisper, holding out my rune pouch.

They clatter and glow, sending off little beams of light that pierce the darkness. The beams fizzle and fall all around, settling in grooves and footprints and creating a pattern of Katla's activity. Everywhere she's been glows a sickening yellow. I see her footprints, pointed at the ends like knives, and smears on the building's doorframe that suggest her brushing against it. Her fingerprints are on the door handle. The whorls of her imprint aren't like a mortal's in any sense. They form a pattern like a serpent's body. I am careful not to touch them.

The markings fade, and there are no other signs of her. Wherever Katla is, it's not close by. I push in the door, peeking inside the murky darkness. The moths flutter inward, illuminating the space, and my heart lurches in my chest. My beloved sister is chained in the corner like an animal.

"Sýr!" I exclaim in a loud whisper. I rush to her and kneel to embrace her.

"Runa," she gasps. "My Runa."

She is emaciated, her ribs visible beneath her dress. Cuts and bruises cover her body and her once long and lush hair is choppy and matted. Katla must have hacked it off for use in her wicked spells. If I ever get the chance, I will cut that witch to pieces. But for now I must try to free my sister. I grab the chains and examine the heavy locks.

Sýr moans. "Stop, Runa," she says. "It's no use."

"No, I won't give up. I will get you out of here." I wonder if her bonds are enhanced by a spell. "My runes can help me break through these. I just need a little time."

"No, Runa," she says. "Look at me." She searching my face with her eyes. "By Freyja!" she exclaims. "Why do you look so old?"

At first I don't understand, and then I remember the disguising spell I used earlier. Taking my runes in hand, I wipe the soft leather of the pouch over my face.

"Better?" I ask.

"Yes," she says. "There is the Runa I have longed to see again. I knew you were coming. I left messages for you. I tried to speak to you, to cross the distance between us."

"Sýr, I want to know everything. I want to sit and talk with you forever. But I have to get you out of here before Katla comes."

Her eyes have a ghostlike sheen to them, as if she's fading out of existence. Is it Katla sucking her life force? Or is it the stone?

"Where is the moonstone?" I ask.

"I have it," she says. "But it is almost drained. Katla draws from it even more when she takes over my body. But she cannot wield it herself. I have made sure of that."

I shudder, thinking about Katla possessing my sister's body. "I can get help. I'll go to the elders. They'll stop her."

"No, you can't."

"But why, Sýr?"

"You have to let things be," she says. "You must leave me and battle Katla in the circle, or else she won't get the stone."

"Wait, what do you mean?" I ask. "You *want* her to get the stone?"

Sýr is shaking and I know she won't be able to hang on much longer. "I don't have time to explain everything, Runa. You have to trust me. We must make sure Katla gets the stone, but it has to be in the circle after it charges in the reflecting pool. It needs to be strong. As strong as possible."

"Where is it? How did you disappear it?" I am getting more scared by the moment.

"I didn't disappear it," she says.

"What do you mean?"

"There's no time now, Runa. You must go. I wanted to see you one last time, sister. My beloved baby sister." Sýr starts to cry, her sobs racking her thin chest, and I throw my arms around her.

"You've grown so beautiful," Sýr says through her tears. "As I always knew you would."

"How can I leave you now that I've found you again?" I cry.

"You must. I am weak, Runa. So weak. Now you are the strong one."

I shake my head, but I know it is true.

"Trust me, Runa. When Katla holds the stone, she won't understand what it is, what it truly is."

"What is it, Sýr?" I whisper.

"It's a time stone, Runa. The most powerful of all the time stones, and so few can wield it."

"A time stone," I say. I pull open my rune pouch and cast my own time stones on the ground.

Sýr gasps. "It's all coming true," she says. "You are who I dreamed you to be."

"What does that mean? I'm so confused, Sýr. I want you back. I want to go home. Our village, our people. Frigg. Amma."

Sýr nods. "I have felt the loss in my heart. When Frigg was killed, I knew my old life was over."

"Sýr, Frigg is not dead. She is under the power of an enchanted dust. If we defeat Katla, then maybe the spell will be broken and Frigg can be saved. Maybe you can have the life you dreamed of."

My sister cries harder, her breaths coming in ragged gasps. "Please promise me," she begs, "that when you return home you will help Frigg. And tell her...tell her she was the only one I ever loved."

I rest my head on Sýr's shoulder, taking in her smell. Still the same.

"Listen to me, Runa," she says. "The runecasters who know the moonstone's true nature are those who've been blessed to hold it and survive. Runa, there is so much you don't know, and I fear I have not prepared you." Her voice is strangled with emotion. "I'm sorry, I'm so sorry. I tried. You must forgive me."

"For what, Sýr?" I ask. I lift my head to look at her.

"For what I must do," she says, meeting my eyes with a sadness I've never seen before.

I shake my head. "No, no. I don't want to know."

"When you were born, we knew you were special," she starts.

"You mean a freak," I say.

"Hush! Special. But—" She hesitates. "There was something odd too. You seemed to shake, like the light of a candle before it flickers out. And then Mother realized that you weren't connected to this time."

I stare at Sýr, starting to comprehend what she is saying.

"Runa, you were still attached to our mother with your life cord," says Sýr. "And you were jumping around in time. You took her with you."

The air is still and silent between us. "What happened to her?" I am terrified to hear the answer, but I must know.

Sýr shakes her head. "One moment you were there in my arms, still attached to Mother, and we were admiring you. Then you vanished, and she vanished too. And when you came back, appearing once again in my arms, Mother did not come back with you."

I swallow hard. I'm dizzy and overwhelmed. "I killed our mother?"

"No!" Sýr says. "She's gone. Lost in another time. And..."

"What?" I ask.

"I thought it was me," Sýr says, her voice quiet. "I was jealous while Mother was expecting you. I dreaded your birth.

And when you both vanished, I thought I had wished you away. It took me a long time to understand. And when I did, I made it my life's goal to protect you and keep you here. With me. In the now."

Sýr looks at me with pleading eyes, begging my forgiveness.

"So every night, when you did the sleeping spell—" I begin.

"It was a time spell," Sýr finishes. "To keep you with me. I was able to do it because I carried the moonstone."

I take all this in. "Could Mother be alive?" I ask at last, thinking back to the vision of her at the entrance to moonwater.

"I don't know. All I know is that you're the one who will wield the moonstone."

"But you've been using it all this time!" I say.

"No, Runa," she says. "I inherited the stone. It was low on power after Mother disappeared, and it has been killing me ever since. Look at me," she says, opening her arms as wide as the shackles will allow. "This isn't from Katla. It's from the stone. And when it is charged in the reflecting pool, it will be more powerful than I can handle."

"If you can't do it, then how—?"

"You must believe," she says, interrupting me. She nods at my runes. "Those," she says. "And that." She looks at my spear. "Those are the tools of a powerful caster. The most powerful I have ever seen."

I gather my runes and put them away, then reach out to touch Sýr's cheek. Gone is the soft, tanned skin that glowed with youth and health.

"I'm scared," I say, not without shame.

Sýr nods. "That's because you are still bound by my time spell. And once I remove it, you will be who you truly are. I'm so sorry I had to do it this way."

A surge of panic goes through me. "What will happen? Will I disappear? Will you?"

Sýr shakes her head sadly. "I'm sorry I hurt you, Runa. I'm sorry I had to keep this from you."

"Sýr, please," I plead. "Let's find another way. It's all I have left of you." I embrace her again, crying into her neck.

Sýr whispers in my ear. "I must take it off now, Runa, and you must fight to stay here and use your own strength. I know you can do it. I unbind you, Runa. I set you free."

As she says these last words, I feel myself falling fast, as if plummeting through the earth. I tumble in darkness, and I'm jolted back and forth by alternating flashes of light. I realize that I am slipping around in time.

How do I stay? How do I get back?

Sýr, I call out with my mind and heart. *Help!*

The bright light of day rushes at me, and I'm sitting on the floor of our dwelling back home. I am very small, and Sýr is a teenager. She feeds me porridge, and I am filled with love.

Back again into the darkness, tumbling faster now. Another flash, and I am an infant, newly born, staring at my mother's face. Darkness. Light. Over and over I fall. Over and over I visit some small moment of my life. Feeding Núna, my raven. Sending Amma's body out to sea. Waving at Father's ship from the shore. Eating shark with Sýr. Casting runes with Sýr. Always Sýr.

Blackness. Cold. A sharp, searing pain in my left side. And then the bright blue sky is spinning past. I land on a hard surface, the breath knocked out of me, and it takes me a long time to sit up. When I do, I recognize nothing.

I am alone on a small hilltop. There is nothing but green fields of tall wild grass as far as I can see. I am naked and cold. Wet leaves cling to my body.

There is a lone tree on the hilltop with me, its branches bare. Sap runs from a gouge along its trunk. As I look at the tree's wound, I become aware of my own injury. My side pulses, and I reach down to examine it. I touch the edges of the wound and then cry out in pain as a hot, stabbing sensation rips through my abdomen. How did this happen? Where am I?

Even as the terror of my wound rushes through me, it is replaced by a new fear. I don't know who I am. I don't know my own name. I struggle to recall something, anything, of what happened before this, but my mind is blank. Did I exist moments earlier, or not? Somewhere deep inside my soul, I know that I was someone. I *am* someone.

I'm lightheaded. The blood runs from my wound, thick and dark, and it smells like death, like bodies festering in the earth, and of long-forgotten things cast into pits. I turn around, and in the distance I see a golden lake and a dark figure standing next to it.

I tumble out of control again. What was I doing? There is something I need to do. What is it? I'm lost. And then, through the fog, a voice.

Runa, the voice calls. *Stay with me.*

Sýr.

The love of my sister calls me back. All I can do is focus on the love. Sýr is my guiding light. In a flash I am beside Sýr once again in the dark room, kneeling beside her bound form.

"Please," Sýr says. She is frantic. "Go! They're coming. You need to be strong."

"No, Sýr, I don't want to leave you."

My runes begin to clatter, and the sound they make is a name, repeated over and over. *Katla. Katla. Katla.*

"Go, Runa, run. When you need me, look for the moths. Today, tomorrow, it will always be the two of us, Runa. Forever," Sýr says, her voice shaking.

I kiss my sister on the cheek. "I will set you free, Sýr. And I will kill Katla."

My runes are reaching a crescendo now, warning me of Katla's imminent arrival. I hurry through the small window that opens into the back lane. Once I'm out, I look inside at my sister one last time.

"I love you," I whisper, before running away into the night.

I sprint through the filthy lanes, crying and desperate to get as far away from Katla as possible. But how will I ever do this without Sýr? How can I be strong enough?

Sýr may have lifted her binding spell, but I feel more confused than ever.

I turn a corner and run into someone hard and unyielding. It's Einar.

He grabs me and whirls us behind a stall, crushing me with his hug.

"Runa!" he exclaims. "Thank the gods. I have been searching everywhere. I found your shelter and your pack, abandoned, and I thought the worst."

I look at him, at the concern and fear in his eyes, and I let him hold me in silence for a while.

"Oski?" I ask.

He shakes his head. "I don't know. Come," he says. "I found a place."

We steal through the lanes to a hay stall, where we collapse in a heap. Einar has brought my pack. He hands it to me.

"I wasn't sure if...you know," he says in explanation.

"If Katla killed me already?"

"No!" he says. "But this place...this place is strange. I feel danger everywhere."

I nod. "I found Sýr."

"And?"

"It isn't good."

He doesn't say anything. And of all the things I love about Einar, this is perhaps my favorite. He knows when to be quiet. When to let things be. He opens his arms, and I lean into him. We stay like this as the night brightens toward day. It may be the last time we ever do this.

"How did you get in?" I ask at last.

"Oh," he says, stroking a piece of my hair, "I thought of you. And then you opened the door."

"Me?" I look at him.

He shrugs. "I knew it wasn't real," he says. "You were like a light in the darkness. And I followed you. As I've been doing all this time."

He gazes at me, his golden eyes dilated wide in the dim light of dawn but as glowing as ever. I lean in and press my lips to his. I half expect him to taste like honey, but he does not. He's warm and spicy, and softer than I imagined. When I pull away he doesn't try to kiss me back, but he doesn't let me move too far away either. He holds me in place, looking at me like he's never seen me before.

"When this is all over," he says, "will you do that again?"

"I will," I say.

He smiles the barest of smiles, and it coincides with the tolling of a loud bell.

The competition is starting.

I scramble to my feet, gathering my things, but Einar doesn't move.

"What's wrong?" I ask.

"I wish we had more time," he says.

I know he is afraid that I might die battling Katla. I am afraid too. But I can't indulge those thoughts. And I need Einar.

"There will be time for us," I say in response.

"When?" he asks.

"I don't know. But I will find a way to make it myself, if I have to."

I swing my cloak on, feeling stronger than I have in a long while. I don't know if it's because Sýr lifted the binding spell or if it's because of the kiss, but I feel alive. I suppose walking into certain death can have that effect on a person.

Einar stares at me. "I wish you could see yourself the way I do," he says.

I smile at him and offer a hand to help him up.

"I think I do," I say. "Now."

I hand him his own pack and pull up the hood on my cloak.

"Whatever happens," I say, "you must take care of yourself. Help your clan. If I can't kill her, then you have to."

He adjusts his pack and draws his cloak tighter, shivering a little, as if he's cold.

"I promise," he says. "I'll see it through."

We stand there, a beam of cold morning light shining through the slats overhead. We've come so far, and it feels like a lifetime since Katla first came to my village to steal the stone.

"Runa, I—" He struggles to find the words.

"Tell me after," I say, turning to go.

I walk away from the stall, leaving him behind. I can't look back or else I'll never leave.

We'll have our time. When we're back on the black sands of home, and the world isn't falling apart around us.

TWENTY-TWO

I weave through the throng as the crowd heads to the battling circle. My face is once again shrouded in false lines of aging. Any caster worth their runes will see through my disguise if they truly look, but I want to go as unnoticed as possible. I've even disguised my spear as a mere walking staff. No need to attract attention to a marbendill's spear in a place where such things are sought and lusted after.

As I walk past stalls and taverns and sellers hawking their wares, I see a large figure, clad in black, with a bald head shining in the morning light. Oski! Did the bindrune tattoo work for them, or was it something else? I watch as they slip into a doorway, casting around surreptitious glances. What odd thing are they doing now?

I follow, peeking through the slats of a dilapidated window. It's difficult to see, but Oski is speaking to someone. Carefully,

I pull open part of the broken shutter to get a better view. There's an old woman, gnarled with time, sitting on a pile of ornate cushions, her skinny legs folded beneath her. She is dressed in colorful robes not of our custom. The old woman casts a glance toward the window, and I jump out of sight.

I strain to hear, but their voices are too low. "Louder," I whisper to my runes, and I cup my hand to my ear. Oski and the old woman's voices echo in my ear, much louder now.

"I have done my duty," Oski says. "I have brought the caster here."

"Yes," says the old woman. "She is close."

They're talking about me! And what is this duty Oski speaks of? Enough! I remove my disguise and barge in through the doorway.

"I *am* close," I say. "And I demand to know what is going on."

Oski recoils in surprise. "Runa!" they exclaim and then rush to embrace me.

I sidestep them and give them a poke with my spear.

"Ow!" they howl.

The old woman laughs, and the sound is like a gurgling stream.

"I demand the truth!" I say, wielding my runes. "Or I will *make* you talk."

Oski cowers away from me. I am stunned to realize they are afraid. They should be.

"You're different," Oski says. "You are not the runecaster I saw last."

"She is unbound," the old woman explains.

I whirl around. "What did you say?"

The old woman sighs. "Child, I have known your family for generations. I have provided counsel to your mother and her mother and her mother, all the way back to Freyja herself."

"How old are you, Mimir?" Oski asks the old woman, rubbing their side where I had jabbed them with my spear.

"No matter," Mimir says.

"I don't understand what is happening," I say.

"The Valkyrie," says Mimir. "I sent them to find you. And to ensure you got here. I have seen things. My family has the gift of foresight. And yours, the gift of time."

"What did you mean about Freyja?" I ask.

"Ha!" Mimir laughs. "You are not a goddess, never mind. A few drops of Freyja's blood in your line. But that is all you need."

"I have Freyja's blood?" I ask.

"I thought you said she was a smart one," Mimir says to Oski.

"Hey!" I exclaim.

"One drop is enough," says Mimir. "But not every child in the line inherits the gift. To wield the moonstone, a charged moonstone, you must have the blood *and* the gift."

There seem to be a great many people concerned with my ability to wield this stone.

"Why do you want me to wield it?" I ask. "Why is everyone so involved with me and with my family and my gifts? If you can call them that."

"Because child," says Mimir in a grave voice, "no one else can do it. And it is vital that you obtain the moonstone."

"But why? To kill Katla? If we get enough casters together, we can defeat her," I argue.

Mimir laughs her gurgling laugh, and I look at Oski, who won't meet my gaze.

"Oski? What is it?" I demand.

Oski shakes their head. "I'm sorry, Runa. There's so much more you do not know."

"Then tell me," I say. "Tell me now."

The bell tolls again outside. I have minutes left before I must be at the circle.

I grasp my runes and hold them in front of Mimir, who recoils in shock.

"Time stones," she whispers. "A time caster with time stones. It has been so long."

"Yes," I hiss. "And I will send you so far back in time that you will not even exist for thousands of years." Even though I have no idea how to do this, the threat seems real enough to me. I feel like I can do it. Somewhere inside of me I know it to be true. I am that angry, and the old woman senses it.

"You must get the moonstone," Mimir says. "You know that it is a time stone. The most powerful of all. And when it is charged and wielded by a time caster like you, your power will be unparalleled."

My heart quickens, recalling my mother's test at moonwater's gate.

"What do you intend to use me for?" I ask, anger rising in my throat. I am so tired of people lying to me.

"I do not intend to use you," she protests.

"Ah, but you do," I say, spitting the words into her face. "Everyone wants to use everyone for something. Katla is using my sister to try to get the moonstone. She's trying to use me. She's using Einar and his family. You used Oski to get me here. And in truth, I used Oski and Einar to get here. Now tell me why *you* want me."

Mimir sighs. "A long time ago the wanderer and god of all, Odin, traded his eye for a drink of water from the well of cosmic knowledge. The same well the stone will be charged in here at moonwater."

"Go on," I say, a chill running down my back.

"The moonstone is not just a stone. It is the lost eye of Odin. If you are able to wield it, then you must return it to Odin himself. He wants it back, and he's desperate. So desperate, in fact, that he sent a serpent, a witch, to retrieve it for him."

I stare at Mimir. "A serpent?" I ask. "You mean to say that Odin sent Katla—*Grabak*—to get the moonstone? All of this is his doing?"

"Yes, child," says Mimir. "Odin is a tricky and fickle god. This we know all too well. Oski knows it," she says, nodding to them.

Oski glowers with anger.

"Then why should I give him back his stupid eye?" I say.

"Because," says Mimir, "if he does not get it back, he will bring about Ragnarok. Everything in existence will be wiped out."

As she says the words, I hold out my runes. This is too much. "Stop," I command.

Time stands still.

I know Mimir has spoken the truth, and I have heard all that I care to. I look at Oski and the old woman, each of them frozen in the moment. It's exactly like back at the elf tavern when I met Píla Ör.

Staring at Oski, I am filled with anger. How could they betray me? I walk over to their frozen form and take the feather from inside their cloak. I wave it. "Goodbye," I say, placing it in my pouch with my runes. "Go back where you came from." With that, Oski disappears in a flutter of black. I stand there for a moment, blinking in disbelief. I didn't expect that to work.

"Oski?" I say, but they do not return. Somewhere in my mind's eye I know that they are waiting for me. Perhaps by the golden lake. They will have to wait some more.

As for Mimir, I reach out and carefully shut both of her eyelids. "When you wake," I whisper, "your eyes will remain closed, and you will not be able to open them." She will also have to wait until I release her from this spell.

I peek from the window and see that the crowd is frozen in place. I slip out the door and walk through the crowd, wandering around people as if they are monuments in a graveyard, and I am aware that if I fail, they will all be as good as dead.

It's tempting to leave things like this, frozen in place, no one moving forward or changing. No one to cause problems for me. What would it be like to wander the world alone while the whole of existence waited for me to start time again? I don't know if my command will last as long as I wish it to or if things will resume their pace on their own. It occurs to me that maybe I'm the one who is out of time, and everyone else is still moving forward as they always were. If that is true, then every world I step into or out of from now on is a different world each time.

I laugh, bitterness flowing through me. I thought I would find Sýr, and she would help end this. Now I can see how foolish I've been. This will never end. Return the eye of Odin? Ha! How could I possibly do that after all the suffering he has caused?

When I arrive at the circle, I see that the Jötnar are all there, lined up in neat rows, waiting for the competition to start.

I scan the crowd and see Einar. He is standing by Ymir's side, father and son reunited. Ymir looks like a husk of himself, like someone painted his skin on and walks around with it.

The council of elders, all female runecasters of advanced age, is in position on the elevated stone seats. I wonder how many of these competitions they've seen, or if any of them have wielded the moonstone. I know of them only from stories. They have discarded their old identities and have taken the names of the three Fates in tribute to their commitment to the forces of destiny. They bear the names of the Fates of time itself. They are Urðr, Verðandi and Skuld. Amma told me all about them and how much they seem to enjoy their status and influence. My amma has never cared for people in lofty positions.

I walk by them, close to their seats, and look each elder caster in the eye. None blinks or moves or indicates that they see me. I'm alone in this.

I do not see Katla or Sýr, but the witch could be present in the bodies of any of the spectators.

The only thing that moves in my frozen world is the reflecting pool. I walk over to it and see that its waters are rippling in anticipation of the eclipse. The red moon has almost covered the sun. It is still moving, so it appears I am not all-powerful with my time stones. Even I cannot stop the moon.

I peer into the sacred water, seeing myself. I look older than I remember, though this journey has not taken the years that seem to live on my face. My one brown eye gives me an odd, somewhat crazed look. It's not much in the way of a beauty improvement, but it is scary enough to intimidate a foe, and I think I'm even happier for that.

I feel a presence behind me. Turning, I spot Katla in the crowd. She is not frozen.

The yellow witch skulks through the stilled forms of the people like a winding serpent, hissing and dragging Sýr behind her like one of the brainless Jötnar. My dear sister is near death. This much I know.

"Sýr!" I call, but she doesn't look at me.

Katla slithers closer.

"Look at the runecaster," she says. Her voice sounds like something slithering through grass. "I am going to enjoy consuming you."

"Is that so?" I say as I touch my runes.

"Back to now," I say, and time resumes in violent relief.

Katla slinks back into the throng, a smile on her face. She has retracted her daggers. For now.

The council elders are startled, but the crowd doesn't seem to notice that they've been out of time.

"What is this?" says Verðandi, the middle elder. "Who are you?" she demands. "Why are you in the circle near the waters?"

I take a step back. "I am Gudrun Unnursdóttir, sister of Sýr Unnursdóttir, and I have come to win back the moonstone for my clan, the people of Myrkur Strönd."

The crowd murmurs.

"Silence," says Urðr. She is the oldest of the council members. "Is that not Sýr behind you? She is the current keeper of the stone."

I step aside to allow the council a good look.

"Indeed," says Katla, stepping forward. "She has defected from Myrkur Strönd and will now fight on behalf of the Jötnar clan. She is our champion now, and we are the current keepers of the moonstone."

"Liar!" I shout.

Katla growls, then composes herself. She doesn't want to reveal herself yet.

The elders are suspicious. "Who are you?" asks Skuld, the third elder.

"I am Katla of the Jötnar," she says. "Wife to the great Ymir."

There is a gasp from the crowd. Katla's name has preceded her.

As I watch, I see Einar sneaking back through the crowd to hide behind a big Jötnar. He gives a gentle nod to me and touches his tattooed arm. He is trying to say we are in this together. I give a slight nod back.

But then Einar suddenly steps forward, and I want to blast him backward or freeze him in time. I do not want him in danger.

"Great council," he says, addressing the elders. "My name is Einar Ymirsson, heir to the Jötnar clan, and I have come to tell you that this witch Katla is an imposter. She has tried to steal the moonstone and in doing so has murdered countless people. My clan is under her spell!"

"Lies," says Katla. "He is a scheming elf and forbidden from the circle."

"If he was deemed worthy to pass through the moonwater gates, then he must belong here," I say through gritted teeth.

"Enough!" says Urðr. "This is unusual. But we must observe tradition. We must first charge the moonstone. For there are hard years ahead, and the clan that wins it will have prosperity."

"And what about the clan that was destroyed by Katla?" I exclaim.

"Silence!" says Urðr. "Though many look to us for guidance in matters of destiny, we do not decide such things."

"So you will do nothing?" I ask in disbelief. "What use are you?"

Several people in the crowd murmur their support. They, too, seem to want the council to act. Amma always warned me about such things. Once people get power, they tend to use it to serve themselves.

"If you won't do anything, then I will," I say, turning to face Katla.

"Yes!" shouts a spectator.

"Fight her!" shouts another. "Kill the witch!"

"I will," I say.

But Einar is faster than I am. He attacks Katla with a poison dart, blown at her from his own mouth. As it zips through the air, I recognize its golden sheen. It is the arrow pin that belonged to his mother.

Katla is faster than us both, and she sees it coming. She skillfully sidesteps the dart and plucks it from the air as it passes. She hurls it back at Einar and it hits him in the center of his chest. He staggers backward, an expression of surprise and pain on his face.

"No, Einar!" I cry out, running to him.

He struggles in the dirt, coughing, fighting to stay in this life. I touch his face and lean down to kiss him. "Hang on," I say. I pull out the rune of Ür and lay it on his chest. I will leave it there, close to his skin, so that it gives Einar a little more time. I hope this will give me a chance to find a cure.

I look up at the council. "Let me have my revenge," I say, "or I will cast you into a never-ending fire." I wield the rest of my runes, emphasizing my threat.

The crowd reacts, some people crying out and hurrying to leave, others emboldened and shouting encouragement to me.

The council confers, and then Skuld speaks. "We will grant you the opportunity to fight for the stone."

"Wise choice," I say.

"Very well, runecaster," says Katla, her voice venomous. "We will battle."

"Bring forth the stone," says the council elder.

Katla kicks Sýr, who struggles to stand. She hobbles forward and approaches the pool.

Sýr meets my gaze for a moment and then looks away.

"The eclipse is upon us," says Verðandi. "The stone must be placed in the sacred waters."

With trembling hands Sýr cups some water and raises it, intoning a spell of revealing. "I call upon the sun and the moon to reveal what is hidden."

The crowd gasps as the moonstone appears in her palms. It is still blue, but it is flickering now and almost inert.

"Charge it," Katla hisses, licking the edges of her cracked lips, flashing me a glimpse of her forked tongue.

It is beyond her ability to hide her greed and desire for the stone, and the council glances at her. I hope they are nervous about her intentions, for everyone's sake.

As I watch Sýr lower the stone toward the reflecting pool, I feel a magnetic pull that I cannot deny. My body, my soul, wants the moonstone more than anything. I thirst for it, yearn for it, and I am ashamed to admit that in this moment I want it more than I want to liberate Sýr. I want it more than I want to bring my mother back from wherever I banished her to. I want it more than Einar's health. I want the power.

The casting circle glows a vibrant red as the moon completes its cycle. It is at this moment that Sýr drops the stone into the water.

The circle plunges into darkness for a moment as the moon completely covers the sun. And then everything is illuminated by the glowing blue of the moonstone emanating from the sacred waters.

Everyone is silent. None of us dare to move as we watch and wait for the stone to recharge. As it glows, blinking in the waters of all knowledge, I remember that this is not a simple runestone, and it is not a prosperity stone or even a time stone. This is an eye. The all-seeing, curse-bringing, lost eye of Odin. And as we all watch it, I have the distinct feeling that it is watching us.

The darkness lifts. The stone glows a steady blue, no longer flickering.

Katla paces on the perimeter of the circle, waiting for her moment.

Urðr the elder steps forward and uses a long staff to scoop the stone from the water. She places it on a small pedestal in the center of the ring.

"The competition will now commence," she announces. "All representative casters may try their magic and cast the rune that will allow them to wield the stone. If they are successful, a challenger may attempt to battle for it. In the end, one will be deemed worthy."

Before any other clans can make a bid for the stone, Katla steps forward, dragging Sýr along with her.

"She will claim the stone on behalf of the Jötnar. On behalf of me." Katla stares into me from across the circle. She knows I will challenge her.

"Don't do it, Sýr!" I shout. "Don't take it! She will possess you as soon as you touch it."

Sýr walks toward the stone, drawn to its brilliant blue. She looks at me and smiles. "It's okay, Runa."

"Indeed," says Katla, hovering behind Sýr. "Take it, Sýr," she hisses. "Hold the stone. Let me feel its power through you." Katla reaches out and clutches Sýr's back, her fingers sinking into Sýr's flesh and disappearing.

People in the crowd back away in fear. "Dark magic!" someone cries.

"Stop this," says Skuld. "One caster at a time."

"Don't do it, Sýr," I beg.

She looks at me. "Always the two of us," she says, reaching out to grasp the moonstone from its pedestal as Katla sinks further into her.

Sýr holds the stone for a moment, mesmerized by its powerful beauty, and then she opens her mouth and shoves the stone inside. With great effort she swallows it whole.

"No!" I cry, at once understanding what this means. Sýr will surely die.

Lit from within by the stone's eerie light, Sýr staggers backward, and Katla falls away from her, releasing her unnatural hold on Sýr's flesh.

Katla lets out an anguished scream as she is separated from Sýr and from the stone.

"Give it back!" she demands. "Stupid mortal."

"The stone," Sýr says, her voice far away. "The eye." She throws her head back, and the blue light shines from her eyes. "No, I don't want to see. I don't want to see." She jerks in violent spasms and cries out in pain.

"Sýr, no!" I run to her, but Sýr holds out her arms and I cannot get any closer. It's as if I am walking against a windstorm, and I can't pass through.

I look at the elders. "Please help!"

They are grim. "We cannot retrieve it," says Urðr.

"Then I shall get it," says Katla. She hurls herself at Sýr, possessing her body and disappearing into her.

The spectators scream as the two become one, and the casting arena bursts into chaos. People run, stomping over one another in their panic, leaving their belongings behind in a desperate bid to flee.

The witch cackles, aglow with power. I must try to separate her from Sýr again.

Before I can think, Katla strikes at me with a blast of energy and I hold up my rune pouch as as a shield. The yellow fire rushes past me on all sides, carrying with it a coldness that I imagine is what death must feel like.

"Blind the witch!" I shout, directing my rune power at her. A bolt of red fire shoots from my runes and knocks Katla back. She recoils, clawing at her eyes.

She recovers in a moment, laughing. "You are weak. You are nothing," she says, and her face changes to reflect Sýr's, then my mother's and then my amma's. "Freak," she spits as she walks toward me.

"Stop," I say, stumbling backward, away from the sight of my loved ones under the control of this evil. Sýr's eyes still glow blue, and I wonder how much longer my sister's body can withstand the moonstone. Wounds and burns appear on her skin. She's smoldering from within.

I steady myself and muster every measure of love I have for Sýr in my heart. I focus on it, remembering all the times Sýr has cared for me. Her lullabies and sleeping spells, the countless hours spent trying to teach me the ways of the runes, the games we used to play on the black sands of home. All our happy memories, and the sad ones too.

Believe. Sýr's voice in my mind is all the encouragement I need.

I grasp my runes, powerful time stones in their own right, connected to me by fate and desire, and I know what to do. I will try to bind my runes to the moonstone.

"I call upon the lost eye of Odin," I intone. "I call upon

the past, the present, and the future. I command you to leave my sister!"

"You are too late," Katla says from within Sýr. "We are one, and I control the stone."

"Never!" I shout.

The three elders, emboldened by my commands, step forward and place their hands on me, feeding their combined energies into me. I am at once several people and one powerful being, and I feel all the fear and desire of these women coursing through my veins.

"Sýr," I say, and my voice sounds like four voices blended together. "Come back to me. Fight the witch."

An image floods my mind, a gift from Sýr. She is showing me what I must do next, but I cannot. "No, Sýr," I say, my voice echoing around the casting circle. "Don't make me do that."

Again Sýr projects the image into my mind. *Please, Runa.*

I try to withstand her plea, as the horror of what she's asking is too much to bear.

Release me.

My love for her is my undoing. I give in. With a scream, I charge forward and plunge my spear into Sýr's stomach as she begged me to do. She falls to the ground, folding herself around the spear and clutching my cloak.

Katla leaks from her, at first more liquid than a whole being. With struggle she regains some of her orginal form, but she, too, is wounded. A thick yellow blood oozes from the gash in her middle. As she tries to rise up and fight, she flops around on the ground, more snake than woman, and my fear of her vanishes. I know now that I am stronger.

"Stupid runecaster," she hisses. "You still believe in good and evil, light and dark. When will you learn there is no opposite to power? We are one and the same. We can join together and rule all the realms."

I hold Sýr, ignoring Katla as she writhes in pain.

My beloved sister looks at me, her face full of love. "I must finish this, Runa," she says. She grabs hold of the spear and plunges it deeper into her abdomen.

"No, Sýr!" I scream.

Sýr pulls the spear out and it clatters, slick with her blood, to the ground. She reaches into the wound with a trembling hand, pulls the glowing moonstone from her stomach, and holds the bloody stone out to me.

"No," I say. "I don't want it. I hate it. Look what it has done."

"You must, Runa," she says. She is growing weaker. "It is your destiny."

"Damn you, Odin!" I cry, directing all of my rage into the sky.

The three elders recoil from me and begin casting runes around Katla. They chant an ancient binding spell that contains the witch in a pool of her own sickly yellow blood.

I place my hand under Sýr's, as I'm scared to take the moonstone outright. I'm not ready to touch it.

Katla groans, surrounded by a magic she is now too weak to overcome. "My stone," she wails.

The stone changes from blue to red, and I understand what is happening now. Sýr has charged the runestone with her sacrifice. It's a power beyond all understanding and far beyond the powers of the reflecting pool.

"It was always your stone, Runa," Sýr says. "You held it even as a baby." As she says this, I know it is true. I remember the stone. I remember playing with it, holding it.

"No," Katla protests, writhing on the ground beside us. The elders have her bound, and she cannot heal herself in this state.

"Swear it will always be the two of us, Runa," Sýr whispers. "Swear it."

"I swear it," I say through my tears. "Always the two of us. Where I go, I take you with me."

"And where I go," she says, "I take you." Sýr takes one last ragged breath and closes her eyes. She is gone.

This casting circle, this city of moonwater, even this island, suddenly seem too small to contain my grief.

I wrap my fingers around Sýr's hand, my flesh touching the moonstone, and as I do the eye of Odin's power flows into me, bringing with it the pain and power of Sýr and every caster who has wielded it before.

The casting circle is engulfed in red light, and in an instant I can see through time. I can see my entire journey. The massacre of my people. The obstacles in my path. The doubt and the pain.

Moving backward, I see my birth. My family. I see myself as a child. Moving forward, I watch as I grow older. I'm alone on a great ship, floating on an endless sea. It isn't the ocean of home, but the bright blue waters of a new place, somewhere I have yet to go. There is a flash, and I see myself walking through golden fields. There are women there, beckoning to me. Sýr. Amma.

When I come back to the present, I am holding the moonstone. It glows as red as my wrath.

The casting circle had cleared of people, but now a few trickle back, murmuring at the sight of Katla dying on her belly. Some quake in fear at the sight of me. Others look at me in awe.

The elders turn to me. "You are the chosen caster," says Urðr.

Katla crawls on her belly. "My stone, my stone, my stone," she chants.

"I am," I say.

I whisper to the moonstone, "You are mine, and I alone command you."

I look at Katla, who once struck deep fear in me but now reminds me of a worm under my feet. "You want this stone of sorrow?" I ask.

"Yesss," she hisses, reaching out a clawed hand.

I hold it out to her and watch her slither. "Then take it," I say.

"Stop! What are you doing?" Urðr protests.

Ignoring them, I lean down to Katla, and as she sneers up at me I dig my fingernails into her right eye socket and rip out the orb.

Katla screams, the sound deafening. I squash the eye in my hand, slimy with her yellow blood, and throw it down into the dirt so I can crush it beneath my foot.

"My eye!" Katla wails, clutching at her face.

"When you see Odin," I say, "tell him I'm coming."

With that I jam the moonstone into Katla's empty eye socket. In a flash of red light, the stone sucks all of Katla's power from her, draining her until she is a withered husk. Her fear is exquisite, and I'm pleased to see that she is still alive. She wheezes, barely clinging to this realm.

"She isn't dead yet," says Urðr.

"Wait," I say.

The stone pulses red, with a blue center in it not unlike the pupil of an eye. I take it back from the hole in Katla's dried-out face, and her life power flows into me, startling me with its intensity. Images of tree roots, hungry serpents and endless darkness flood my mind. I taste blood. So much blood.

I use the stone to crack free one of Katla's exposed fangs. I will take this with me on my journey to find Odin. Perhaps I will stab him with it.

Standing over Katla's shriveled form, I hold the stone high. "I banish you," I say. "You will live out eternity in pain."

I wave the stone, and a large hole opens in the ground of the casting circle. It is filled with boiling magma, red and black and hotter than the realm of Hel.

"You will be forgotten, Katla," I say. "You serpent, you slave of Grabak. In every lifetime, I curse you. You will never know love. You will be forgotten. So shall it be. Until the end of time."

I kick Katla's thin body into the hole, and she sinks beneath the flames with a weak scream.

"It is done," I say, and the hole closes over.

Daylight returns to the casting circle and, with it, life to the Jötnar. Now that Katla is dead, they are released from her spell of control. They look around in confusion. My heart surges with the hope that my clan will also be freed from its death-like sleep.

I struggle to shake off my rage. I am still consumed by it and have to will myself not to set everything ablaze.

Ymir cries out when he sees his son on the ground. "Einar!" He rushes to hold him, lifting his head.

The sight of Einar is enough to pierce the darkness within me. I hurry to him and kneel beside his limp body.

"Please tell me he isn't gone," I say to Ymir, as I place my head against Einar's chest. The slight rise and fall of Einar's breathing tells me there's hope.

"Einar!" I shake him. His eyes flutter open.

"Tell me how to cure you," I say. "Your poison. What is the antidote?"

"Asta," he says, his voice weak. "Asta cure."

Asta. Of course. The flower he gave me. I reach into my cloak and pull out the bundle of dried asta flowers. There is no time to make a tea, so I crumble a bit of the bud and place it in his mouth. He chews and tries not to gag. I lay my runes on his chest and ask them to protect him, then gather water from the reflecting pool for him to drink. No one stops me.

He comes around and requests more asta. Finally he is revived enough to sit up on his own. "You kept it?" he asks, clutching the bundle of flowers to him.

"Of course," I say. "It's the sweetest gift I've ever been given. Now eat some more." I keep feeding the asta to him until I am sure he will recover. Then I leave him to be reunited with his father.

Einar clutches at my hand. "Wait," he says.

"It's okay," I say. "Your father needs you now. And I must tend to Sýr."

The elders move out of my way in respect as I walk past.

In death, Sýr is as beautiful as ever, her dark hair splayed out on the soft dirt of the casting circle. I drape her with my cloak, wrapping her tight so she isn't cold, and then lie on the ground next to her. When I am ready, I will take Sýr home to Myrkur Strönd. I will bury her broken body, and I will make sure my clan has been released from the spell. But for now, in this moment, I need to lie here with my head on my sister's shoulder. I sing to her the same soft songs she used to lull me with as a child. No one dares disturb me.

TWENTY-THREE

When I am ready, the Jötnar, led by Ymir and Einar, help me transport Sýr's body back to Myrkur Strönd. I want to get home as soon as possible.

The journey home is much faster with a warrior party leading the way, and we are well protected and supplied now that I have the moonstone. I don't have to think when using it. If we need enough fish to feed us, all I have to do is stand by a stream and the fish appear, ready to be scooped. If we have a bit of moss for soup, I can expand it with a touch. The moonstone seems happy to be at home in my pouch with my other time stones, and I can feel them chattering to each other and growing off one another.

We are connected now, and I know I cannot give the stone back to Odin. It is part of me, as my runes are, as much a part of me as my own eyes. I haven't even begun to explore the stone's potential, but I feel it pulling at me, wanting me to incite it to travel through time. But I must stay here, stay now. I need to deliver Sýr home, and I need to help my clan.

Einar, still weak from the poison dart, hasn't left my side on the journey home, though we haven't spoken much. We've suffered great loss, and my heart aches in mourning for Sýr. There's something else different between us, and it's hard to decipher. Before I claimed the moonstone, I was like a child. Yes, I had come a long way, learning much on our journey together, and I'd thought I knew who I was and what was important to me. But things were simpler then. Find Sýr, defeat Katla, win the stone. Somewhere along the journey Einar fell in love with me, but now that I have become the keeper of the most powerful time stone in existence, the eye of Odin himself, that love seems like a frivolous dream.

The moonstone has peeled away the silly concerns of my childhood and the insecurities that have plagued me along my journey. I don't care about my weird eyes anymore or my wild hair.

We reach the place where our clans separate, arriving sooner than Einar is ready for. He must travel back to the Jötnar village with his father to help put things right. They need to rebuild after the devastation Katla has caused, and to heal. I need to do the same. I use my stone to provide them with supplies, amassing piles of herbs and grains and wild game. The large Jötnar warriors will drag it along the path on a sledge made from felled birch trees. They built a smaller sledge for Sýr's body, and I must pull it home now, completing the final leg of the journey alone. Einar offers to come, but I refuse. I am strong enough to do it on my own.

I have promised to care for the Jötnar as they rebuild, and emissaries from our respective clans will exchange more supplies once we are settled. There is even talk of combining our people, with Ymir as chief of his bloodline and me as leader of mine. In our clan's tradition, this task would fall to my father, but even if he were here, there is no doubt that I would be the one to lead. I hold all the power, as I hold the moonstone.

I stand at the same crossroads I encountered at the start of my journey, gazing at Einar, neither of us wanting to leave. I take this time to study his face, the pointed eyebrows, the soft lips, the golden eyes.

"I will come visit by the next half moon," Einar says, closing the distance between us. "If I am able to wait that long."

I smile, even though I don't feel much like it. "I'll count the days." My voice comes out flat, and I wonder if he notices.

"What of Oski?" Einar asks. He's been avoiding the question, knowing how angry I still am.

"I know where they are," I say. "They are safe."

"Can you forgive them?" he asks.

I sigh. "Yes. Because it's what Sýr would have done."

Einar nods, but he looks troubled.

"What is it?" I ask.

"Why not go back now that you have the stone?" he asks.

"You mean back in time," I say.

"Yes," he says. "Back to when Katla first tried to steal the stone. Why not undo all of it? That way Sýr would be alive."

"Because," I say, "that would mean undoing you. And Oski. And it would mean undoing me too. Things have worked out the way they were meant to, I think." I look at my glowing rune pouch. It would undo this, I think, not wanting to say it out loud.

"What will you do now?" Einar asks.

"I will bury my sister," I say. "Help my clan rebuild."

He leans down as if to kiss me, then hesitates. "I still have that poison in me," he says.

"I'll risk it," I say, pulling him to my lips.

This kiss is different. It's not the timid, sweet kiss we first enjoyed. And it's not full of love and hope and dreams either. This is a goodbye kiss, and I wonder if he knows how final it is.

When we part, Einar presses some asta flowers into my palm. "Just in case," he says.

I take it, placing it in my cloak next to my heart, and watch him walk away from me, more beautiful now than he's ever been. I wonder if everyone is this beautiful when you know you will never see them again.

He glances back, unable to resist another look. "Remember me," he says, with his sad smile. "If we're not in the same place. Or the same time."

"Don't worry," I say. "I know how to find you."

The Jötnar leave, their lumbering party kicking a swirl of dust on the road. I look south to where my home waits beyond the foothills. The sun is high in the sky, and we are entering a time of endless light. I will be returning home with the dead body of my sister, but I will also be returning as the salvation of my clan.

I gather the rope in my hands, hook it over my chest, and lean into it. The weight of my sister follows me all the way back to my village, and by the time I reach the rock on which I used my own blood to draw a protection rune for my clan, I am exhausted. I could have used my moonstone to lighten the load. Perhaps I even could have made the sledge float. But sometimes it's better for things to be difficult. Sometimes work is the only thing that soothes.

Looking out over my village from the hillside, I see that the survivors of the slaughter have emerged from their long sleep, and since awakening they have begun to rebuild our burned-out village. Piles of bodies wait on the shoreline for a burning ceremony, and I see where my amma died and where everything changed forever. The place of my childhood is no more.

I don't announce my arrival. I simply walk down the hillside into the village and let people begin to notice me. I have no words to say, and I feel suddenly weak, as if my power was all a dream.

The remaining villagers approach, crowding around me, and I am overwhelmed by their need. I take my moonstone out of the pouch and hold it high. It glows red with a blue center. It still exists.

People hurry over to me from their homes and their work. I hear their gasps, their cries of relief to see the stone shining bright, like a beacon of hope and prosperity. And then they descend on me, wanting to touch me, begging for help. It is now that I relate to what it must have been like for Sýr all those years. The immense responsibility she must have felt. She had to die for me to understand.

"People!" a familiar voice shouts. "Make way!"

It's Frigg's voice. I drop my spear and my pack and run through the crowd until it parts and I see my old friend, my sister's true love.

She sobs when I reach her and scoops me into a tight embrace.

When she finally releases me, she does so with a question in her eyes. "Sýr?"

I shake my head. "She's gone. I'm so sorry."

Frigg seems to crumple in on herself and falls, kneeling in the mud.

I place my hands on her. "She wanted you to know," I say, "that you are the only one she has ever loved."

I turn to the crowd. "Sýr Unnursdóttir is dead," I say. My voice cracks under the pain of the words.

There are cries and murmurs, but all eyes remain fixed on me. No one moves.

"I have returned in her place. I am the keeper of the stone now. And I...I will try to live up to her legacy."

There are no cheers, no celebrations. This is a time of mourning. We are all broken from our losses.

I close my eyes and imagine the village as it was. I conjure the dwellings and the tools, the supplies piled in baskets, the clothing and leathers hung to dry. I see the fish curing in the shacks. I hear the sounds of life that once echoed in this place.

"I vow to restore the village," I say. "I will work to help rebuild dwellings. I will provide food. Better days are coming. But now I must bury my sister."

They make way for me as I retrieve Sýr's body. Frigg follows behind, sobbing.

I will do what I can for my people, but I cannot bring anyone back from the dead. I don't know how. But if it takes me until the end of time, I will find a way. I will give my people, and Frigg, back everything they have lost.

We take my sister up the path to our little dwelling on the cliff. It's here that we will bury her. I will make sure she has the best spot, near the herb garden and overlooking the sea.

Frigg has lost much of her strength and size, and her eyes are ringed with darkness. When I ask her what she experienced during her enchanted sleep, she declines to answer, saying that she doesn't want to think about it.

As for me, I know who I am now, and I know what my destiny is. I will find Odin. I will show him his wayward eye. And then I am going to kill him with it.

TWENTY-FOUR

Frigg digs the hole, and together we bury Sýr. We smooth the dirt with our bare hands, crying and leaning on each other, and afterward we sit beside her grave for two days. We don't eat or sleep.

Finally, we get up and say goodbye, though neither of us wants to leave her.

Frigg turns to me. "Bring her back, Ru, please," she pleads. "Use the stone."

"I can't now," I say. "I don't know how. But I will. One day I will."

The villagers have let us be, and from a distance I have kept watch over them. I will cast spells to supply them with fish and bread and whatever they need. I have heard some of them sending off their dead loved ones with parties.

The mead is flowing. They are healing. People need to move forward, as I do. But without Sýr I feel untethered.

"Now I am alone," I say to Frigg.

"No," she replies. "I am here. Before Sýr left for moon-water, I promised her I would look after you always. You are my sister now, as you would have been if...I had married her as I intended." She pauses a moment to steady herself. "We wanted to leave. We were going to take you, as Sýr always said you longed to journey, to sail and see the world. Now she is free, at least."

We clasp hands and then embrace, and I know what Frigg says is true. I promise that I will return, and Frigg vows to watch over the clan while I am gone. She will be my new guiding light, drawing me back to my home.

Once I am alone again in my little dwelling, surrounded by the things I used to share with Sýr, I know that I no longer belong here. It is too small a life now to contain me and everything I am capable of. I must go. I must honor Sýr by leaving. I know where I am going, but I need something first.

I stand outside Amma's hut for a while, trying to muster the courage to enter. Her home had been partly burned down in the siege and now, stepping over the threshold, it feels sacred. It's like being inside a secret only my amma and I know.

Much of her beloved scrolls and belongings were destroyed, but there's one thing I came for. Picking through the charred wood, I make my way to the hearth and brush off a pile of ash. It's here. Amma's special scroll. The one that maps all the waters of the known world. How long I have admired it, coveted it, and dreamed of using it to sail away.

With trembling fingers, I pick it up and unroll it to see that it is still intact and readable. Holding it feels like a gift.

"Amma," I say, "I will bring you with me. Maybe I *will* find the next great land."

It will be hard to leave the place that reminds me of my family, but I must.

Father has not returned, and there is still no sign of him or his sailing party. I know in my heart that he is alive, because I saw it in a vision. I saw my raven, Núna, flying through a storm, the ring I placed on her foot dropping into the ocean. I saw my father's ship floating aimless and lost in the desolation of the great fog. I saw him aboard, starving but alive. He hauled in a fishing net but found nothing to eat. A trinket caught his eye. The ring. I know he recognized it, for it is the ring he gave to my mother. I believe I will find him somewhere on my journey. There is still hope.

But before I leave, I need to find Oski.

Taking the moonstone out of its pouch, I place it on the ground in front of me and cast my runes around it.

"Take me to the Valkyrie," I say.

The room floods with red light. Gone is the swirling white confusion of my past experiences. I feel in control now, and I can see around me with clarity. There are many paths snaking out from this one, some stretching into the future and some stretching into the past. There are pathways running parallel to me. When I look into them I see myself as if in a mirror, except the image is different. I wonder how many variations of me exist through time? How many lifetimes could I live?

"Oski," I say, and the name echoes throughout the timelines until one from the distant past aligns and I see all the way to end of it, like a drawing of light at the bottom of a well.

I move forward, and in a rush of red light I find Oski standing alone on a green hill beside the golden lake. I reach out my hand, and they take it.

"Home," I say, pulling Oski with me, and I see myself sitting in my dwelling with my runes and the moonstone before me. We move forward, and now we are back in my room.

Oski is shaken. This Valkyrie, once mighty, seems vulnerable as they look around in confusion. I stoop to gather my runes and the moonstone, and they step back to make space for me.

"I have brought you back," I say. "Shouldn't you thank me?" The anger drips from my voice, and I struggle to contain it. When I'm mad the stone grows hot, and I don't know what it will do.

"Runa," Oski says. "I am sorry. I did what I was fated to do."

I walk outside, desperate for the sun and the openness and the sea wind on my face. Oski follows me.

I turn to them. "But how could you lie to me? We had an oath."

"I'm sorry. I upheld our oath. I helped you to moonwater. I wanted to keep you safe. And when we started our journey, I didn't know you. And now I love you," they add.

I don't want this to soften my heart, but it does. "I understand," I say at last.

"You are the human family I have always longed for. I hope you can forgive me."

"I may," I say, trying to suppress a grin. "But you owe me."

Oski laughs. "Of course, runecaster. Forever."

We sit in the sunlight, our legs dangling over the cliff. The ocean is calm and clear. The endlessness of it grows inside me.

Oski asks what they must, for they know me well. "When will you be leaving us?"

I sigh. "Now," I say. "I must find Odin." I don't reveal my true plans, but something tells me they know.

"You mean to return it?" Oski asks. "Dangerous journey. Maybe you need a former Valkyrie to come?"

"No," I say, my voice firm. "Please, will you make another oath?"

Oski nods. "Anything."

"Stay here," I say. "And protect Frigg and my clan until I return, or until my father does. I know he is alive. And my raven, Núna. Please feed her worms when she comes home."

"I will," they say, unsheathing their sword. "In the name of Chooser of the Slain, I vow it."

"Thank you," I say, and we sit in silence for a long while.

I take a final breath of the salt air and rise. I have my moonstone, my runes and my spear. I need nothing else.

"What about Einar?" Oski asks. "I don't even know if he is alive."

"He is well," I say. "Rebuilding. Which is what you need to do while I am gone. I have cast spells to sustain the clan in my absence. If you need me, I will know."

I turn to go, this time planning to walk westward to the wilder shores to secure a ship.

"And Einar?" Oski asks as I walk away. "If he needs you?"

I turn back. "Tell Einar..." I trail off, thinking. "Tell him I couldn't wait."

Oski nods, a sad look on their face.

"But tell him there will be time for us," I say.

As I set off alone, with Oski watching over my home, I think about Einar and how disappointed he will be when he finds out I am gone. My choice isn't to abandon him. My choice is to live for something bigger than myself. Something bigger than our love.

I walk, my feet toughened by so many miles, so many days, of journeying. It feels right to be moving again, to be leaving this past behind me and forging headlong into an unknown future. Time itself is always moving, and I must move with it.

If I had to choose a time to live in forever, then I would choose the one that is closest to my heart. I'd choose the one with my sister in it. I'd choose my amma. My friends. My love.

But time is slippery. It does not stay the same. I can only watch it flow like a fast-flowing river trapped under a glacier. I cannot control its direction. Not yet. One day I will unlock the secrets of time, and I will find a way to defeat death itself. If it takes a thousand lifetimes, I will find a way.

The horizon glows blue and gold, and I know that somewhere on the open water I will meet my destiny. Through the wisps of cloud that dot the sky, a lone bird flies. Its path is aligned with mine, and it cries out to me in a raven's voice. I watch its black wings, furious shadows that beat away the past, as it it soars into the sunlight of a new day.

Stay with me.

Acknowledgments

This book would simply not exist without the support and hard work of some very special people. I am so grateful to everyone at Orca Book Publishers for taking a chance on this fantasy about an odd girl named Runa, and for giving me a platform to write speculative fiction for teens. It is an actual dream come true.

I'd like to give special thanks to illustrator Song Kang for her amazing artwork on the cover and throughout these pages, and to designer Rachel Page for creating a thing of beauty that so wonderfully expresses the vision we had for this story. I had such high hopes, and you delivered.

None of this would have been possible without the tenacity, guidance and enthusiasm of Tanya Trafford. Every writer should be so lucky to work with a gifted editor who is a champion for and protector of their work. (But you can't have her because she is mine.) Thank you, Tanya, for breathing life into this project, and for trusting me, and for really getting it. By Freyja, we did it!

My family and my friends are the inspiration for everything I do, and I'm so proud to explore my Icelandic heritage in a book that reflects all the things I wanted in a fantasy novel when I was a teen. This book is for my sister, who always protected me, for my best friend, who loves runes and weird magical stories as much as I do, and for my daughters, who I hope will be inspired by Runa's journey—and her courage to be herself. To Robert, who has always supported me in this work, I'm so proud to be able to finally share this with you.

This book was written in memory of my grandparents, Gudrun and Eyolfur.

To whoever reads this story, I wish you enough light to find your way. *Ratljóst.*

Brooke Carter is the author of several books for teens. She lives with her family in Maple Ridge, British Columbia, where she is hard at work writing the Runecaster series and searching for the perfect cloak.

Read on for a sneak peek from

BOOK TWO in the RUNECASTER SERIES

As the current keeper of the moonstone, Runa Unnursdóttir is the only caster powerful enough to return Odin's lost eye and restore the balance of the world—although she'd love to do anything but. In fact, when Runa sets off on the journey she's always dreamed of—sailing across the open sea—she does so with the lust for blood. Odin's blood.

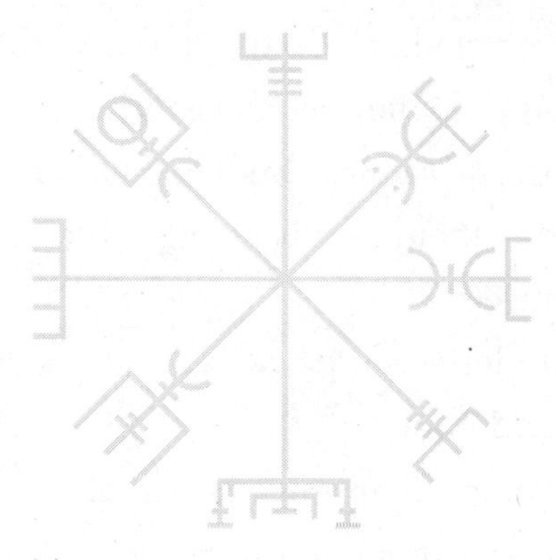

The soft bed beneath me is made of layer upon layer of greenery that smells of tea and herbs. It induces a sleepiness that I fight hard to shake off. The cave boasts a neat collection of tools and implements, clustered in piles and on ledges of stone. There are baskets, rope and drying fish.

A piece of fish steams on a plank of wood next to my bed. I pick it up and smell it, but the salty scent of the ocean makes me gag. I retch up more salt water until nothing but bile comes out. How did I survive underwater for so long?

I try standing up, but my legs are weak, and my body feels like it has grown twice as heavy. The dying embers of the fire in the center of the cave cast a soft glow around me, and a blue light floods in from the mouth. The competing warm and cool tones combine in a colorful wash that undulates along the walls like waves.

The slapping sound of wet footsteps echoes, and Oski appears in silhouette at the entrance. I watch as their pale face approaches in the dim. Their long red hair hangs in shiny sheets, and their black feathered wings unfurl from their wide shoulders. They are so beautiful.

I feel a profound sadness knowing Oski's wings and hair will be taken from them. Is it in another life? Is this the same Oski or someone else?

Oski comes closer and places a hand over my heart. The hand is cold, and I jump.

"Who are you?" Their voice is rumbling and low. It is a calming sound, and at once I know I am safe, even if somewhere I am not supposed to be.

"You know me," I say. "Somewhere, sometime, you know me. I am Runa." My name squeezes out of me in a puff of air.

"Runa? A strong name for such a weak being." Oski chuckles.

"Where am I?"

"Nowhere. My prison." Oski opens their long arms, indicating the cave.

"How do I get out of here?" I ask.

Oski's smile vanishes. Their dark eyes narrow.

"You shouldn't have been where you were, and you shouldn't be where you are now."

Oski picks up the piece of fish at my side and tears into it.

"Look," I say. "If you hadn't rescued me, I'd have been eaten by that...monster." I shudder, refusing to let my mind recall the image of the gaping mouth. All those teeth.

Oski tilts their head to the side, questioning. "No, that was Jörmungandr. Not just a monster."

"Truly?" I ask.

"Yes." Oski smiles. "Isn't it beautiful?"

"Beautiful?" I scoff.

Oski throws down the half-eaten fish in disgust. "Jörmungandr is a pure creature. It lives in loneliness in the golden waters. It must kill to survive. You know nothing."

I am transfixed by Oski's glowing anger. They are as incandescent as a flame.

"I'm sorry," I manage. "It's just, I was afraid..."

"Of course. Your kind is always afraid. But I am a Valkyrie, and I don't get scared. At least, I *was* a Valkyrie." Oski drifts off, a sad look on their face.

"What are you doing here alone?" I ask gently.

"Ah, banished," Oski says. They let out a loud belch.

"Yes, but why?"

Oski shrugs. "I don't remember well. Keep forgetting. But it had something to do with the woman I love."

"Yes," I say excitedly. "Wyrd! You love Wyrd."

Oski takes a step backward. They look fierce. "How do you know about her? Are you a witch? A spy?" They pull out their sword again, and I raise my hands.

"No, no. I'm a friend. But in the time that I know you, you don't have all this hair. Or wings. And...you also lost your horse." I try to remember everything Oski told me on our journey to moonwater. But my memory is fading. I wonder if it has something to do with this place. I feel like I could sleep forever and just forget everything.

"Ah, my horse, yes. He had a shock of black mane that

was always in his eyes, and he would never let anyone brush it back or braid it. He felt as though he was charged with lightning!" Oski's smile fades. "I remember his death, when Odin struck him down. His black coat was shining with rain. He died in the mud."

"Oski, I'm so sorry."

"Why? He wasn't your horse," they say.

We stare at each other in silence for a while.

"Oski," I whisper. "Are we dead?"

"No." Oski frowns. "I don't think so."

Oski watches me, their head cocked to the side.

"Oski, I have another question."

"Já."

"Do you have any clothes? I'm very cold."

"I find things," Oski says. "They wash up onshore. From other realms." Oski rummages around in a basket and produces a long dress that looks as though it was made for a Valkyrie even bigger than Oski. "This will have to do," they say, handing it to me.

I slip it on over my head and am grateful for the warmth, but the arms droop off me, and the bottom of the dress pools around my feet.

"Here," says Oski. They pierce the extra cloth with their sword and then tear at the fabric until the dress is short enough for me to wear.

I roll up the sleeves and try not to think about my beautiful cloak lost out on the ice, frozen solid and alone.

"Well," says Oski. "You look fine. And I suppose you are

someone to speak to, at least. Eternity is so boring, já? Do you have any mead?"

I stare at them. "No, Oski. I don't have any mead. I don't have anything. But I would love some water."

"Bah, what good are you?" Oski waves their hand at me before fetching a jug filled with water. They pass it to me, and I grab it, drinking it down greedily. The cool water soothes my raw throat.

I stop to breathe. "Oski," I ask. "How are you here?"

"I think I'm always here. I don't think I will ever be free."

"But how are there two of you?"

"There are two of me? Where?" Oski pulls out their sword. "I will destroy the impostor."

"No," I say. "Not here. Another you, in another time. Another place."

"Well then, Runa. Does that mean there is another you?"

Their question stuns me into silence. I drink my water, and the shadow girl's face looms in my mind.

I spend a long time sleeping. Dreams of Núna, my beloved raven and my lost friend, dominate my mind. She flies through the golden sky, squawking a warning to me as she alights on the lip of the cliff. She takes flight again, and it's as if I can see through her eyes. She shows me the golden sea below. I can see the moonstone in its depths. It is waiting for me.

I wake with a start and try to clear the sensation that a veil covers my eyes. Núna has shown me the way. I must retrieve the stone.

Oski appears suddenly. "I have looked into the reflecting sea," they say. "I have seen things."

"You can see things in the sea?" I ask. My heart pounds.

"Yes, when it wants to show me."

"What did it show you, Oski?"

"I know who you are now. You are the runecaster. You're the one responsible for the end of the world."